Also by Adrienne Nash.

Crime

'The Cellar'

'A Time to be Brave'

The Trudi Novels

'Trudi'

'Trudi in Paris'

'Trudi et Simon'

'Trudi after Simon'

Art.

'Wide Skies' a history of Art in Norfolk and the Norfolk and Norwich Art Circle, 1885 to 2003. With statistics by Brian Watts.

Trudi et Simon

By

Adrienne Nash

Chapter 1.

It was a dull day in late June. The sun had risen at four thirty but the Normandy landscape was covered in a sea mist which had crept in from the Channel. From my bedroom window, in Chateau de Beauvonne, I was able to see only as far as the stream that ran through the bottomland.

It was my wedding day, my secret wedding day and I need to explain, why our wedding, my wedding to Simon de Beauvonne, was to be secret.

Simon had married Catherine Schüster in September nearly three years ago, because she could give him heirs and I for obvious reasons, could not. That I could not conceive was and is a matter of supreme regret to me, but many natal women also cannot bear children. It must be the biological aim of every female to reproduce, to carry within their womb another human being for nine months, and welcome a baby into the World although some resist the instinct and others through quirks of nature cannot conceive. It is important to someone with an estate, whether land or a fortune, to leave heirs.

Right from the start, Simon's marriage to Catherine was agreed by them both, to be a marriage of convenience. In return for bearing his heirs, Catherine was to receive €5 million, but she had reneged on the agreement, having become accustomed to being la Comtesse, mistress of the Chateau Beauvonne. She had also been somewhat jealous, or severely miffed that Simon was in love with me, a twenty-year old transsexual woman. To be fair, I can see her point.

In making this marriage bargain, Simon had made a terrible mistake in picking an ambitious and ruthless woman. A spurned female is a bitter enemy, capable of almost anything in revenge. Catherine hated me and had threatened that she would drag Simon through a scandalous divorce, naming me, with the aim of keeping the children, twins André and Adèle and little Sébastien. She really had no interest in the babies, did not display any affection for them or any maternal instincts. Her intention to deprive Simon access was an act of vicious spite, her trump card to secure her portion of his estate.

As so often happens, when children are used as a weapon, tragedy followed and Catherine was found at the bottom of the Chateau's marble staircase. She had died four months ago.

At first Simon was suspected of causing her death, but his mobile phone records, showed that he was at least one hundred miles away at the time. Indeed, one of the calls to his phone had been from me. I later found out what had really passed that day.

Catherine should have been at the hairdresser but on her way there, she received a call to say that her stylist had reported sick, so she returned unexpectedly. Simon was caught in the act of staging a robbery at the Chateau, in which he was taking all the evidence Catherine had amassed connecting him with me. As Simon escaped, Catherine had fallen down the marble staircase and had died on the way to hospital. Later on the same day, Simon had left the road in his car and lay trapped in it for sixteen hours. They had to amputate his gangrenous leg to release him from the wreck. He was in a coma for days and I sat by his bed for sixteen hours a day, talking to him and using other ways to wake him.

Much later, I discovered that it was not he who had replied on the phone but his cousin Gérard. I had not yet discussed this with Simon, because just as he had recovered from the crash, he had a heart attack.

There was to be no one at our wedding except Simon and me and two of our friends, Annette, the new Beauvonne PR guru and Gérard, Simon's cousin who I had put in charge of the day to day running of the fashion house while Simon recovered from the heart attack.

The wedding had been advertised at the Mairie for as short a time as possible, under Simon's name, Simon Chartrand, rather than anything to do with his title or the Chateau of Beauvonne. Euros had changed hands to make sure that the notice of wedding had not been seen, except by the Mairie staff. I had signed the forms, a Certificate of Celibacy and Certificate of Custom Law in secret too.

After the wedding, we drove straight back to the Chateau. I wore the wedding ring on my right hand, until such time as we would have our church wedding next year with all the accoutrements. At twenty-three, I was a married woman in France, not only married but married to a Count and able to give myself the title Comtesse or Countess should I wish to. I didn't want to be so ostentatious, in fact I disliked intensely such titles, as did Simon.

As a terrific bonus, I had three lovely children, who would grow up, I hoped, to call me mother. Life was sweet, sweeter than I had ever thought it would possibly be, except that my beloved Simon was recovering from a crise cardiaque and had lost a foot, all in a few months. That was a tragedy. Even though Catherine hated me and showed no affection for her three lovely children, her death was also a matter of regret, a deep sadness, at least to me.

Nevertheless, I glowed within. Simon is without doubt the kindest, sweetest person. He is handsome and desirable. He is not only the most cultured person I know, but the also the wisest and most gentle, except in bed.

His recovery from his heart bypass had been slow. Five weeks after his crise cardiaque, he was still weak. We had not made love for three months. I understood the reasons for this but our love making was an affirmation that he really loved me and also that I was truly the person I purported to be, a real woman, female in form as well as mind.

The four of us returned to the Chateau after the short ceremony. I wanted to yell out to everybody that I was sitting beside my husband in the back of Gérard's BMW. However, it had been my wish that nothing would be known of our marriage until we had the large church wedding in a year's time, when everyone connected with us would be invited. I wanted a respectable interval between Catherine's death and our nuptials. This wedding while delighting us both, was primarily for the security of the children should any further tragedy befall Comte Simon de Beauvonne, my husband.

University had finished for the year and it was summer break. It had been a year of hard study again, and I and my flat mates, Élise and Jean Luc, completed the third year successfully. Next year we would all start our externship actually working in a hospital, training in the various disciplines, learning the arts of interrogation and diagnosis and the work of the various departments.

The summer break had come at the right time. Running Simon's enterprise in a caretaking capacity and being a student had made me infinitely exhausted.

The July forecast was for settled hot weather, and the mistiness had been part of that syndrome, damp cool air off the ocean meeting the heat of the continent. I hoped to ride everyday and recharge my batteries and occupy my other time with the children and Simon. I would go to the Maison Beauvonne once a week, to make sure that all is well and I hope that Simon will feel well enough to accompany me.

We four and Sophie the children's nanny and Sabine, Simon's second cousin who is now his estate manager, have an intimate dinner. Yes it is special, the chef having been asked to make a celebration feast for he knew not what. I had worked it out with him, Lobster Thermidor, salt meadow lamb followed by fresh fruit brulée. The salt meadow lamb comes particularly from the Mont St. Michel district, not far from us, and is served on a bed of beans with a sauce made from the lamb's juices. It is delicious. We also had wilted spinach and crispy broccoli spears from our kitchen garden.

We all retired early, mostly because Simon still tired easily. I went to my bedroom that is next to his, and bathed, my third shower that day. I examined myself in the mirror. I saw a lithe athletic body, my waist is like that of most girls these days when the hour glass figure has all but disappeared. I am a small size ten, even an eight in somewhere like M & S. I usually have blonde hair, straight and shiny, ending six inches below my shoulders, but sometimes adopt other styles and colours. I think I am attractive, others say beautiful. In some lights, and from some angles, I can see what they mean, but subtle makeup and a careful maintenance programme helps turn heads.

I put on a beautiful fine black silk nightdress, which hardly disguised my assets, then slipped into Simon's bedroom. He was still in his bathroom. When he appeared, I am already in his bed, the covers drawn up as far as my waist, pert breasts pressing against the flimsy silk of my nightdress. Despite the fact that we have been lovers over the last three years, I feel apprehensive. Will Simon want to make love or will he be frightened to? Sex does not mean a great deal to me, except with him. My only other lover has been Ellie, but of course, lesbian sex is quite different. I have been thinking of this day for the last three years and have built it up in my imagination. Had Simon been well, I would have felt no fear, but as he now is, I would have felt disappointment, even if he had the best reason to refrain, his state of health.

Simon entered the bedroom, clad only in his PJ trousers. He switched out the lights bar the bedside lights. He looked at me curiously, with a look of uncertainty, an expression I had not witnessed on his face before.

As he entered the bed, I took hold of his arm. 'It's time to make love, my husband. I will do all the work, you just enjoy me.'

To my surprise I found that he was already erect. I stroked him then took him in my mouth until he came, surprisingly quickly. While he was still erect, I lowered myself on to him and pump up and down, riding him in a canter, careful to not put weight on his chest. His scar shows white and the stitch marks are clear. Again I was rewarded by his climaxing, even though I had not achieved an orgasm. It was enough, that he at least was having a normal sex life again and that I was the one pleasing him.

I kept him inside me, while we kissed and he stroked my hair and ran his hands over my body. 'Do you want to go again?' he asked.

'No chérie Simon. It is enough for you tonight, but more often now if we are careful. Exercise is good for you, oui? And I want you, so much Simon. I have missed this so much.' He used his hands to caress my body and it was even more sensual and arousing through the diaphanous silk. Eventually we fell asleep. I orgasmed in the night, waking as the dream brought me to a climax. My panties were wet. I fell into a contented sleep again.

I was up early, leaving my beloved in bed to rise when he felt rested. I was meeting Sabine and we planned to ride round the estate, making notes of what we are going to do. We had put a map of the estate on the office wall and marked all the fields on it. Sabine was checking all the crop rotations and planning for next season.

Sabine had already convinced me to buy three hundred Border Cheviot sheep from Wales to run on the parkland, and she wanted to make a trip to Wales where she had found a herd for disposal. The plan was then to put them with a Texel ram. I just did not have the energy to do everything, so I had to delegate as Simon, my control freak husband would not do.

My career is medical. That is what I have worked at for the last three years, as a medical student at University of Pierre et Marie Curie in Paris, part of the Sorbonne. I am determined to complete the course that will take another six years at least to become a registrar. It was hard work, but I love it.

Another thing I had to do, is become a French citizen, for the sake of the children, to make sure that no distant relative will disqualify me from inheriting the de Beauvonne estate, should anything further happen to Simon. By marriage I had to wait five years from the date of the wedding and then I might be given citizenship after a further wait of eighteen months. As a resident, I had already completed three years, so I aimed to put in the papers as soon as the five years had expired. I would of course, retain my British nationality.

These heavy matters are not what I would have thought about a year ago. Then I was a privileged carefree student. A year later I had so much responsibility upon my young shoulders. I was therefore pleased to be meeting Sabine, a woman just three years older, and wise for her years, to see how she would go about reorganising the estate.

When I arrived at the stables, I found her ready with her horse, but she had left me to fetch my Arab mare Sheba and to tack and saddle her. 'If you ride,' she says, 'then you do everything for your horse.'

When I was finally ready we rode out. It was a big task to map the whole estate. Sabine had a saddle bag in which she has equipment, a map of the estate, A4 sheets of each field, and a camera. We rode in a circle doing the outer fields first, using the estate tracks, Sabine telling me what she intended to do as we progressed. At lunch time, we rode out of the grounds to a small café in a village and ate an unsophisticated meal of beef soup with veg floating in it and pain de compagne, followed by coffee.

We rode back in. Sabine started a conversation of a more personal nature.

'So, mon ami Trudi, you have married him?'

'Why do you say that?'

'There is not much which is secret in this small society. Why?'

'Why, what?

'Why have you married him?'

'I see I have to be honest with you Sabine, but you know, all our conversations are confidential?

'Do you need to ask? Of course!'

'Simon believes that he may not live long, after his heart attack, one never knows, he may live a long time or not. He is frightened that the children would be left orphans, and so I am now their step mother and guardian and I will make sure they are protected and loved.'

'I approve. But you still love Simon too?'

'Of course. Sabine, we plan a big wedding next year, and I want you to be dame d'honneur. Will you do that?'

'Bien sûr. Where?'

'The Basilique Saint Thérèse, Lisieux. Everyone will be coming, about five hundred guests. Oh Sabine, I am so glad you will be with me. I will need your help. Sometimes I feel so young, too young and I have a panic that I can't cope with all this. At least I think I now have Gérard earning his money and Annette too. I want all your family there, all the family, and of course, most of the fashion staff and connections. We are selling the rights to a magazine. I am also inviting all my family and friends from school days as well as from University. There is so much to do.'

'I will help all I can, for your sake. You have my love and best wishes.'

We completed the survey by four and sat in the office discussing the plan. Sabine would write it up and then we would discuss it with Simon. Sabine thought that she could double the profits, using contract labour for the ploughing and harvesting.

I had tea with Simon, before going to help Sophie Maynard put the children to bed. Tomorrow I would ride early, alone, leaving Sabine to get on with her work. I would then spend time with Simon and the children.

Dinner was a quiet and casual affair. Again I was washed out and we retired early. I slept with Simon. He cuddled me and kissed my neck, a lot, which I loved, and he rested a hand between my thighs. I slept until well after dawn.

Chapter 2.

I saddled Sheba and headed off across the park, turning into the forest and cantering the long drive. The woods were silent. Sheba and I shared this world, the only sound that of her hooves hammering on the pine needle strewn floor with the scent of the pine trees in our nostrils. Sunlight flickered through the trees as we pounded along. We slowed to a walk in a glade and passed through a cloud of dancing gnats. Sheba snorted and threw her head up. OK Sheba, I say and off we went again at a slow canter, leaving the bugs behind. I turned and headed west down a path I had not used before and found it led down to a stream. We stopped and contemplated it. The bottom looked like sand, the water was clean and clear and I let Sheba drink, then we headed across and up the bank. We took the rise and emerged into open country of fields and A pheasant called in alarm. Sheba's ears flicked far off a church and a couple of houses. I turned and we headed back.

When Sheba was fed, watered and groomed. I went up to change.

I found Simon having his breakfast. He looked better today, quite fresh and I saw some of the old business-like Simon.

I kissed him. 'How do you feel about taking the children to the seaside today? The weather is fine and will be hot and they can play on the beach. I will have cook prepare a picnic. If you get tired you can have a nap there or we can come back. And you can stroll the sands and get some fresh air. We can buy fish for dinner too.'

'It is a splendid idea, but we take Sophie too so that we can stroll, like honeymooners on the shore.'

Sophie had herself and the children ready in thirty minutes. We packed them in the Landrover and I drove north until we came to Lion-sur-Mer. We parked and while Sophie shepherded the children, Simon and I unloaded everything and made camp on the sand. Simon strolled the promenade while we showed Adèle and André how to dig in the sand. They were really too young, but they tried and enjoyed it. They loved dancing in a pool and looking for sea creatures too. We ate the picnic, and with the children having a nap, Simon and I strolled the sands, hand in hand.

'Dear Trudi, I am sorry that I cannot do more. I do not know what I would do without you. I hope to be more active soon, but I am so proud of the way you have taken over and become mistress of everything.'

'Mon cher, it is what I should do, as your wife, until you are recovered and you will be. So you approve of what I have done? Sabine, Annette and Gérard?'

'Of course. Trudi you always have good judgement. I was too weak with Gérard and I am impressed with Annette's work now. Sabine, we shall see, but you know her family do not like me. Perhaps, as she is your friend she will do well. I hope so.'

'Tomorrow Simon, we go to Paris for your check up at the clinic. We will stay overnight at the mansion, I have asked Madame Gameau to have it ready, then the next day we go to Maison Beauvonne. I need, we need to be sure that everything is OK. I hope you feel fit enough?'

'Oh yes, it will be good to see the business. There are things to do.'

'Such as?'

'I need to see that Gérard is not thieving and he is pulling his weight, but not interfering with the designers.'

'Simon, you mean he steals?'

'That is why he is no longer an accountant. He is family, so I gave him odd jobs rather than see him starve.'

'And I put him in charge of the day-to-day running of the Maison. Oh Simon, I wish I had known.'

'Do not panic. I limited how much he could draw a cheque for at the bank, and he knows that if he steals from me, then that is the end. He would go to prison for sure, I would make certain. We grew up together, he is like a brother, but he is the black sheep. I just want reassurance that he is behaving.'

We returned to find the children asleep under the sun shade. Sophie was reading a book. We lay for a while. Then it was time to pack up. The children were fractious from the heat and would be better in the air conditioning of the Landrover. We played nursery rhymes. Pomme pêche poire abricot, Frere Jacque, Alouette and some I did not know. Simon played conductor. It was a merry ride home and the children giggled to see their father so happy.

The next morning we drove into Paris and straight to the Pitié Salpêtriere. We were early and sat for a while waiting for Professeur Rousse. We were called and Simon was connected up to the ECG machine. Rousse entered and watched the trace. He moved two of the sensors, and listened to Simon's heart with his stethoscope. Then they injected Simon with some dye and he went into the scanner. I waited apprehensively. At last it was all over. We saw Rousse in his office, the same office he had warned me in.

'So Simon, your protégé is looking after you?'

'Very well, thank you Professeur. I could not be in better hands.'

'Well, your trace looks good. We need to analyse it further but the scan is fine and everything is as I would expect. I see no reason why you cannot resume your previous life, but not to excess. No more jetting around, crossing time zones and eating God knows what. In future you need to be more careful. You have a weakness there and we will continue to monitor your heart for the rest of your life. Exercise is good, but again not to excess. You ride I see and ski, but again, not to excess. Plenty of walking at a reasonable pace, that means somewhere between a stroll and a trot. Fresh air, a diet which is fat free, lots of white fish, chicken, a little lean beef from time to time. Moderation. For now I leave you in the hands of Médecin Trudi.'

He rose and we were dismissed. We left the room and were in the corridor, when he called me back.

'Close the door please Trudi. You need to look after him. He must not work too hard. I do not think he is in imminent danger, but the results could be better. I see you have an engagement ring on your hand. I hope that he will make the wedding, and he will if he is good, but the advice I gave him was serious. He needs to be careful. Getting the balance right, is the trick, between doing nothing and doing a lot. Good luck and good fortune with your externship. I will keep an eye on you and I am at your disposal if you need advice.'

I found Simon sitting waiting in the corridor.

'Why did he call you back?' Simon asked.

'He wanted to talk about my externship. He looks forward to having me on the ward with him, he says.'

I drove to the apartment. For dinner we went to L'Ecume a good fish restaurant in walking distance.

Over dinner I say, 'Simon, I need you to teach me as much as possible about Maison Beauvonne and the Estate, in case, you know, you get sick again.'

'Trudi that is only sensible. Tomorrow we look at the books and the designers can tell you about the materials. You must ask as many questions as you like. I can tell you too, about our shops in New York, Hollywood, Tokyo, Beijing, Shanghai and Singapore. What has happened about a salesman to look after them?'

'We are interviewing next week, now you are stronger. We pick up the list tomorrow and go through the CVs at home.'

Simon smiles. 'So the Chateau is now home?'

'Am I wrong?'

'No, just that is the first time you have called it home. Who would have thought when we met that you would call it home. How long ago was that?

'It is six years Simon. Six unbelievably exciting years. You have given me so much, shown me so much, yet I still feel like a little girl around you. I still know so little.'

'Non, you are worldly wise, instinctively, and you soak up information. I am so proud to have you as my wife.'

'Really. I mean, with my history, my origins? You could have anyone.'

'I have you Trudi. Beautiful, and clever, loyal and you are not greedy. And I love you, for you. Do you spend all your allowance?'

'No, I save about half. I take rent from Élise, about seventy per cent of what she would pay, because she can afford it, but take nothing from Jean Luc who is poor. Perhaps one day I will need some money and I will have it.'

'I want to make love tonight.'

'That will be fun Simon.'

We had a lobster salad and baby new potatoes. We walked home through empty summer streets hand in hand. It felt as though the old Simon was back. Even his limp was minimal. I hated Catherine Schüster, even though she had died. She had brought this disaster, putting him under so much pressure.

We reached the apartment and it was still light.

We went straight to bed. This time I let him do with me as he would. I loved when he took charge and manipulated me like his automaton. I giggled, with ecstasy and love. Thank God he was back. I needed to have one strong person in my life.

Chapter 3.

We were at Maison Beauvonne by nine-thirty. First we called on Gérard. He showed us what he had done. His purchasing skills looked good. Simon was impressed at some of the prices. Also all the arrangements had been made for the autumn show, a new venue, twice the size of the old one. He showed us the guest list drawn up by the designers, and Annette. I recognised names of footballers and pop stars, opera singers, racing drivers and their wives and girlfriends, and of course the fashionistas and journalists and politicians. In particular the big stores were on the list, Harrods, Saks, Bloomingdales, Harvey Nicols, Selfridges, Galleries Lafayette, Franck et Fils and others from the World's capitals. Simon was pleased.

We then turned to the short list Gérard had prepared for a salesman, or rather a representative. We decided to take all applications and study them at the Chateau.

We moved, all three of us to see the designers. Simon looked through the designs for haute couture and ready made. Both designers asked Simon if I was available to do some modelling. I said I would love to and they showed me the designs they had in mind for me. The first was a readymade design, a skirt suit, fitted peplum jacket but with a slanting zip and absolutely figure hugging. The skirt hem was four inches above the knee. The next was a diaphanous tea dress, in pretty pastel print, full skirted, just on the knee, with a plunging back that lay in a swag across my lower back. The last was a full-length silver dress, boned bodice, and figure hugging until it swirled out to a pool of material around my feet. I could not understand how they could cut it to fall to that shape. We then went through all the designs and Simon was pleased. As each dress was inspected it went back into security, because spies were numerous, particularly from China. Venetian blinds protected view from the windows.

    The five of us went for lunch at the Kok Ping just off Rue Byron. Annette joined us and Simon said how pleased he was with the press coverage she had achieved over the past month. We took a taxi to the apartment and picked up my Mercedes. We were home by six.

    I escorted Simon to his room. I made for the nursery. André and Adèle played happily in the bath and Sébastien bounced in his cot, standing, holding on to the sides and yelling. Soon the twins too were in bed. We sang Frere Jacque, then looked at a picture book of animals, and they settled down. I kissed them all goodnight. I was beginning to feel like a real parent.

    We two had a light supper and were in bed by nine. It would be another busy day tomorrow, looking through the applications and making sure the short list contained all the right candidates.

I was up at seven. I decided to have a half hour jog and set off. As I passed by, I saw that Sabine was already in the estate office. I returned and ate a plate of cereal for breakfast then showered and dressed in a blouse and skirt.

I heard Simon on the move and found him half dressed. We kissed. He clasped me to him as he had before he became ill. How I loved his possession of me, to be enfolded in his powerful arms. Weakness welled up in me and I could have let him hold me tight to his chest forever. Reluctantly I released myself, kissing him on the lips as we parted.

'Simon, I love you so much. I want you to know. My life since knowing you has been so full of beauty and love. You must know that.'

'I hoped it was so Trudi, ma fille douce, I loved you, really from the moment we met.'

'This morning Simon, we must go through the job applications, and make sure everyone we want is on the short list. There are forty and a short list of fifteen, so we have work to do. Then I will send a letter to the short listed candidates asking them to attend for interview. Simon, will you let me be involved in selection?'

'Of course. If anything happens to me, then you will be in charge, so you must help make decisions.'

'Nothing will happen Simon, but I am now your wife and I want to be involved in everything, not just a surrogate mother to your children. Catherine just wanted to sit here and be the Comtesse, but I want to be a doctor but also a partner in your business.'

'So it shall be Trudi, bien sûr.'

As soon as he had eaten his light breakfast, we went to the study. It was an easier job to sort the applicants than I had thought. Some were completely inappropriate, even though the head hunting company was supposed to have sorted them. We had looked at twenty, numbering as we went and putting them in different piles, when I came across a name I knew. Wally Harding, my old school chum and protector. He had been working for a Spanish based high street fashion chain, with shops throughout Europe and the World. He was not on the short list, probably because of his age. I showed it to Simon. Wally had not gone to university, instead going to Scotland to work for a thread maker. He left there and joined the multiple. He had risen quickly.

'Simon, I know this man. We must include him. He is someone we can trust.'

'Of course. I do not promise we will hire him, but we will certainly give him a chance.'

We looked through the rest and the no hope pile was soon the largest. Of the fifteen that had been in the original short list, we threw out five and brought in Wally and a Dutchman who worked for C&A. I was doubtful about the latter, but it would make no difference if we saw him.

I typed the letters, signing per pro Simon de Beauvonne and posted them off.

That done and out of the way, I went to the estate office and looked for Sabine. She was not there. I was disappointed. I enquired of the stable hand and he told me that Sabine had ridden out to look at an area downstream from the small lake.

I quickly changed and saddled up and went in that direction. The sun was high in the sky and the temperature had risen sharply from when I had jogged around the grounds. As I rode the sun beat down upon my shirt and thighs. Sheba snorted and puffed. She was frisky and skittish this morning. I was a bit frightened. I had not had her in this mood before. Luckily she settled after a short canter and we trotted for a few hundred yards. I found Sabine photographing and measuring an area of sedge grass and reed.

'Allo Comtesse,' she said laughing, 'so you thought to check up on the staff. Well here I am on the job. You can help me if it is not too manual for your soft little hands.'

She held Sheba's head as I dismounted, then kissed me unexpectedly on both cheeks. 'How are you Trudi?'

'I am very well. Somehow, I manage to do all I must do.'

'You have so many responsibilities, with Simon still recovering.'

'Yes but every day now he improves. We went to Paris for a night, to see the heart clinic and to check on Maison Beauvonne. Then this morning, we sorted through applicants to take over Simon's globe trotting. Something new each day, which makes life more interesting and exciting. By the way, don't call me Comtesse please.'

'Of course not in public.'

'No never. You are my friend not a servant, not that I want anyone to call me Comtesse. I am Trudi, and even in jest as now, no. I want no barriers between us. So Sabine chère amie, how are you progressing with the grand plan?'

'As soon as we have measured up here, then I am done. I have written up a preliminary outline of changes I want to make. Simon has neglected the estate and devoted time to the Maison, but I know that I can make good money out of 3,200 hectares, even though the forest covers 500 of them. That too needs managing, and we can take out some timber and replant. That will give us a bit of working capital. Then we sell the machinery and bring in contractors. Yes we need some tractors and trailers, but the ones we have are good. You will see. When do I put my ideas to Simon?'

'How about tomorrow morning? We are not doing anything.'

'Bon. Now just help me make these measurements and we are finished.'

After lunch en famille, we played with the children on the lawn. It was good to see Simon with them at last. Until now he had been a remote figure in their lives, either away or rowing with Catherine, leaving the children with Francoise and the black queen. Now here he was lying on the grass, holding the twins up in the air and making them giggle, pretending to chase them. Sophie also enjoyed our company and I had warmed to her as I had come to know her. She was very good at her job. I would miss her over the next two weeks because she was going on holiday to her parents. I just hoped she would be coming back. I took the opportunity to speak to her.

'Sophie, how are you here? Are you happy?'

'Oh yes. It is a wonderful situation, but of course, I do miss the city at times. This is the most rural position I have held.'

'Well when I am back at University and Simon has recovered we will move to Paris to the house there. There is room for the children and you. So that will be a change and you can do the things young girls like us like to do. We could go to clubs together and see some shows?'

'That sounds wonderful. But the children, in the evening? Who would look after them?'

'I am sure that Élise my friend or Madame Gameau will baby sit. It will take some of the pressure off. Above all, we value you and want you to be happy. If there is anything, speak to me rather than Simon, I do not want him worried with such things.

'Now, you have money enough for your holiday? How do you go to Strasbourg?'

'I take the train. But I need to get to the train station. If you would take me?'

'How else would you get there? Of course I will take you, in fact if I take you to Chartres, it is just over an hour to Montparnasse. On your return, phone me and we will arrange a time for me to pick you up.'

'That is really good of you Mademoiselle Trudi.'

'Non, Sophie, Trudi oui!'

'OK Trudi, merci bien.'

Sabine presented her grand plan next day. Simon sat mute, it was plain to see that he was sceptical that

Sabine could run the estate, but he let her run through her plan and suggestions for the future uninterrupted. That was good of him, because he had run the estate, and in a way, her new methods could be considered a criticism of his management.

When he heard the costings and savings he sat up.

'So how much for the disposal of the machines Sabine?'

'Market price less fifteen percent commission, for all the harvesting equipment would be approximately €550 thousand..'

'And contractors for our harvests will cost how much per year?'

'About €250 thousand. But we would not have depreciation on machinery, nor repairs and maintenance. If we added those to the €550 thousand, it means a saving of seven or eight hundred thousand.'

'Then there is the forest. We can take out over a million Euro's worth of timber, without harming the forest. Then we replant with hardwood for the future and some fast growing soft woods to mature more quickly. I want to turn that useless bottomland into a lake. Aesthetically, it will be a picturesque feature, visible from the terrace. We could also sell fishing rights. We ought to employ a gamekeeper to look after that and to have a pheasant shoot. People pay a lot of money to shoot and of course it is good to cultivate business contacts. Perhaps you will think about that.

'This has been an arable farm, but I would like to run sheep on the parkland around the house which at the moment, is more or less fallow. I know we make some haylage and sell it, but I think a flock of 300 will make much more. I have seen a flock for sale in Wales and I know of a shepherd too. Then there are some new crops, peas, rape and even flax that we can grow. All involve us in little work and are valuable crops.

'Whatever you decide Simon, then I will abide by what you say, but I think this plan will pay, even with three new staff members.'

'Sabine, I am impressed. I was not convinced but Trudi said you could do this. She was right as usual. Go ahead.'

'We need to discuss salary mon oncle. I would suggest a basic salary of thirty thousand and ten percent of the profits I provide over and above the average of the last five years. Is that acceptable?'

'Shrewd. The women around me are shrewd. I shall have to be careful.' He rose from his chair and kissed Sabine three times. 'It's a deal. Now, a spot of lunch and a bottle of champagne I think Trudi. Now what else have you up your sleeve to make my life easier? Soon I will have nothing left but to be le Comte.'

'Nothing else Simon. Now you can be the managing director, delegating and making long term plans. Is that not better than chasing around like a fly on a horse tail?'

'I hope so Trudi.'

Chapter 4.

Life after that was easier. I had arranged everything, delegated what I could so that Simon in future was the managing director, not everything from super salesman to office boy. I had collected around us people we could trust. With the imminent appointment of a representative my changes would be complete. Trustworthiness, that is the asset people have to possess above all. My one doubt now was Gérard.

Life at the Chateau was sweet. Simon regained his joie de vivre, Sabine set about finding contractors to do the main work of the farm, ploughing, harrowing, etc and harvest next year. This summer would be the last harvest using our own plant. Sabine on reviewing her plan found that the workforce was large enough, it just meant a bit of retraining. No hiring and no firing.

She took off for Wales, a fat cheque in her bag to buy the sheep, and she would travel back with them in the transport, making sure they were fed and watered on the way. The Texel ram had already appeared and was in a small paddock alone, not knowing that he would soon have his work cut out. He better succeed, he had cost nearly €10,000.

Plant had arrived to dig out the new lake. First they piped the stream around the site, before digging out the considerable sized lake. Then it would be clay lined and planted up. Sabine certainly had vision.

The contractor also arrived to select timber to take from the forest. He walked it with me in the absence of Sabine, selecting mature trees, some French oak, chestnut and ash and of course sycamore, the weed tree, as well as thinnings of birch and various evergreens. He painted their trunks with various hieroglyphs so that his men knew what to do. He would also advise in replanting.

Harvest began, first the winter barley then the wheat. Potatoes were topped so that the tubers grew rather than the foliage. Sabine returned with the sheep and they were unloaded on to the parkland. The ram looked interested.

I was glad she was back. I could again devote time to Simon and the children. Once a week we tripped into Paris. Everything was running smoothly. The first week in September was the time for the fashion show, and all was seemingly ahead of schedule. This was to be the largest show ever for the brand, the first time that the readymade lines had presented a full range. The difference between haute couture and the readymade was Simon explained, not only the materials used but the cuts used less material and the clothes were wearable everyday wear, the inspiration coming from the pavements of Chelsea, Bayswater and Sundays on Camden Lock, as well as some American influences from LA and New York's Greenwich Village. The show had signed up thirty models to show the nearly 200 designs. It was ambitious.

The beginning of August and the weather broke. Rain poured in from the Atlantic. Sophie was back and we took off for Paris for a week to see how we all fitted in. Madame Gameau was all too pleased to see us and fussed over the little ones. Sophie was thrilled with the situation and the layout of her rooms and those for the children. Simon and I were free to interview the representative applicants.

We started on the Wednesday afternoon. The first three were all in their early forties, only one of whom was presently engaged in fashion. Simon was probing, business like, armed with a stock of questions. I was left to enquire into their private lives, wives and partners, children and how those family responsibilities affected their business life. The first ten were all French. Only two really impressed, a woman who had been a buyer at Lafayette, and a man who was the representative for the perfume side of what is probably France's premier haute couture house.

On Thursday we had the remaining five. Number twelve on the list was Wally. His size impressed and he was dressed immaculately. I remembered him coming off the rugby field, the collar torn from his shirt and blood running down from a gash on his knee, mud caked shirt, shorts and arms.

He shook hands with Simon. Then looked at me, with that little gesture he made, his trade mark, pulling his head back as though needing to focus. 'Trudi? C'est vous?'

'Oui. Tell us, about yourself Wally. You have family, a girl friend, wife?'

'A girl friend. She lives in Madrid.'

'And is a wedding likely to be planned?'

'We have been discussing engagement. Her family are exerting some pressure.'

'What nationality is the lady.'

'Isabel is Spanish, she studies art at the University.'

'And would you both move to Paris if we wanted you to.'

'Well, we discussed this before I flew up here. Yes, we could, well after she completes her course next year, but I could live here and commute weekends.'

Simon took over, asking what he thought of the haute couture trade and how he saw the high street developing. How would he feel about spending a week in the USA then going to the Far East? Did he understand that he was representing the headquarters of haute couture as well as selling the readymade? He didn't but he did not see that as a problem. What languages did he speak? Spanish, English and French.

'Are you worried about your relationship if you are parted for two weeks at a time, travelling the World.

'Ah, that's the tricky one. One never knows. Isabel says that it would not be a problem, but I don't know.'

'What happens if we hire you, then Isabel complains that you are away too much?' I ask.

'I do feel sure that she and I can work something out. Really. She knows that my career will ultimately define our income and standard of living.'

'How much do you really want this job?'

'That is the easiest question. I really want it. Beauvonne has a reputation in the trade as at the cutting edge, going into the ready-mades as well as couture. I want this job, make no mistake about that.'

Simon asked a lot of questions about his work for Z....

Simon finished his questions. 'Wally, I have just one more question. Are you staying in Paris tonight?' I asked.

'Yes, then flying back to Madrid tomorrow. I am on my own time for this interview.'

'So are you free to have dinner with us? As an old friend?'

'That would be really good.'

'Perhaps you would come to our house at say 6.00? Then we will go out to eat.' I passed him the address.

'It is such a pleasure to see you again Wally. À bientôt mon ami.'

When he had gone, I said to Simon, 'You don't mind if we take him to dinner tonight?'

'No, but we must not mislead him into thinking the position is his.'

'You don't like him?'

'Oh I like him, and as your friend that is valuable too. However, we have three to see as well as the others on our short short list. Let us see what happens with the last three.'

Only one was vaguely in the frame, so we had realistically a short list now of three.

We left for the mansion at four, still undecided whether to call people back or to make a decision.

Simon went to his part of the mansion. I went to mine, to pick out something to wear for the night. I asked Simon to book a table at FL, which I heard was good.

I went through to find Simon again. 'Mon cher, I cannot decide what to wear. Can you choose for me?'

'So you can impress your old school chum?'

'Oui. Remember, when I last saw him, I was dressed as a school girl. Before that, I was dressed as a boy. Simon, I need to impress him, to look really feminine. Please help me?'

'Of course. But I am telling you, he makes me feel jealous and I am not giving him the job.'

'We'll see. I like him, yes, but I love you. He is the past and you are my future. You are not really jealous?'

'I could be, but no. I know you love me. Let us see what you have in your wardrobe.'

He selected something I had never worn, a cream fine wool dress with V neck and a plunging back. Yes, it was perfect. He pulled shoes and an evening bag from their nests.

'You will have to tape me Simon.'

'Your breasts or your posy?'

'Oh Simon, don't be foolish. Somehow, with this young man who knew me as a boy, I feel the need to prove something. That is all.'

'I know, I understand. I was joking. Come, I will tape your pretty breasts so you look gorgeous.'

When Wally was shown up, we were already dressed. I had put my hair up and was wearing my diamond cuff. Simon had demanded smokey eyes, so there I was looking, actually to use Simon's word, fabulous.

'So this is where you live?'

'No. This is the town house. We spend time at the Chateau in Normandy also.'

'And you are in the fashion industry now?'

'Oh no. I am a medical student. When Simon became ill, I had to take charge, there was really no one else.'

'But I thought he was only your benefactor?'

'Wally, you used to be my confidant at school. Now I will tell you things that are still confidential. Simon and I are married. I am still studying medicine, but Simon has been ill, so I have been looking after things until he is back on his feet. And as his wife, I need to know the business in case, well you never know what might happen. Come, see the children, they are just going to bed.'

I took his hand and led him to what had become the nursery. We found Sophie with everything under control, Sébastien in his cot bouncing and the twins in the bath. I turned and found two pairs of eyes watching me with smiles on their faces, Simon and Wally.

'What?'

They looked at each other, and nodded. 'A natural,' said Wally, as I caressed Sébastien and picked him up. I was so pleased but pretended not to notice. I placed a towel over my shoulder to protect the dress and patted his back. I was eventually rewarded with a burp. I put him down and danced him in the cot.

'Simon, can Sophie come tonight, if Madame Gameau will baby sit? It would be good to have a four and keep her happy too.'

He shrugged, 'Whatever you wish.'

I could not lend her a dress as she was two sizes bigger, but she had a reasonable frock to wear. With the children safely tucked up and Madame sitting watching television, we went to the restaurant. The rain was lashing down again, and not too many people seemed to be out. Café FL was full. Simon had of course been given a splendid table.

We sat and Simon ordered aperitifs. Sophie and I had daiquiris while they drank old fashioneds. I was worried that Simon would overdo it, but he poured half his into Wally's glass.

I asked Sophie about her holiday. She told me something about her home and the small farm they had growing apples and pears outside Strasbourg. Meanwhile I watched as Simon and Wally chatted as though they were old friends. I caught a few words about école, school, and knew they were talking about me. I did not mind. I trusted Wally and I trusted Simon. They could say what they liked.

Simon chose fish, as a starter and as a main, asking me if that was healthy enough. I chose to have a dish from Indo-China. Wally ate steak. Over the coffee, Wally spoke in English so that Sophie would not understand.

'I can hardly believe that you are here, looking so Parisian, so chic Trudi. Simon, you have a remarkable protégée. This girl is one in a million. If you had known her before, then she would actually dazzle you now.'

He started in to tell the tale of my ordeal before the board of Governors. 'She soon had them eating out of her hand Simon. That is how she is.'

'Oh I know. There has been only one person who disliked her, and she is dead. She will make a fine surgeon, I have no doubt. So, what other secrets can you tell me. Let us go to the bar and leave the ladies here.'

'Simon, be careful. Remember.' I say bossily.

'I remember. I have coffee.'

'One cup only Simon, then water.'

Sophie and I chatted about the children and I watched as Simon and Wally talked. I was so pleased they seemed to be getting along. At eleven, I said that we should be going home. Wally took a taxi to his hotel and we three another to the mansion. Next morning we all settled into the Landrover and took off for the Chateau.

On the way Simon and I chatted. 'I like him.' Simon said.

'Wally? I am so pleased. Un homme fidèle. A man you can trust, and he is young and keen. Are you thinking of offering him the position?'

'You want me to?'

'I know him. He is a hard worker and if he says he will do something, then he will. We could depend on him Simon.'

'You can write to him tomorrow and tell him the good news. I think he will do nicely. He can start as soon as it is convenient. I would like him to move to Paris. Perhaps Gérard can find him a flat. We offer him what he earns now plus twenty per cent as a starting salary. And hope he accepts.'

'I'll phone him Simon, if you don't mind?'

'Of course, but you follow it up with a letter. It has to be legal.'

When we reached the Chateau, I phoned Wally.

'Wally, we want you to work for us. The position is yours and I hope you take it. The salary is what you have now, plus twenty per cent, as a starting salary to be reviewed. Of course there are the benefits I think Simon discussed with you, health insurance, a Paris flat, and a car too. He asked me who pays for your Madrid flat? Oh, they do. Can you stay there, when in Madrid? OK, we will pay that too. We want you to agree, but you can have the weekend to think about it. Wally please, say yes. I'll speak to you on Monday. Oh, I am emailing all this to you.'

'I think I am coming on board. Trudi, really nice to meet you again. Just think you are a wonder. I will email after I speak to Isabel.'

I would keep my fingers crossed. I knew he would do the job well if he took it, and it was someone else I could trust. Gradually everything was falling into place in case something happened to Simon. Gérard was my one worry.

Chapter 5.

I received the contract back Saturday morning, signed. Wally was on board and it was a great relief. He phoned mid-morning.

'So Trudi. I gave my notice this morning and was instantly dismissed on a month's severance pay, but with the caveat that I cannot work for a month.'

'Wally I am so glad that you are with us. It will be hard work, but we will look after you. Why don't you come and stay for a week, while you have no work. Bring Isabel. We go to Paris once a week too and that will be a chance for you to see the Maison and what we are doing. Speak to Isabel then give me a ring to talk about when you are coming. Oh, and by the way, I did not select you, I mean it was not my influence. Simon asked me to appoint you. We are both really pleased.'

'No need to ask Isabel, she is here, listening. How about if we come Friday?'

'I just need to look at my diary. No, Wally, we go to the Maison on Thursday and get back Friday evening. Is it possible for you to come Wednesday? How will you come?'

'We can do that. We will fly to Paris, then train, I am not sure where to.'

'Take the train to Chartres and I will meet you there. When you are about to board the train at Charles de Gaulle, phone me and I will drive to Chartres to pick you up.'

'You can do that?'

'Why not? Bien sûr, mon ami. À bientôt.'

It would be interesting to see Isabel. I pictured a small, petite typically Spanish woman, with curly black hair. I would soon see.

Annette and Gérard arrived for the weekend. They had not been since before Simon's heart attack, but I gauged he was now fit enough to have visitors. The warm weather had returned, and we planned a picnic at Arromanches. Sophie readied the children and we packed them into the Land Rover with their toys, and everything else into Gérard's BMW.

The day was fine, a slight breeze across the beach, and far off out in the Channel a few cotton wool clouds floating by. Out in the bay were the relics of war, from the landings of 6th June 1944, nearly seventy years ago. I would want them removed, for they are a reminder that thousands died upon this now peaceful shore, and the lapping waves on that fateful day, foamed pink with the blood of young men. They are meant to remind us of these heroes who gave up life to rid Europe of a terrible tyranny and perhaps the futility of war, but the message seems lost, for we keep volunteering for fresh wars. Old men and their families return to these shores, remember and weep while others shrug.

I could not ponder these sombre thoughts for long, for the twins were already taking off down the beach to the water's edge, Sophie in pursuit. I joined the chase, leaving Simon to gather up little Sébastien. Together, Sophie and I stripped the twins of their bottom layers. We danced the children in the wavelets. We went back to find that Annette and Gérard had selected and arranged our camp, erected the windbreak and spread the waterproof rug. Sophie dressed Adèle while I dressed André in their tiny costumes and we applied lashings of sun block and put their sun hats on. Sophie then attended to Sébastien and he was soon crawling after his brother and sister, to interfere with their efforts at making sand castles. To my surprise, I turned to find Simon too, changed into swimming shorts, his artificial limb bared for all to see, and he was soon digging an ambitious moat round what was to be a castle. I stripped down to my bikini and helped. Annette lay reading, Gérard ambled off to look at the town.

The sun was really hot and I purchased a sun hat at a stall a few hundred metres away. I sat watching Simon and Sophie, engrossed in their castle building, the children doing their best to fill pails with sand to make castle towers. Simon saw me sitting and went to the encampment, pulled a large camera from a bag.

He asked me to pose and positioned me in ten or so different poses, then took photos of the children and all of us, singly and together.

Gérard returned with a bag of ice creams which he issued to us all. We sat eating them, the children with ice creamed faces, Simon giving himself an ice cream nose to amuse them.

We ate lunch, smoked salmon, garlic crevettes, small patties and salad. Simon held Sébastien while he had a bottle, the first time I had seen him do so. I said that Seb needed a nappy change and he should do it. At first he refused, then gave into me. Afterwards he said it was not so bad to do. Actually I think he was quite proud to have done it. I wanted him to interact with his children more. I borrowed the camera and snapped away.

I realised that we were being snapped by a guy in T shirt and jeans who had parked a motor cycle on the promenade. I took no notice until Simon spoke. 'Annette, go and see who that is with the long lens there please. If he is from the press, we invite him to take nice shots rather than bad ones. Bring him down here please.'

Annette did as bidden. She returned with the fellow, a chap in his thirties I supposed. He produced a press card announcing that he was from a British agency. He had been on route to Dieppe when he was tipped off that the Beauvonnes were on the beach.

Simon took him aside with Annette and they looked at what he had taken. Then he was allowed to take new shots, natural poses of the party, particularly of Simon and I and the children, but of the whole party too.

Simon asked him which magazines he would sell to. He named a few, British, French and German. He would let Annette know which ones were publishing.

We packed up at four, before the children became too tired. We would be home just after five, in time for their baths and supper.

The next three days Simon spent much more time with the children, while I rode all one day with Sabine and then alone. She was impressed with my progress, but said I must learn to jump as well as just hack about.

'At least you no longer look like a sack of potatoes,' she said, with a grin.

Wednesday morning I checked that Wally's room was ready. Then I checked with the chef that he was ready for the guests. I found Simon in his study.

'Simon, you need to think what you are going to do with Wally in Paris. Have you?'

'It is all taken care of. Tomorrow he will just have a look, meet people, see the processes. We will give him a diary of the events and schedules of work. I will tell him about the shops abroad, and what he should look out for. When he starts properly, then I will give him a month in the Maison, working in each department and he and I will need to visit in LA and Tokyo. Then he should be able to take that over. In that month we will have the spring show too, so he will see all the panic and excitement.

'Tomorrow perhaps you will, as well as being chauffeur amuse Isabel. We will lunch at Ladurée. Then in the evening, I have booked a box at the opera.'

'Oh Simon, how lovely. What is it?'

'Madame Butterfly, I think it will appeal to you.'

'What about after? Should we go to have a light supper.?'

'I leave that to you to organize Trudi, but of course.'

'Which opera house is it?'

'Palais Garnier. It will take your breath away. I will dress you, for it is very grand and I want you to be even grander.'

'Oh, oui. You have a surprise for me?'

'Wait and see!'

'Palais Garnier is just near home. I will find a restaurant though that is memorable for our visitors, yes?'

'Trudi, you may do what you like, I know we are in good hands.'

I booked Ze Kitchen Galerie, a fusion of East and West. It was over on the left bank but had a good reputation and I had long wished to try it.

A call came from Wally at 3.00. They had arrived at Charles de Gaulle. I set out in the Mercedes. I was casually dressed in a silk shirt and light grey tweed mini skirt, my hair loosely tied in a bun with a leather clip and what looked like a wooden knitting needle. My makeup was done, though not overdone for the country setting. I wanted to give the impression of a young Countess, rather than a model.

I drove the familiar route, finding no traffic until the outskirts of Chartres, but there was no difficulty in reaching the station. I looked at my watch, the train was still ten minutes away. I locked the car and waited on the platform, having checked my appearance. I so wanted Wally to see me at my best.

The train flowed smoothly to a stop. I waited as people pushed by then saw Wally. The girl by his side was dark haired, but her hair was as smooth as silk and shone as only nearly black hair can. She was actually quite beautiful, with slim legs and arms. I walked towards them. Wally stopped before me and dropped the suitcase to the ground. I kissed him on both cheeks and then one for luck. He introduced me to Isabel and I took her hand. It was rather limp and I was instantly disappointed. I kissed her on both cheeks too.

'So good to see you Wally. The car is just outside. Did you have a good journey?

'It was fine. How far do you have to drive?'

'An hour, but this is the best way to come, via Chartres. Anyway, you can see a bit of Normandy as we travel. Have you been to France before Isabel?'

'Oh yes, but not here. To Biarritz and Aix-en-Provence.' Her French was not too bad, a bit guttural.

Wally helped her into the back seat and put the luggage in the boot. He sat beside me. We were soon out of Chartres and lost the traffic. Wally sat half turned towards me. I sensed him looking at my legs. Good. I liked that.

'Trudi, it's a long way from school.'

'A very long way, it has been quite a journey.'

'Do you mind talking about the past?'

'I don't mind with you, because we all have to have a past, and that is mine. Actually, it was a lot of fun. I enjoyed being different. I would rather have been born female, but, well, I had no choice. I presume you have told Isabel all?'

'No, not all. The bare facts. She has just whispered she does not believe me, so that is a compliment to you. And I cannot believe it either.'

'Nor can I Wally. It is all a dream I think. I was so lucky in meeting Simon. Does Isabel know Simon's relationship to me?'

'No. I thought that was confidential.'

'Yes it is. Thank you.'

We drove in silence. For a time, but I still sensed him staring.

'Another fifteen minutes, then we are there.'

'Is it a big house, a farm?'

'We have over three thousand hectares, about seven thousand acres. The house is large, yes. You will see.'

I turned north onto the Rue de la Chateau then left into the drive. As we rounded the shrubs near the gate, the Chateau came into view.

'You weren't kidding were you. How many bedrooms are there?'

'I haven't counted them. Your room is all ready, so I will take you straight up if you can manage the luggage. Then come down for some tea. Dinner will be at eight, so it is a little way off yet. Don't be long, and perhaps, not too much unpacking because we go to Paris tomorrow and stay overnight.'

I showed them into their room. 'I presumed that you would share a room? If not I can ready another.'

'No, it's fine we share, but not at her parents' house.' He grinned.

'Good. I will see you in ten minutes, bottom of the staircase and turn left through the blue and gold doors.'

I went to the kitchen and waited while the chef made tea and put some cakes on a plate. I finished the tray off with plates and forks, cups and saucers. I carried it through.

As I backed through the door of the salon, I saw them descending.

Simon was sitting waiting for us. He rose as I entered and took the tray as though I was too weak to carry it. Wally and Isabel entered and Wally did the introductions. I knelt on the floor and poured tea to their taste.

'Tomorrow,' said Simon, 'Trudi will drive us to Paris and you and I will spend the day at the Maison Wally, while these girls do whatever they want to do. In the evening we are going to the opera, Madame Butterfly, so I hope you have handkerchiefs. It is a dress up occasion, so I hope you have something to wear. Non, oh well, I think we can find a dress for you, Isabel and I daresay I can lend you something Wally. It is at Palais Garnier, very old, very grand, lots of gold leaf and Trudi will look like a princess, so we do not want to let her down.

'On Friday we will spend some more time together at the Maison then return here. I hope that meets with approval.'

'That sounds just wonderful Simon, thank you,' said Wally.

'Ah Trudi, you remember the photographer on Sunday? Well the pictures are now in Paris Match, so you must buy some copies tomorrow.'

'Of course I will, but will Annette not have done that?'

'Oh yes, of course, well just in case. I must remind her about the UK and Germany too. Well I am going to get ready for dinner. We have plenty of time, but I may just have a short rest or read. I will see you all later.'

'How is he?' Wally asked when Simon had closed the door.

'He is getting there. It has taken a time, but I think the old Simon is coming back.'

'So what brought this on?'

'He was put under a great strain by his wife. There were rows and he was working very hard also. He devoted all his time to promoting Beauvonne around the World, but did not really have the support in place here. Then Catherine died, fell down these stairs, and died on the way to hospital. At the same time, he crashed on the way to the chalet in Courchevel, where he was going to escape all this. They had to cut off his leg, actually in the car to get him out and because it had gangrene. He was in a coma for five days. I sat by him all that time. After that,' I nearly broke down remembering, 'after that, he was accused of causing Catherine's death. Luckily, it was proved by his mobile phone that he was over one hundred miles away. So I do not find it surprising that he had a heart attack.'

'So you picked up the pieces?'

'I had to. His cousin Gérard was not really earning his keep, so I gave him a proper job, as office manager, leaving the designers free to design. Our PR, Annette had to sharpen up. You are the next step, Wally. But here too, I have put his niece to work as estate manager. Sabine has been to agricultural college and has a degree. She grew up on her father's farm, but he will not let her do anything. So she now manages the estate and has big, revolutionary ideas of how to make profit from this. Yes it made a profit but it was small and the place is untidy. I expect big things.'

'So you made all these appointments?'

'Yes, until you. That was really both of us. It was good that I knew you and invited you to go to dinner. He liked you. That is the truth. I have gathered about us people who I trust and to take the pressure off Simon. There are now three people doing what he did. I will go back to being a medical student in September, and live in Paris most of the time having I hope, put the business on a better footing. We hope for big things from you, but you have to balance effort with relaxation Wally.'

'So, you are not Wally's boss?' Isabel spoke English slowly.

'Oh no. I have just been here for Simon, while he was ill, but everyday now he gets stronger. When we return from Paris, I will show you round the estate, and we can go to the beaches, perhaps.'

'My grandfather died near Caen,' Wally said, 'I would quite like to see his grave.'

'Of course. If we go to one of the British cemeteries, they have a list of all the graves and where they are.

'Isabel, I don't think you will have a dress for the opera tomorrow. You must be a size smaller than me. So we must remind Simon to find something. He will find you a dress suit also Wally.

'Now I must go and help put the children to bed. Do you want to come or perhaps you would like to go to your room and freshen up?'

'We'll come and see the children.'

We found the children at play after their tea. It was therefore bath time, and while I bathed Sébastien, they and Sophie played with the twins.

I dried Sébastien and we watched while Sophie put the twins into the bath. Wally thought he would help and the twins thought they would splash him. He retired before he was soaked. I got Sébastien settled, then helped Sophie.

We sang Frere Jacques, which we had been teaching them.

I kissed them all goodnight and left them to Sophie.

I quickly changed and went into Simon. He was relaxed on his bed, reading.

'Are you OK Chéri? I ask.

'Oh yes. I am fine. I was just thinking about tomorrow, mapping out what I am going to show Wally. And you, what will you do with Isabel?'

'I don't know. Simon, we need to lend or give her a dress for the opera. Have we something here or at the Maison?'

'After dinner, I take her to the archive. Do you remember when I took you there all those years ago? When we first met. I gave you a green dress to put on.'

'I remember. I was so in awe of you. I was a little girl then and you were so grand.'

'And now you are managing everything. What would I have done without you?'

'Perhaps I have brought this on you. If you had not had me to think about, then you might have been happy with Catherine.'

'No. Do not think that. Why do you think Catherine brought Francoise here as nanny for the children?'

'Because she was an old friend?

'No, because she was an old lover. If you had not been in the background, I would have looked elsewhere for what I was not getting from her, The result would have been the same.'

'Simon, what happened that day, the day of your accident, the day she died.'

'You are so astute my Trudi. Life was intolerable. You can imagine how we spent the evenings here, those two kissing in front of me. When I protested, she would immediately threaten divorce, threaten to drag our names through the court and boasted that they would take the children too, as well as the Chateau. I don't think they could take the children nor the Chateau, but the whole atmosphere was intolerable.

'I decided to go to the chalet to escape. She threatened me, saying she had all the photos of us and some letters. Gérard and I cooked up this plan. Francoise and the children were going to the doctor. Catherine, going to have her hair done. It was a golden opportunity with the staff off, to take all her 'evidence' and her jewellery to make it look like a robbery. Gérard took my car, leaving me his. I left the Chateau and when I heard Catherine's car, I went back and took everything. They phoned her in her car to cancel the appointment and she came back.

'I was caught in the act, on the landing. She was like a tigress. We fought, I struggled free. She ran after me. I was half way down the stairs. I heard her fall but I did not look back. I did not see what happened, only a cry like a banshee from behind me. I ran through the forest and got in Gerard's car and drove like fury.'

'And when I phoned, I spoke not to you, but to Gérard. I knew it was him. And my phone call and another from New York, established your alibi. Why did you not tell me this?'

'Because I did not want to involve you in something so dreadful.'

I stayed silent. I was thinking. If he knew she fell, and he still didn't look back. I tried to put myself in that position. He was halfway through a plan, trapped by it. I did not know what I would have done, under that pressure, in those circumstances. I loved him. I could not judge him.

I kissed him. 'Thank you for telling me. Come, we must go down to dinner. Don't think anymore about this. I love you Simon. You did what you had to do. It was bad luck that she came back.'

'It is another reason for me to be indebted to you. I think I have paid dearly for marrying her.'

'I think so too. Cette salope! (That bitch).' I spit the word out.

Chapter 6.

Next morning, I roused the house at six. We were all in my Mercedes by seven thirty, having had to wait ten minutes for Isabel. It was annoying and I was fairly silent on the drive, as a result. Simon sat in the back with Isabel and Wally in the front beside me.

After about seventy-five miles of my monosyllabic replies, Wally chuckled. I looked to see what he was laughing about. He was smiling at me.

'Qu'est-ce que?'

'You Trudi. No longer meek and malleable. Une femme formidable. You do not like to be crossed, do you?'

'It's over. No, you know I am a stickler for time keeping, even if it is not essential. But OK Wally. You are right, I am no longer the little shy girl.'

'You were never shy.'

'Oh yes I was. Inside I was jelly, but you know at school, if others see a weakness, they will play upon it. You remember that evening, the first evening when I appeared in the refectory as a girl. Was I cool?'

'I'd say. We didn't know how you could do that. We all said amongst ourselves. To suddenly appear as a girl amongst a lot of silly boys? That took guts. Yet you did not even blush. I would have wanted to hide.'

'Inside I was jelly. It was my self-belief, in me, as a girl, and the euphoria of at last being the person I wanted to be, rather than pretending to be a boy, that carried me through. Even now, at times I am still shaky. I know you, I know Simon. Isabel, knows about me, but I do not know her. I feel at a disadvantage. I hope to get to know her today.'

'What are you going to show her?'

'I don't know. What she wants. Tour Eiffel, I hate it, the crowds and the height. It makes me giddy, but if she wants, and everyone should once. Or Musée d'Orsay, Louvre, Centre George Pompidou, Notre Dame, Montmartre and Sacré Coeur. We lunch together at Ladurée on the Champs, so we will have to taxi about. And Simon has to find a dress for Isabel for tonight, we must not forget, because my dresses will fall off her she is so petite.'

Wally took my hand and looked at my varnished nails. 'Still can't believe you. You were an interesting chrysalis but a beautiful butterfly.'

'Thank you Wally. That is the nicest thing to say. You are my second favourite man. It is great to have you here. I am so pleased.'

We enter Paris and cross the Pèriphérique and then straight to the Arc de Triomphe. I park at the rear of the Maison in Simon's space.

'Simon, une robe pour Isabel, premier, oui?'

We go to the salon, and Simon asks them to find Isabel a dress. He dictates the colour and the length, for he alone knows what I am wearing. They find her a burgundy dress, slim fitting, one shoulder and reaching to the floor. It is a good fit, largely because the back is a stretchy material. She is overwhelmed. I see a tear appear in the corner of her eye and Wally gives her a quick cuddle and a peck on the lips.

That done, the men depart. I suggest we go to the d'Orsay, my favourite, because it has all the Impressionists, including two Van Gough self-portraits. We can return to climb the Arc if we have time before lunch as the restaurant is close by. Our lunch table will be large, we four and the designers and the senior dress makers and Annette and Gérard. Simon has also asked Annette to have the press there, so they can advertise the appointment of Wally.

Isabel and I head off and enter the Orsay easily. There is so much to see, and sometimes a painting will interest one so much, that one just sits and considers. Such a one was La Toilet, the rear view of a nude woman looking in a full length mirror. I sit and stare. It is unremarkable, yet it fascinates. Isabel is overawed by Millet. We find we have some favourites in common.

We taxi to the Arc and have time to climb to the top behind a fat American, loaded down with three cameras. We smile at each other behind his huge arse. From the top we can see in every direction, La Défense, Sacré Coeur, Notre Dame way down beyond the Champs Élysée and the Tuilleries, and the Eiffel. We come down and stroll to Ladurée. We are first. We freshen up and are shown to our table. Simon and his party troop in. There is lots of kissing and hand shaking, and Simon arranges the table, me at one end and he at the other, Wally on his right and Isabel on his left. I have Gérard and Annette next to me. Simon is in an expansive mood, the, most lively I have seen him for months. We eat different dishes.

The press turn up and they take lots of photos, then we pose in different numbers. I hold back, because I am really not part of the party but Simon insists that I come in to pose with him and Wally.

It is after three by the time we are finished and we split up. Isabel and I go to Sacré Coeur, see the dim interior and stand on the spot from which Hitler surveyed the conquered city. We take tea at L'Eté en Pente Douce, just down the hill from the Basilica.

We arrive home at six and Simon and Wally arrive just afterwards, with parcels.

I tell Isabel that if she needs anything, she must ask. I show her my apartment and tell her she can use anything from my wardrobe.

Simon came through to my bedroom. 'Here is your dress. Opera Garnier, is full of gold leaf, so you have a silver dress. I would like you to put your hair up if you will. I have brought your diamonds too and the diamond headdress. You will look like a goddess among earthlings. I shall be so proud.'

'Do you not think this too ostentatious, Simon?'

'When you see Opera Garnier, you will see ostentation. And you are representing Maison Beauvonne. When you are ready, I will help with the dress. You will be the most beautiful woman among all.'

I showered and did my hair, piling it up in a knot. I made my face, knowing that he would want smokey eyes, but I put a bright blue eyeliner on my bottom lids, to emphasise the colour of my eyes.

Dressed only in panties, I called Simon.

'Let me see your posy.' He said, his eyes twinkling.

'I think you are feeling better,' I replied then dutifully lowered my panties.

He chuckled. 'So delightful. I think you should go just as you are. Everyone would be so envious. However, we don't want to be arrested. So the dress.' He held it for me to step in. It was a heavy fabric of silver thread. I wriggled in and he pulled it up to my mid riff. He taped my breasts skilfully, double sided tape to my rib cage, then pulled up the boned front and fastened the one shoulder piece. He knelt and put my silver platforms on, then my jewellery. Finally he wound the diamond string around my piled knot of hair.

Only then would he let me look in the mirror. My appearance was so far removed from student medicine Trudi Nash, that it took my breath away.

'Good eh!,' he chuckled. 'We see what your friend Wally says when he sees you, oh and little Isabel.'

We entered the salon and found them waiting.

Wally did one of his double takes. 'Wow, who *are* you?'

I laughed. 'It amuses Simon to make me his doll, to dress me up. But there is a purpose, I represent Maison Beauvonne, so exotic haute couture is what he likes me to wear. At least he is not making me wear a cage on my head as was popular four or five years ago on the runway.

'Isabel, you look charming. That colour really likes you. Have you everything? By the way, the opera is very sad, so you need a handkerchief or two. Have you a handkerchief Wally or perhaps you won't cry?'

'I don't think I will cry, but here,' he produced a hankie. 'I feel like crying when I think back five years, and remember. They should see you now.'

'Perhaps I will go back to school and give a talk. That might be fun.'

Jerome drove us in Simon's limo, even though it was only a few hundred yards. He would pick us up afterwards and whisk us to the left bank for dinner.

Palais Garnier was so Phantom of the Opera, and when I said so to Simon, he told me that the play was modelled on this theatre. I had the sudden thought that Simon was the Phantom to my Christine. Somehow I did not mind. We met Annette and Gérard in the foyer with lots of kissing. How I loved this ostentatious affection. We turned heads, which was what we were supposed to do. A photographer snapped us, and we were on our way to the box, Simon holding my arm while I held the heavy skirt above my toes.

In the box, expensive chocolates appeared. I tried to resist, but they were delicious. I sipped a glass of champagne for it was going to be a long night. When the lights dimmed and the opera opened with Pinkerton marrying his fifteen year old bride, Simon reached for my hand and held it tight. He raised it to his lips, savoured my perfume and kissed it. I felt myself dampen. Here before me was an older man seducing a young girl for his own amusement while far away on a foreign shore. But there was no parallel here. I knew that Simon simply adored me, and I adored him. It was so good to have my Simon back. I placed our hands upon his firm thigh.

I saw Wally was watching us, but he was also holding Isabel's hand.

In the interval, we ladies went to the toilet. Isabel was full of it, excited and smiling more than I had seen her do. I was pleased that at last she was coming out of her shell. I was beginning to see what Wally saw in her.

The last act took place. Poor Ciocio gave up her baby to Pinkerton and his new American wife, then took her life. I did cry, even though the whole extravagant production was faintly absurd. I noticed Wally comforting Isabel too.

Outside the night was dry, fine and warm. I let my white faux fur stole slip and carried it in one hand. We were whisked off to Ze Kitchen Galerie. I chose Thai broth, followed by roasted Guinea fowl, followed at length by ginger icecream with a chocolate sauce. We all enjoyed the Michelin star food.

I was very tired when we reached home. Simon helped peel the tape from my skin. I removed my makeup and fell asleep in his arms. I so loved this sensuous

Frenchman with his whims and demands. I loved being his plaything. I had an erotic dream.

Chapter 7.

In the morning, Wally and Simon were again at the Maison. Isabel wanted to go to the Louvre, so we walked down to the Seine. We passed the morning there easily. Isabel made sketches of some paintings while I wandered, feeling I was wasting time. I would rather have been at the Chateau or even in the hospital.

We found Simon and Wally at the Maison. Simon had ordered in some light snacks for lunch. Afterwards I drove us all to the mansion where we picked up our luggage before heading out to the Chateau. I almost breathed a sigh of relief when I turned into the drive.

I told Wally that I would see them before dinner. I flew upstairs to the nursery. I needed to reassure myself that Sophie and the children were well. I felt neglectful of them. I don't know what had brought this feeling of insecurity on, or why I felt so tired of company. All was well. The children were eating tea, and Sophie seemed happy.

I went to my room. On a whim I changed into riding gear, descended the back stairs and out into the stables. I saddled Sheba and set off across the estate. Coming to the forest drive, we cantered along. Sheba was skittish, having not been ridden for several days. I turned and rode the other drive which quartered the forest, then trotted along an estate road which ran the length of the North side. I decided to see what Sabine had done with her lake site and turned that way, the track running through an end of the forest until it emerged near the river.

As I exited the forest, a pheasant rose in front of Sheba's feet. She reared in fright, flinging me from the saddle, my right foot still caught in the stirrup. In alarm, her eyes white with terror, Sheba turned to look at me and took off. Then my world blacked out.

When I came to, I was in a vehicle. I passed out again. The next I remember, I was being placed in a bed. A pain shot through me from my collar bone, and it must have been that that brought me round. My head ached and so did my right thigh. I saw Simon looking at me and tried to raise my head, but pain made me gasp again.

'Trudi, do you know who I am?'

'Of course Simon. What question is that? Where am I and why do I hurt?'

'You fell off Sheba. We didn't find you for three hours. Now you are safe in hospital, but you have a fractured skull and cheek bone as well as a collar bone. You have to lie still.'

'Sheba, is she all right?'

'She is safe. Sabine caught her and looked after her.'

'I am sorry Simon.'

'No Trudi mon amour. Everything is all right. You just have to get well. Everyone sends their love. I have to return to the Chateau to look after your Wally, who also sends his love, and I will see you tomorrow. Now you have to be good and rest and do what the doctors tell you. I would kiss you, but I am not to, with your injuries. They say that you will mend completely, but you have to take care. Now I am going.' He kissed my hand and was gone.

I went to sleep. I woke several times in the night. I remembered a nurse looking at me, but the rest was a blur, except for the pain.

Morning came. I watched the dawn develop, but fell asleep again. Noises woke me and I realised that there was someone in the room. The nurse informed me that I had a catheter and she was changing the bottle that collected my urine. She also told me that the canula in my wrist would probably be removed later. Meanwhile she replaced the bag feeding plasma into me.

I was alone again, and dozed. I was woken by a nurse who brought a jug of water and a glass. I was to drink a glass full every hour to protect my kidneys.

Simon appeared. He held my hand and spoke softly to me. 'We are taking you home tomorrow. Have you seen your face? You have a black eye, but the doctor says that there will be no lasting injury. Thank god.'

'And Sheba?'

'She is OK. I think I will sell her. Arabs are too high spirited.'

'No Simon. I forbid it. It was not her fault. I love her. I forbid you to sell.'

'Why did you take off like that, without saying anything. What made you do it?'

'I don't know. I just felt trapped. I am twenty-two, yet I am having to behave as though I am ten years older. I am a student, I should be having fun, yet I have had to look after you, through two crises, and run and reorganise your business and the estate. I just needed to get away for a short time, to let go, to let off steam.'

'I thought you enjoyed taking charge?'

'I did, I do Simon. I enjoy everything about Beauvonne. I love it as I love you and the children. Somehow, on the way home, I just felt so trapped. And I confess, I find Isobel difficult. I think she dislikes me, because, you know, my past.

'Sometimes, I would just like to go to a club with a young girl friend, drink something disgusting and dance.

The sort of thing I would have done had I gone to Cambridge to study.'

'Oh Trudi, I did not understand you felt like this. I am sorry.'

'No don't be sorry. You have given me everything, including your love. And I love my life with you. I suppose I was having a sort of breakdown, trying to shake off all the responsibility. *I* am sorry.'

'But you regret having to do all this?'

'No Simon. Je ne regrette rien, like Édith Piaf, but it has just been too much in too short a time. I feel worn out. I have to get back to being a medical student, but I also want to be your wife and lover as well as mother to the children. I cannot run your business and the estate too. I have let you down.'

'No, never could anyone have done all you have done for me. No Trudi. It will be better now. We have Wally, Annette is doing good work, even Gérard. And Sabine has great plans. You laid the foundations. I am now so much better, you can relax and be what you want to be, anything as long as you remain my lover and love the children.'

'That is easy. Now Simon, je suis fatigué. I must rest.' He held my hand. I never saw him go. When I next woke, it was I saw by my watch, nearly five in the afternoon.

The next day the doctor said I could get up and walk about. If I had no headache, I could go home, but first they would scan my skull. They pronounced me fit enough to travel, but no riding, no violent exercise and if I had any headaches or blurred vision, dizziness or nausea, to return immediately. I phoned Simon and he left to pick me up. I looked a mess, my face swollen and blue turning a nasty shade of green.

To my surprise Simon arrived with Wally and Isabel. Simon insisted on taking me to the car in a wheel chair. A TV camera was at the door as well as a few photographers. Was I that famous? I waved to them and we moved on. I could imagine the headlines, 'Beauvonne Another Tragedy', 'The Curse of Beauvonne'. No doubt Annette was not missing an opportunity. Well that was fair enough.

'I will phone my parents tonight and tell them,' I told Simon as we sat in the car while Wally drove.

'I already have, but I am sure they will like to hear your voice.'

'That was thoughtful of you Simon. I will email everyone else. How are the children?'

'They are fine, but you can't play with them yet, just in case they hit your face, and you can't lift them with your arm in a sling. Nor can we make love.'

'And my Sheba?'

'She is safe. Do not worry. I would not dare send her away.'

'Thank you Simon.'

'I have a surprise for you, at home, well two surprises.'

'What?'

'It is a surprise. You have to be patient.'

Wally and Simon helped me into the Chateau. They took me into the salon and sat me down. A box was produced, done up in a red ribbon. I pulled the end and undid the knot. Inside I found a kitten, a beautiful tortoishell, white, ginger and black. It was tiny. I lifted it and kissed its head.

'You said you would like a cat, so there is a cat. Sophie will look after it in the week.'

Isabel entered with a dog on a lead. It had a brown and white hairy face and a black saddle. It's face was alert and it made straight for the kitten sitting in my hands. It sniffed the kitten and wagged its tail.

'I thought you might like some little friends. The kitten has no name, but the dog answers to Tasha.' The terrier immediately pricked up her ears and wagged her tail. 'Of course the kitten will have to stay here, but you can take Tasha to Paris. Madame Gameau will look after her in the day. It is my get well present.'

'Thank you Simon. They are lovely. I'm sorry everybody, but I think I have to go to bed. Can I have them in my room please?'

'Of course. I will arrange it while you get ready.'

I lay in my bath, relaxing in the warm scented water. I felt weak and tired.

Simon came in and helped me out of the bath. Tasha was behind him and followed by the kitten.

'Mitzi,' I said, 'the kitten's name is Mitzi. She is bold.'

Simon caressed my body with the towel and helped me into pyjamas, easier to get on with my broken shoulder than a nightdress.

Simon tucked me into bed. Gently kissed my forehead and sent Tasha to her basket which had been placed beside the bed. I put the light out. I could hear the kitten moving about and chattering. I fell asleep.

When I awoke, I could tell it was well after dawn. I looked at my watch and found it was eight o'clock. I had slept for thirteen hours. I looked but there were no animals in the room. I slipped out of the bed carefully. I managed to shower in a fashion. I set about dressing myself. I could not wear a brassiere, it hurt too much. I managed to dress in my favourite cream silk shirt and grey slacks. I put on my sling.

I examined my face. It all seemed to be in the right place. The swelling looked less than yesterday. And the last of the black was turning a horrible shade of yellow. There was nothing I could do with make up to improve it. I would just have to suffer the indignity. It would be the first morning for over five years that I had not done my face.

I dried and straightened my hair as best I could, my collarbone hurting with each movement. I combed it across the damaged side of my face. I walked down the stairs and found everyone in the salon.

'Bon jour,' I said brightly. 'what are we doing today?'

'Ma Chérie. First you eat breakfast. We have waited for you. Now come.'

'Where are my animals, Tasha and Mitzi?'

'They have just gone to the kitchen to have their food. I will fetch them. Now, today a proper breakfast, an English 'all day', with bacon, egg, sauté potatoes, sausage, tomato and mushroom. You have hardly eaten for four days. That is not good. Then we thought to drive to find Wally's grandfather's grave if you feel well enough.

'Of course. I can take Tasha too.'

The breakfast was gorgeous. I realised I was really hungry. I had seconds of bacon, even though it hurt to chew, and finished the potatoes and mushrooms.

'Feeling better?' Wally asked sardonically.

'I was hungry. How soon do we go?'

'In half an hour, we should all be ready,' Simon said.

I went to the kitchen. I found Tasha in her basket and Mitzi cuddled up with her. It was perfect. Tasha was licking the kitten clean.

I attached Tasha's lead and we went upstairs. I put on sensible walking shoes and found a coat. I looked at my face. I tried doing things with a chiffon scarf. Nothing seemed to work. There was no disguising that my face was a mess. I tried hats. In the end I selected a wide brimmed navy straw, ripped net from another hat and applied it to the straw with nail glue. It was not too bad. A navy bag completed the outfit. Tasha and I descended to the vestibule, and as there was no one there, we went out to the car. The air was already warm, the sun high in the cloudless sky. The others came out.

'We were waiting in the salon Trudi,' Simon said.

'I needed some fresh air. Simon, can we go via the estate office. I would like to invite Sabine to dinner tonight.'

'Anything Trudi.'

'I want to thank her for finding Sheba, and I want to hear how her plans are going.'

I found Sabine in the office. 'I want you to come to dinner Sabine, tonight, if you are free.'

'Where else would I go. You are OK?'

'I will be. So, see you tonight, my friend and you can tell me how things are going.'

Simon drove us to Caen, where I had been in hospital. We stopped at the first cemetery we came to, Saint Charles de Percy. We waited as Wally looked at the records. His grandfather was in Ranville Cemetery which was between Caen and the coast.

We found the cemetery close to the Church. It was enormous. Wally found the grave easily from the records. His grandfather had been a sergeant in the Parachute regiment. There were hundreds of white crosses.

Wally knelt at the grave. I saw him praying and when he rose, I could see tears. Isabel remained apart. I felt tears rising too.

I turned and left the cemetery. I saw no purpose in sorrowing over what had happened seventy years ago, however dreadful. For Wally it was real, but not for me. It was all terrible, hundreds of thousands dying for the decisions of a handful of aggressive dominant men. It was despicable. We should hang the leaders and save the thousands I thought.

I returned to the car and released Tasha. We walked round the church and down the lane. I heard a car coming and stooped to pull Tasha behind me. I could not pick her up. Instead I bent down with a grimace of pain. She climbed upon my knee. I saw it was Simon.

'Trudi, what are you doing? I was so worried when I found you gone.'

I entered the car, taking Tasha on my knee. I struggled with the belt and Wally leaned over and helped me. I thanked him.

'I have seen all that death and destruction, young men's lives thrown away by too powerful men. I could not stand it. It was only fair to take Tasha for a little walk.'

'In a few moments, she can run on the beach.'

'Oh no, I will not release her. She does not know us well enough yet. No, we will walk with her Simon.'

We all walked the beach at Arromanches. I could see that Wally was absorbed with his thoughts of the war, and all those soldiers landing on this beach, thinking about those events of June 1944. I was also affected. One could not see films like 'Saving Private Ryan', or the series 'Band of Brothers', without knowing what took place and how hellish it was.

I wanted to run with Tasha, but my collar bone hurt and a sudden movement also made my face throb. I knew I had to be patient. Simon took my hand as we walked the almost deserted beach. Wally and Isabel lagged behind, deep in conversation. Tasha pulled at her leash, wanting to run, excited by sea birds.

'So my wife, dear Trudi, how are you today?'

'Sore. I ache. My upper thigh is blue. My collar bone hurts unless I am very careful. And my face!'

'The sling helps?'

'Yes. The doctor said they may give me a different one when I go back next week. I don't think I will be modelling this autumn.'

'No, certainly not but by next year. And it is very good publicity.'

I looked at him and saw he was laughing. I smiled back.

'Why did I not think of that.'

'We are all over the papers today. A page of us at lunch, showing Wally joining us and then a page of you before and after, coming out of hospital. Then a lot about the curse of Beauvonne. Also, a British TV company wants to do a documentary piece on you. You need to think carefully about it. Only do it if you want to and we have to make sure that we retain the editorial rights, meaning that it says what we want it to, concentrating on the heroic side, of overcoming adversity, not oooh a transsexual woman!'

'How long have you known about this?'

'From after your accident. That is what triggered the interest. What is your feeling?'

'My first instinct is to say no. I need to think about it. It could be a can of worms. On the other hand, if I control what goes out, it might be good, even inspirational, like the Paralympic games. I don't know Simon. I value my privacy. What do you think?'

'I also think it could be inspirational, but our privacy is involved. I leave it to you.'

'No Simon, it concerns you. Yes no one knows we are married but they will next year and then they will dig everything up. Oh, but then they are going to anyway, aren't they?'

'Yes, they will.'

'Simon, will you mind everyone knowing you have married a transsexual? You have to be truthful, because this really matters. For me, I think I have always been female, but with the wrong bits, but other people will not think that. I know people. This sex thing goes so deep within people's psyche and understanding. People even get annoyed if their pets are called by the wrong gender. It runs that deep. Even Wally sometimes.......and I feel Isabel does not look at me as a woman. Wally of course remembers me as a boy, Isabel has only heard about my past, yet what she sees, the princess at the opera, does not mean as much as my birth as a boy.'

'Is that why you ran away on Sheba?'

'Oui, yes, I think that was something to do with it. And everything had just got too much. I don't like Isabel, I find her moody. I tried to amuse her but received no thanks. It is impolite. My birth is something I can never live down, and when it is known we have married, something you can never live down either. That is why so many transsexuals are not 'out'. They keep their past a secret because the revelation changes perception. I can be as feminine as the most feminine woman, but that past will always follow me.'

'Trudi, you know what I think of you. I don't care what others think. You look like a woman. You think, god help me, like a woman and act like one. I have enough money not to care. If Maison Beauvonne collapsed tomorrow, I could sit on this estate and survive. I have three healthy children and a beautiful wife. Now do you think you can bear to be kissed?'

'I think so, if you are gentle, my husband.'

We stopped and he held my head gently in both hands. 'Never doubt that I love you,' he said, and kissed me gently on the lips.

Wally and Isabel had caught us up. Wally was all smiles, but Isabel seemed out of sorts.

We turned back. 'I think we need some lunch Wally. There is a little place here which I think you will like.' Simon said.

We ambled back to our starting point and onto the land. We were soon at Le Celina. It was an uninspiring exterior, it might have been a seaside restaurant anywhere. The proprietor soon found us a table and welcomed Tasha too.

'What do you recommend then Simon?' Wally asked.

'I think lobster for me. And Trudi?'

'Oui mon cher.'

'Sounds good to me.' Wally turned to Isabel, 'Do you know what you would like or do you want Trudi to translate.'

'Would you like to have fish or meat Isabel?' I ask, helpfully.

'Oh I don't know.'

'Very well.' I translated everything, dish by dish into English and Wally translated into Spanish. Finally, she decided on a rare steak and salad. The food arrived and it was surprisingly good. The lobster arrived in two ways, half as thermidor and the other half in a tomato and brandy sauce. The steak for Isabel was large, she pecked at it, but said it was good.

On the way home, we drove through Caen, scene of a long three month siege after D Day. Most of the ancient city had been destroyed, Simon told us, which did not make the British very popular there. What was the alternative? In the end the American breakthrough threatened the city from the south and the Germans were forced to escape or surrender.

'So Wally, tomorrow is your last day with us. Is there anything you want to do or see?'

'Well, the Musée des Beaux Arts in Caen and of course, The Bayeux Tapestry, I think Isabel would certainly be interested in them.'

'That sounds a good plan. And I think Trudi will like it too?'

'Oh yes. That will be nice.'

We arrived home at four and took tea in the salon. I walked round to the office to see Sabine, Tasha running along beside me.

She was busy on the computer. Her face lit up when she saw me. 'Ma chère Trudi. Comment ça va?'

'Oh fine. I'll be glad when we are alone again. I like Wally a lot but Isabel........ Anyway, I just want to make sure you are coming to dinner tonight.'

'Of course. So are you starting to feel better?'

'Yes thank you. By the time I go back to Uni, I will be fine.'

'Well, do not feel bad about falling off Sheba. We all fall off and if a pheasant gets up from under the horses feet, anything can happen. You just have to get on again as soon as you are well.' She fondled Tasha's ears. 'Keep this beast away from my sheep, won't you.'

'Of course. I think I need to introduce her to them, teach her not to chase them. How is the work going?'

'Do not worry Trudi. All is under control. Simon has given permission to sell the machinery as soon as harvest is over and I have appointed a contractor for next year. Now you run along and don't worry. I see you tonight.

I spent the next hour and a half with the children. I looked forward to spending more time with them in the future.

I showered and changed with Simon's help, ready for dinner.

Chapter 8.

Dinner was quite merry. Isabel was much more affable and actually tried to tell a Spanish joke. It did not work in translation, but we laughed dutifully. Sabine was her usual self, poking fun at me in her sisterly way. Her father was she said, surprised and jealous at the turn of events that had given her this job. Now she had a feeling of self worth that had been missing. I was so glad that I had given her this task and that Simon had concurred.

The meal was my favourite, duck, with a plum sauce. We started with a leek and potato soup and country bread and finished with chocolate and ginger ice cream. After coffee, Simon insisted that I go to bed. I went to my room, taking the animals with me and a cat tray for the kitten and also some food that was placed inside a wooden fruit box with a small door cut in, so that Tasha did not wolf it down. I watched them settle down in the basket together, then extinguished the bedside lamp and went to sleep feeling much happier.

I awoke to find Mitzi nuzzling around my face, purring merrily. I turned carefully. And she sat on my chest as I stroked her rough kitten fur. The bedside clock showed seven-thirty. I decided to bath and carefully pushed back the covers, Mitzi climbing over them to get to me. I extricated myself and ran a deep hot bath with oils and salts. Simon found me and insisted on gently washing me, much to my delight. I giggled as he washed my clit. He kissed my hair. I wanted him then, but in my condition it was impossible. He raised me out of the water, so gently, then towelled me, applied deodorant, and combed my hair and through. Kneeling he kissed my posy and tongued me, gripping the cheeks of my bottom in his strong hands. I moaned and caressed his head.

'Come,' he said, 'time to get ready. I give you two more days, then we find a way to make love. I need it and so do you.'

When we entered the salon, our guests and Sophie were already there. Simon fetched champagne, a magnum.

'I propose a toast. To the newest members of the Beauvonne household, Wally and Sabine.' We drank.

'I would like to propose a toast,' Wally said, 'To my dearest and oldest friend, Trudi and a quick recovery and revival of your spirits. And to Simon for bringing me aboard.'

By the time we had finished the meal, we were all very merry. I suffered quite a lot of joshing from Wally and Sabine. Sophie remained respectful and protested amiably over some of their taunts on horsemanship.

Sabine grew serious. 'You are quite right Sophie. This girl, my friend Trudi, learnt riding more quickly than anyone I have known. The accident could not be avoided, certainly by someone as new to riding as she. I propose a toast to the first lady of Beauvonne, who has carried it on her back while Simon was ill. It was a great feat to do.'

Simon gave a big here,here, as they all did. Throughout the meal though, Isabel had remained fairly mute, answering Simon's questions about her life as briefly as possible. I wondered whether her diffidence was shyness or, she just could not be bothered.

'What time is your flight on Wednesday Wally?'

'Sixteen forty, so working backwards, we ought to leave here about eleven.'

'Simon, I will drive them to Chartres. Do you want to come?'

'Of course. I could not let you drive all that way alone as you are. Then next day, we go to Paris and we take the children and you too Sophie. We will stay over the weekend. Sabine too, come Friday night. I would like you three girls to go out on Saturday night, there is a concert and I can get tickets. I will baby sit. It is time I did more with the children.'

'Sabine, say you will come, please.' I say.

'I would love to. What is the concert Simon?'

'Someone called Ed Sheeran. He is English, but they say he is quite good.'

'Simon, he is brilliant. Thank you.'

I looked at Wally. He seemed amused again. I gave a quizzical look. He just shook his head.

'If you will excuse me, I just want to walk Tasha round the Chateau before bed.' I left the table and collected Tasha, exiting via the kitchen. We walked around the Chateau. I was surprised to find Wally on the terrace.

'What are you doing here?' I ask.

'Waiting for my old friend. Hardly had a chance to speak to you alone. Wanted to say, well,' he stopped suddenly less than his normal confident self. 'I knew you as the shrimp of a boy playing rugby. People like me would pick you up and fling you out of the scrum. But you always had guts, more than a good number of chaps. That hasn't changed. You've still got more guts than most.

'As far as the rest is concerned, your persona, your look, everything, you are every inch a lady. Sometimes you have caught me smiling and you frowned. I was smiling because, there is no trace of the gauche small boy. I cannot believe what my eyes tell me. Thanks for bringing me aboard the good ship Beauvonne. I know you did have some influence there. I shall move to Paris within three weeks. Isabel will not. I asked her to but she has refused. Funnily enough, I am not that upset.'

'Oh Wally. I am sorry.'

'No, it doesn't matter. Anyway we are both too young to settle down. And if I am travelling the World, what would she do? I am looking forward to this new challenge. But most of all, I want to say this, if I can ever be a support to you, no matter what, confidant, shoulder to cry on, I will be there.'

'Thank you Wally.' I kissed him on the cheeks then the lips. He did not flinch away.

He took my hand, 'We better go in.' He said.

Chapter 9.

As we went to bed, I told Simon what Wally had said.

'Well that will please you,' he replied.

'What?'

'That he is leaving Isabel in Madrid.'

'Not if it broke Wally's heart. I have not taken to her it is true, partly because she is so diffident, I cannot get near her. She says little, I say something and nothing comes back. That is the only reason. I am not happy but, more relieved. I find her difficult.

'No, I am pleased with how he sees me. I was wrong, thinking that he was laughing at me. He was just bemused, trying to marry up what I was and what I am. He is still a good friend.'

Simon patted my bottom. He had never done that before. I didn't know what it meant.

'Cuddle me, Simon. I love you. Good night darling husband.'

I was asleep almost immediately, his arm wrapped around my midriff. So comforting. So possessing.

I awoke late. There were no pets and no husband. I felt bereft. I rose quickly and showered and dressed. Things were getting easier. Positions of my limbs that had hurt three days ago, no longer did. I was on the mend. The bruise on my face had decreased in size and colour. I tried a bit of makeup. It was a small improvement.

Dressed I went down to the salon and found everyone there.

We ate a continental breakfast, some cold meats and boiled eggs and bread and croissants and lots of coffee.

We set out for Bayeux where we saw the tapestry. It was impressive but the place was very busy. We lunched at a little café outside Bayeux, three main dishes to choose from, a place frequented by local French, working people. There were two stews and some cold sausages and meats. It was good plain country fare. We moved on to the Musée at Caen. It was we found a good gallery, with paintings from every century including some nice Impressionists.

We returned to the Chateau and took the children out for a little walk to see the sheep. The ram had been doing his work, leaving a trail of blue dye on his wives as he went. Tasha seemed not that interested in sheep, which was a relief. We walked back to the Chateau, the twins running ahead, letting off steam, falling on the long grass of the paddock and getting up again.

Simon carried Sébastien there and back. Then surprisingly he went up to help at bath time. I stayed with Wally and Isabel, chatting until it was time to get our selves ready for dinner. I secretly thought that it will be nice to have just family to amuse after tomorrow, but I was also looking forward to the weekend.

Departure day for Wally and Isabel dawned with rain clattering against the window panes. I snuggled into Simon and pulled the duvet around my shoulders. I found that it was weighed down by Tasha at the bottom of the bed and Mitzi in the hollow between Simon and I. Sensing that I was awake, Mitzi crawled across the folds of cloth and bodies until she reached my face. I was greeted with a wet nosed kiss on my nose and a purr like an engine.

Again we had the large English breakfast, which Simon remarked, we would take to the chalet when we went skiing. Today, I was more picky, just having one egg and a piece of bacon, followed by bread and marmalade that mother had sent over.

Isabel was again very subdued, but that was understandable. They packed my Mercedes and I drove them to Chartres. It was an easy drive with little traffic. Some showers came through, crossing the flat land like net curtains, then the next minute we were in dazzling sunshine, the water droplets shimmering, almost blinding in their intense refracted light. The sky changed from dark blue to azure and back. Simon and Wally chatted about the work ahead, Simon promising to draw up a programme.

We saw them onto the train. I kissed Isabel on both cheeks and wished her well with her art. I kissed Wally on cheeks and lips.

'Be careful,' he said as he stepped into the train. We saw them through the window, Isabel preoccupied, arranging herself, while Wally mouthed I thought, see you soon, then they were gone. I took Simon's hand.

'Simon, can we go to Lisieux? I would love to see where we are to be married.'

'Of course. A charming idea.'

I drove northwest through open country on country roads, Simon's hand resting on my thigh. It was cosy and delightful.

The Basilica was enormous. I felt intimidated before I entered. But inside, I found a very ornate and well lit chancel unobscured by great pillars. I took a leaflet describing the place and found that St Theresa was only twenty-four when she died. On her deathbed, she said, 'I only love simplicity. I have a horror of pretence.' I wondered how she would have applied that to me. I also found that it is France's greatest place of pilgrimage after Lourdes. It was so grand.

We spend an hour there, largely in silence. I was overawed, even as an atheist. There was no doubt that it would be a wonderful site for a wedding.

We exited into strong sunshine and sat on an ornate terrace outside. 'Simon, are we really going to be married here?'

'Why not?'

'Because St Theresa hated pretence.'

'Where is the pretence?'

'Well we are already married. And Simon, I am not a believer. I would go through with the wedding ceremony, because you want it, and so do I want the grand event. And this Basilica, it would be a wonderful setting. But there is the pretence. And Simon, my past.' I burst into tears.

'Ton passé sanglant,' (Your bloody past), 'never let me hear that again, never do you understand?'

He pulled me to him, jarring my shoulder, but I was more concerned with his anger than my physical pain. He wiped my tears with his handkerchief and kissed my forehead. He gripped my head between his hands and looked into my eyes. 'You were never a proper boy, you understand? You may have looked like one, but I doubt you looked a very convincing one, but inside you have always been female. I want you to agree that we will be married here. You as an atheist should not take the words of these religious people so much to heart. I love you and I believe you still love me. That is what is important. That is the truth. No pretence unless it is with you.'

'Of course not Simon. I love you to the depths of my soul. Have I not shown that over this past three years? We will marry here. It will be magnificent. Just sometimes, I do not feel worthy of you.'

'Ma petite biche, you are very frail at the moment. You have carried a heavy burden. Now I will look after *you* again. We must eat something too.'

We strolled into the town and had soup in a small café. From there we drove straight home.

We both climbed the stairs to the nursery. We took the children into the garden and showed them the flowers and the bees at work. Then we went to see the horses and allowed them to stroke Sheba, who was looking out of her box.

'Simon, I know the nursery has always been upstairs, but could we not have it downstairs? There is a room in the West that is unused. It appears to have been a small sitting room. It would be nice to have the children nearer us, and for Sophie too.'

'I like the idea. It was my mother's sitting room but we will have it renovated.'

Chapter 10.

We took the Landrover to Paris as it had more room for Sophie and the children as well of course for Tasha. Thursday was spent at the Maison. Annette showed us the latest news coverage of Beauvonne. There was a full page of me, from my fall on the catwalk to exiting hospital with my bruised and ugly face. They even had one of my impromptu news conferences of four years ago in Venice. At least they had not dug up any of me as a school boy. Luckily, I thought, there were none, bar a large one of the whole school when I was fourteen, and that was blurred. *My family did not do photographs either.* There was also some video footage on You Tube. Gérard seemed to have the office under control. The designers were happy too and all the projects were on schedule.

We were in Jacques Paquet's room. 'Jacques,' Simon said, 'I want you to design a wedding dress for Trudi. Whatever she wants, but I do not wish to see it at all. You liaise with her at all times and keep it apart from all the other work. I hope it will be something classical, flattering, beautiful. There is no budget, I leave that to the two of you. This is confidential too Jacques, but we are to wed in July next year, so there is plenty of time. I am inviting everyone here. Tell no one until I give permission.'

'Of course patron. I will do some designs. Trudi, perhaps we can discuss now, what sort of thing you want, while Simon is in the salon?'

Jacques and I talked designs. I wanted something with classic lines, nothing bouffant, no frills, a bodice with tiny pearls and a skirt which flowed out in a graceful flare with a chapel train in silk organza or chiffon. Jacques promised to make about five designs for me to choose from.

I returned to the mansion and Sophie and I took the children out to lunch. It was wonderful to be with another young woman and with Sébastien and the twins. I was so glad to be able to help Sophie. Three little ones was a big job, which she appeared to cope with easily, but I wanted to keep her happy. I liked her, I admired her skills too. We had a super time with them, doing very little, but showing them everything we came across. It was the first time the twins had seen boats. We took a short boat trip from Notre Dame to the Eiffel, then a taxi home. Simon arrived just afterwards and helped with their tea and bathing. In the evening we adults went to Franco's for pasta leaving Madame Gameau in charge.

Franco welcomed me like an old girl friend. Then he welcomed Simon, pointing to his leg and saying no one would know. It was then Sophie's turn. Franco turned on his most oily charm and I watched as she blushed.

'Franco,' I said to distract him, 'what have you that is special today?'

'Everything is very special, special for you Mademoiselle Trudi. You soon get better eh. No we have very special today, osso buco. You know what is. Oh yes Monsieur Simon, you know. It is veal shanks, cooked very slowly in white wine. So tasty. Also is very special, carne pizzaiola, cook slowly too.' He smacked his lips and grinned. 'Also all the pasta dishes, Bolognaise, Arrabiata, Puttanesca,' he flourished the menu.

Simon spoke first. 'Well I think we have anti pasti, a selection. Then I am having osso buco.'

'I will have the same.' I said.

'I would like the pizzaiola please,' Sophie said.

'And to drink?'

'What about that Italian champagne. It is dreadful Franco, but we will see if it has improved.' Simon said teasingly.

'Is not dreadful. Is better than champagne. Very beautiful wine. And water, Mademoiselle Trudi always ask for water. Minuto.'

He departed.

The wine arrived, then the anti pasti. We started in. We all seemed hungry.

'So Sophie, tell us about your parents. They have a farm?'

'Yes, pears and apples. It is not too bad, a living but they will never be rich.'

'So what made you become a nanny?'

'I just like children. I started as a teacher of kindergarten, but it was not personal enough. I love babies so looking after Sébastien has been a real treat. They are lovely children.'

'Thank you Sophie. I hope so.' Simon said, 'Their mother was not interested in them. She left them to her nanny entirely, and I did not like her. I did not trust her and one has to have trust in a nanny above all. I can say, we are very pleased with you. Very pleased. Trudi said to me weeks ago now, that we should get a girl from the village to assist you. How would you feel about that?'

'I would like to have a little more time off, perhaps a day and a half a week. The worst thing is that I have no transport of my own if I want to go into Caen or Alençon.'

'Simon we can do something about that can't we?'

'It is remiss of me. You can drive the Landrover, we don't normally use it. You have to work that out with Sabine who uses it day to day. And there is a girl in the village, you could train.'

'And Simon, my Mini is here too, unused for nearly a year. We can have that checked over and take it to the Chateau to use. It is right hand drive, but that should not be a problem.'

'That is a good idea. We will have it serviced. You can use that for personal use Sophie.'

The osso buco was quite special, very greasy but exceedingly tasty. Sophie seemed to enjoy her pizzaiola too.

It was Friday morning. I went with Simon to the Maison and walked around the workrooms meeting people and chatting, my injuries still very visible, but since all those pictures in the press, the real life me was an improvement on their expectations of my appearance.

As I passed Jacques office, he called me in. He had five rough sketches of a wedding dress. I could not believe he had worked so quickly, but then he was a professional of the first rank in fashion.

The first was not what I had asked for at all. A skin fitting bodice with pearls and embroidery was fine, but the skirt was layers of almost transparent white chiffon, ending in points all around the skirt like petals of a flower.

The second was a design exactly as I had specified, like a drawing from a 1920s brochure, clean flowing lines, but a fitted bodice, the skirt flowing out from under the bust.

The next was a really straight dress fitted on the waist and over the hips and it would show my rear to effect. I might win rear of the year with that.

The next was a sheath column, brush train dress with two shoulder straps and fine tight lace sleeves, again in white chiffon.

The last had a much fuller skirt. They were all lovely. I closed the door, so no prying eyes would see or overhear.

'Jacques, they are all incredible. I am spoiled for choice. You know me, which do you consider will suit me best?'

'Personally, I love number one, but also number four would suit you too. Those are my favourites for your figure, and they are different from what one finds in the market place. What do you like?'

'Yes certainly those two, I think are my favourites. Number two is nearest my brief. But it is such a difficult decision.'

'You don't have to make it now. There is plenty of time. If you are not sure about these I will do some more.'

'No, no more. It would just be more confusing. And I want to make a decision now. If I delay it will just be putting it off. First tell me honestly, which one you think would suit me best, between one and four.'

'I still love number one. It will be so floaty. You will move as if on a cloud, yet I think it will be easy to manage. The material is really light. Now if you like, you could have the two shoulder straps from number four with the stretch lace sleeves. There is nothing worse than a bodice which gradually works down your body, so you are continually hitching it up and feeling uncomfortable.'

'Then that is what I want. Number one with the top of number four. Oh Jacques, thank you so much.'

'I have your measurements on record, so I will have it made up. No one except me will know it is for you. When it is ready, I will call you for a fitting. The staff will just think it is for a show.'

'Jacques, you are such a darling. This has cheered me up no end. Now tell me Jacques, the changes I made here, with Gérard, is that working? Be honest.'

'It is OK. He has taken a lot off my shoulders.'

'That's good, but if there is anything, and you feel you can't tell Simon then tell *me* Jacques.'

'I have to say, for someone so young, you are very business-like and astute. You sense that I am unsure of Gérard.'

'I have to be aware of other's emotions to survive Jacques. What is the matter?'

'I do not know, except I think he drinks too much and I chanced upon a telephone call about horse racing. It may be prejudice but I do not like betting.'

'Thank you Jacques, for telling me. Then we must keep our eyes and ears open or he could take us all down.'

I found Simon in the vault, looking through the finished dresses.

'So my Trudi, you were a long time with Jacques. You have chosen the dress?'

'Yes. How did you know.'

'Why else would you be locked in his office all that time?'

'Well it is done and it will be a triumph of the House of Beauvonne. And you will be proud of me, the most beautiful bride you have ever seen. I am making a list of guests on my side.'

'We have eleven months!'

'Yes and people make arrangements. I want to make sure that everyone who wants to attend, has not made a prior arrangement. We should send out the invitations the beginning of December.'

'You are right. You will be pleased to know, that I have been able to secure the Basilica fifteenth of July. So you see, I am on the ball too. Anyway, I am finished here. Let us go home. We can take the children out and allow Sophie an afternoon off. Is that agreeable?'

'Of course, it is excellent. Where shall we go?'

'The big wheel on the Tuilleries, and they have some small rides for little children too. Come mon amour.'

It was like being a regular married couple, just the two of us and the three little ones. Simon pushed the buggy and the children walked holding my hands. My shoulder throbbed, but it was worth the pain. The twins walked all the way without complaining. When they saw the big wheel, they jumped up and down with excitement. Simon went on with them while I looked after little Sébastien. We went on the small roundabout, but he did not seem too impressed. The twins loved the roundabout, Adèle choosing to sit in a cockerel and André a nice red car.

We took a taxi home. On the way we stopped to buy food for a meal. Sabine would be arriving and she too would need a meal. I planned to cook steaks, with baby potatoes and spinach. We would have smoked salmon and a small salad to start. I bought some bread and croissants too, as well as coffee and milk. We had wine and everything else. It would be the first meal I had cooked for Simon, so it had to be special.

I marinated the steaks in red wine and garlic and placed them in the fridge and prepared the rest. I phoned Sabine at five. She was just leaving, so we could expect her just after seven. Simon and I put the children to bed after giving them tea. Bath time was a delight, lots of splashing and experimenting with bubbles, plastic ducks and a boat. This was a very special time, an intimate time for Simon and I, the very first day I had felt we were a real family. I loved these small children as though they were my own, and seeing that Simon was no longer the aloof almost Victorian father, but a real 'dad' instead, gladdened my heart. From the dark days of a week ago and my accident till now, seemed an age in the difference in my state of mind. I was positive again, able to see round difficulties rather than finding an impassable barrier.

The children safely in bed, I took clothes for tomorrow through to Simon's bedroom because Sabine would use my room. Sophie was in the old nursery suite with the little ones. She walked in just after seven with several shopping bags.

'You have been spending then Sophie. Have you had a good time?'

'I spent all the money le Comte gave me. I had so much fun.'

'Good Sophie, you deserve it. We had a good time being parents too. I loved it. The children are in bed and Simon is sitting reading, with the monitor on, so all is safe and you do not have to worry. I am cooking dinner and we will eat as soon as Sabine arrives. Do you want to show me your purchases?'

She showed me all she had bought, two tops, a jumper, trousers and a dress. 'Never have I spent so much money.' She said.

Sabine phoned to say that she was inside the périphèrique. Another fifteen minutes and she would arrive.

With Sophie home, Simon was free to come through to the kitchen. I preferred the kitchen in my apartment to the rather antiquated one in the un-modernised part of the house. I asked him to lay the table, which he did without protest. I wondered whether he had ever done so before. The doorbell buzzed and I answered the intercom. I pushed the button to let Sabine into the lift. I welcomed her at the top and showed her to my bedroom. I told her dinner would be at eight.

I started to cook. Simon loitered, wanting to know if I needed help. 'Yes Simon. Perhaps you can open a bottle of wine for us. What a privilege for you tonight, with three young women to hang on your every word.'

'I think you are becoming impertinent Trudi.' I looked up not knowing that he was joking, 'I told you two days ago, that tonight I would make love with you. So I hope you are ready.' He goosed me, then circled my waist and placed his hands across my abdomen. I was immediately aroused. I craned my neck back, turning my head towards him like a cat caressing to get food and he kissed me on the lips. I wanted to ditch the dinner and have him then and there.

I placed the starter and called the girls to eat. As they chatted to Simon about their day, I cooked the steaks, all rare as is the norm in France and carried everything in. I served the meat and left them to take potatoes and vegetables.

Simon cut into his steak experimentally, looked at the colour and nodded. He took a mouthful. 'So, you can cook Trudi. Is there anything you can't do?'

'Yes, stay on a horse Simon, that I have found, is a bit difficult.'

'No but this is very good. I compliment you.'

'Not just a pretty face, is she Simon?' Sabine said.

'Oh certainly not. I knew that when I first met her. She is very special.'

'Anyway Trudi, your face is looking much better, the swelling has mostly gone, it is just the colour now. You will soon be our princess again.' Sabine said.

I thought she was poking fun, but I could see no sign of that by her expression.

'I hope so Sabine. I shall not be on the runway next week, which is a shame, because I love it.'

'Oh I think you will. I have found masks for all the girls, so there is no reason why not. I have turned adversity into an asset. Masks will attract attention from the media. You will show the dresses already made for you I hope.'

'What a super idea Simon.'

'And that TV company are still interested. Have you thought about it?'

'No, it had gone out of my head. I am prepared to talk to them and find out what they want, but I want your lawyer involved to make sure my, our rights, are safeguarded.'

'I find it amazing that you can discuss such grand matters at your age Trudi,' Sophie said, 'I would not know where to start. I would be terrified.'

'Oh well Sophie, I have been in the news since I was sixteen, so one learns. And it can be a good thing too. Sometimes, it is better to throw them a bone than try to hide. I remember Princess Diana. She used to court the press, even though they liked to look for cellulite on her legs. It was not until she went with that Egyptian / nobody she tried to hide from them, and then it ended in tragedy. If one is famous, one has to accept it and all that goes with it. I am at the moment, newsworthy, so there is no point dodging. However, if I want to go shopping, then I might put on jeans and dark glasses. Simon, I think if you would, I will invite the film people here to discuss it with us both.'

'Of course, I will phone tomorrow and try to arrange for next week when we are in Paris for the show. Actually, when I think about it, we would be better to stay here, rather than return to the Chateau just for one day.'

'Yes. Sophie could come to the show. And why don't I take Tasha on the runway? That would cause a stir Simon?'

'You can try at rehearsal, see how she reacts. If she behaves it will be good. She will need a bath and a sparkly collar and lead.'

'And you Sabine. Can you stay for three days? Go home Thursday morning?'

'I think so, if that is agreeable to Simon? I do not want to take advantage.'

'If that is what Trudi wants, then I am sure Sabine that you can arrange the Chateau work by phone, this once. We will be going out to dinner in the evening, so you both need dresses. I would give them to you, but you are both larger than our models. Over the next days, you need to buy a dress each, a cocktail dress, long or short, not too short, but a bit special. I will pay.'

We chatted about what we would do tomorrow. Neither girl had a great knowledge of Paris and they wanted to do all the tourist things, the Eiffel, Notre Dame and Sacré Coeur, the Pompidou, and Orsay, L'Arc de Triomphe and strolling Montmartre or the banks of the Seine. It was decided that they should do that together tomorrow, meeting us in Montmartre at L'Eté en Pente Douce for lunch, because we had the concert in the evening.

Simon and I made our excuses and retired early. We showered together.

'I told you two days ago, that you had two days. Now is the time. I am going make up for lost months, and I am going to fuck you rigid. On your knees and blow me.' He grabbed my hair and sent me down to his suddenly erect penis. I grabbed it and sucked slowly. I bit him. He responded by showering me with a jet of icy water, I flinched and bit again, then sucked him rhythmically until he came. He raised me up and penetrated me, his hand between our abdomens, fingering me, his other hand running up the crack of my behind. His teeth sank into my neck and I was immediately lost, overpowered, willing to perform anything he asked. He rammed me against the shower tiles, even their chill having no effect against the fire of our passion. My master, my idol was back, making me dance to his tune, manipulating his puppet. The water poured upon us, our lips met and parted. I bit his chest and moaned as I came and he would not stop. I pleaded but he would not stop he was like a train quicker and quicker, even the water seeming to join in the rhythm and I came again.

At last he stopped. He cuddled me in the warm stream of water, holding me firmly in his amazingly strong arms. At last we parted. Separated he washed me down again, gently, massaging me carefully. He dried me. He wrapped me in my dense fleece dressing gown and carried me to bed. I fell asleep almost immediately, his arms wrapped about me.

I awoke to find him on one elbow, watching me. As my lids fluttered, his hand rose slowly up my inner thigh. I giggled. He mounted me, fingered me apart and played with my clit. He entered me and I flung my legs around him and gripped hard, stopping his slow rhythm for a few seconds, then I allowed him to continue. I gasped as he thrust deeply. All the time he stared into my face, watching every expression. I craned up as best as my collarbone would allow to receive his kisses, and our lips joined and he sucked my tongue. I thought he was going to consume me entirely. He came, gasping then slowly continued until I climaxed too, my back arching, my muscles contracting. Only then did he stop. I gasped and he laughed.

Tasha exploded on to the bed, followed by the twins with Sophie in hot pursuit, knocking at the door and waiting for an answer.

We had hurriedly parted. 'Who is it?' Simon asked.

'Sophie. I am sorry, they escaped.'

'Do you want them?'

'For their breakfast. Sébastien has had his. Now it is their turn. They are bathed and dressed.'

'Come back in five minutes Sophie please.'

Adèle was inserting herself into the bed, while André was content to bounce on the bed. Tasha rolled on her back between us. We romped with the children for a few minutes, until Sophie returned.

As soon as we were alone, I slid from the bed and locked myself in the bathroom. I showered alone, before opening the door and allowing Simon in. He looked at me quizzically.

'I shut you out, because I am sore. You have made up for lost time all right. Now I need a day's respite.

Chapter 11.

The girls disappeared and we amused the children with simple things we had to hand, drawing, making a house of cards, playing hide and seek. There was lots of shrieking and laughter, and the morning passed quickly. We took a taxi to Montmartre, L'Eté en Pente Douce and met the girls there. They had found time to buy dresses, so the sight seeing had taken a back seat. We agreed to take their shopping home with us. This was a typical French restaurant, most tables outside, under an awning or a plane tree. It was busy and happy. The food was inexpensive and tasty.

The girls left to go to Sacré Coeur, just up a flight of steps and we took a taxi home. We played with the children, Sebastian staggering about and the twins romping about. I fed them and we had bathed them by the time the girls arrived home. Together we settled them in bed, singing Frere Jacques and reading a story of the little red hen.

I dressed for the concert. Leggings and a mini dress, very large dark glasses and lots of foundation to hide the bruising on my cheek and the green around my right eye. I dispensed with the sling. I asked Sabine to look out for me if we were caught in a crush. I was a bit nervous, worried about my collar bone.

The theatre Le Trianon was not far from Place Pigalle. The theatre was not imposing, sandwiched between a Souvenir emporium and a hi-fi shop. We showed our tickets and were soon inside and found that we actually had seats in the circle, not so much fun but better for my physical state, still a little frail even after two weeks.

The show started late but when it got under way, the crowd was soon gently rocking, even the seated fans were up and dancing. It was super. Sabine and Sophie had never been to a concert before, and we all emerged bubbling with excitement. We managed to grab a taxi and I took them to Willi's for a late night snack, then home to bed.

I fell into bed, cuddling up to Simon, having covered him with kisses for giving us such an excellent evening. It had been such fun to be out with two young women.

Sunday and we woke late. The children found their way into our bed. It was delightful. Their little bodies felt as hot as water bottles. Like cats, they seemed to think they could just climb over us at will. I had a job to protect my shoulder.

We got up, and while Simon was showering and dressing, I helped Sophie with the children. Sabine appeared, bleary eyed in cream coloured pyjamas.

We ate breakfast together. Simon suggested that we all take a boat trip to the Eiffel. The girls could go up while we ate lunch there. He told them it would take nearly three hours of waiting to go up, so we might not wait for them.

We ate an indifferent lunch not far from the Eiffel. We walked the children into the Champs de Mars, Simon carrying Sébastien on his back. Returning to the river, we spotted the girls just leaving the Tour. We all took a taxi home. I prepared a simple meal of spaghetti Bolognese and the girls went out again. We went to bed early.

Monday, we left the girls to do what they wanted while we had a lazy time with the children. We walked down to the Tuilleries and back. Sophie was home in time to bath and help put the children to bed. Tomorrow was the rehearsal. I wondered how the models would take to the masks imposed due to my fading disfigurement.

I need not have worried. Most were quite solicitous, especially my friend La Poulette. Tasha, bathed and resplendent in diamante, behaved herself, in fact was quite a hit with the girls. La Poulette asked if she could bring her standard poodle she had named Madonna after the pop star. Simon said it would be all right, but to come early before the show and see how the bitch performed on the runway and how the two animals got on.

It was the morning of the show at last. The two dogs seemed to like each other, so there was not a problem. Madonna's collar was twice as much bling as Tasha's, being two inches wide and covered in Swarovski crystal. Her tail ended in a pompom and she was clipped out immaculately. Tasha looked the poor relation, but had a charm that the poodle could never achieve. It was character versus looks.

Sabine and Sophie had a peep behind the scenes and afterwards took their seats on the back row. It was a big show, the largest number of dresses Beauvonne had ever shown, because they now had two full ranges. It would take two hours from beginning to end and Simon had allowed for a coffee break for the guests.

My face was done and the facemask fitted. Tasha was very good, curled up at my feet and waited patiently while my hair was done. Eventually we made our way down the catwalk, to oohs and aahs from the dog lovers. Then it was back to change for the next dress. After the interval, I was dressed in the wedding dress, the mask removed, but a white makeup completely covering my face, rouge eye makeup and lipstick applied, and I looked like a window dummy. Tasha had to stay with Simon while I pranced, showing the dress. At last it was the finale, all the girls going out on the catwalk at once and lastly me, and Tasha followed by Simon and the designers. The roof came off and the cameras flashed making Tasha bark. Still dressed, we all descended to the floor and mingled with the customers. Madame Dufour was there as usual and offered her congratulations on my recovery.

A young man of around thirty approached. He presented his card and I read the name, Alex Cummings from Odyssey TV.

'Trudi, I am coming to see you about a TV programme. I know now is not the time, but your journey is extraordinary, so we are really interested. I shall phone you to make an appointment. I hope you will agree.'

'Well Alex, it depends on the terms, but we are willing to discuss it. I hope we can do business but it depends on the terms and the money, I am afraid. I plan to give the fee to charity, so it is not for myself, but of course the amount matters. Anyway, I look forward to hearing from you. Now if you will excuse me, I have to circulate. I hope we have some paying customers. Au revoir.'

After changing and having all the exotic makeup removed, I collected Tasha and returned to the villa with Sophie and Sabine. I was very tired and excused myself and went to bed. I slept for four hours until Simon came home.

Chapter 12.

I awoke to find Simon sitting on the bed.

'Darling, you were tired, eh? Are you able to go to the dinner?'

'Oh yes. I was tired, I don't know why. What is the time? Oh, four hours sleep, I must have needed it. It is you, wearing me out in bed.'

'You did very well today and so did Tasha. It was good having the two dogs there. The newspapers have picked up on it. The headline in one English paper reads, 'Bitch Wars'.

'So it was a successful show?'

'Very, I think the best ever, and far better than I dreamed possible. The readymade lines are selling well and also the haute couture. Much of the credit goes to you, for your reorganisation and the guest list. You certainly shook Annette and Gérard up. Now darling girl, you have two hours to get ready, and of course, I am going to dress you. I have a surprise as usual. I am going to shower now so the bathroom will be vacant for you. Perhaps you will make sure our friends will be ready on time and they have everything?'

I rose and put on a gown. I found the children were already in bed. The girls were doing their hair.

'I am sorry Sophie. I went to bed and slept and left you to attend to the children.'

'It is fine Trudi. Sabine helped and they are now fast asleep. We leave here in an hour and a half, isn't it?'

'Yes. Simon and I have to be there first to welcome everybody. He says the show was very successful, so we are very pleased. Thank you for all your help, both of you. Your support of me has been very special. Have you everything you need?'

'Oh yes. We are buffing ourselves up. I expect you are going to dazzle us though.'

'I have no idea. Simon is dressing me, so I am like a doll. But I love it, letting him do as he likes with me and having a surprise. Is that very shallow?'

Sabine had come in on the conversation. 'Of course not. You have more than enough strength. I can understand exactly. I look forward to a surprise.'

I left them and went to see if Simon was finished in the shower. I found him in trousers and shirt sleeves.

'If you would do your hair and not straighten it. How wavy would it be?

'How do you want it Simon?'

'I want it wild, like it was when we went walking in Lincolnshire. Do you remember?'

'Yes but it is longer now and I won't cut it.'

He took out his phone and dialled. He spoke quickly. He closed his phone with a smile. 'OK. Nancy from the show will come to dress your hair, so if you wash it and leave it, then I get you dressed and Nancy will be here.'

I showered and moisturised. Simon waited in the bedroom. When I entered, he was ready with the dress. First he gave me a black brassiere with thin straps and seed pearls sown into the cups. The panties matched. Sheer black seamed stockings and my black suspender belt completed my underwear. Then he produced the dress. The bodice was sheer black chiffon with two wide shoulder straps, which ended in a v neck at the front and plunged to just above bra level at the back. There was a peplum of black ostrich feathers ending four inches above the knee, then the full length skirt extended to ankle level, again in sheer black chiffon.

'Oh Simon, I love it. Why haven't I seen this before?'

'Because it has been made especially for my darling girl. Now before Nancy arrives, I thought you can cover your face on the bruised side, with makeup. I will do that for you.' He sat me down and worked like an expert, not allowing me to see what he was doing. When I finally saw what had been done, I found my left face was covered in my usual foundation and made up with dramatic smokey eyes. My cheeks were deep vermillion. The other side was covered in matching vermillion and purple, in a swirling art nouveau design. My lips pouted, again in vermillion. It had a strange effect on me. I didn't know whether to smile or to cry. It was unbelievably sexy, almost depraved.

He painted my nails in matching vermillion, gluing a small crystal in the centre of each one. He was just fitting on my five inch platforms, again covered in diamante, when Nancy entered.

'Ooh la la,' she said. 'So, what am I going to do?'

'I thought swept up, then wild, or ringlets cascading down her face.'

'I think the latter. Oui Simon. I can do it, quite easily.'

She set to work, spraying and hot tonging, pinning, until it was done. I hardly knew where I had gone. I recognised myself, but I was also someone else. I looked and turned and looked. I was a fabulous creature. The dress was absolutely beautiful, and it was great to wear. I finally decided that I felt wonderful. I thanked Nancy. We had ten minutes before the limousine arrived. I went through to get the reaction of the girls.

'Wow,' said Sabine. 'He has gone to town on you.'

'You don't like it?'

'Trudi, on you I love it. On me I would hate it. I would feel so out there, uncomfortable. But for you Trudi, in your position, yes it is perfect.'

''C'est magnifique,' was Sophie's only comment.

The limousine delivered us to the Olympia half an hour before the guests were expected. Simon went on inspection, making sure everything was ready and just as he wanted. We welcomed each and every guest, all the models who were able to attend and all the staff and our best customers. Annette and Gérard arrived nearly last, Annette was full of what the media said, and she told us, there was a cameraman and some reporters here tonight. I recognised Alex from this morning, though he seemed not to recognise me. It was not surprising, with the strange makeup and ringlets cascading down my face.

I stood beside him after the last guest entered. 'Bon soir Alex. I hope you enjoy the evening, even if you are working.'

'C'est vous Trudi. Of course it is. Let me get some shots, in case you decide to do the programme.' He signalled the camera man and the crew. They took some shots, before dinner was called.

I hardly ate. I watched Simon from my end of the table Jacques on my left and Gérard on my right. I could not wait to be with Simon. He made a speech, thanking me for my support in his recent illness and thanked all the staff too.

The group started to play and people took to the floor. I found Alex next to me.

'Not dancing Trudi?'

'No, I do not know how I managed to get through today with a broken collar bone. I am content to watch and see everyone enjoying themselves. So Alex, who owns Odyssey the TV company?'

'I do, well my family have a lot of money in it. But we are making money doing fly on the wall documentaries and biopics.'

'When are you having a meeting with us?'

'Tomorrow, Simon says, before you return to the country.'

'May I ask how old you are?'

He grinned. 'No, I am thirty. How old are you Trudi or is that a question I should not ask a lady?'

'Touché. I am nearly twenty-four.'

'You are much more mature than I was at your age.'

'Are you recording me now?'

'No. I would tell you if I was. We are not that sort of company, well not with people like you. Word would soon get round and we would be out of business. You don't trust people a lot do you?'

'No. I have been unlucky once or twice. But mostly I have met and been with nice people. So what editorial rights would I have over what you say about me?'

'We want to give an honest account of your life so far, but I don't want to say things that are particularly sensitive or regretted. We do not plan to do warts and all, or a mockumentary. Nor will it be a hymn of praise. I think your story is one of inspiration to those afflicted with your problem and will also serve to make your plight more understood by, well normal people.'

'I look forward to seeing you tomorrow then Alex. Please excuse me, I have people to see.'

I found Annette. 'So are you well Annette?'

'We are both very well Trudi. Gérard has found himself. He was wasting his life, now he gets up in the morning with a purpose. And how are you?

'I am fine now. I was in a bit of a bad way when I came off Sheba. But since then, the pressure is off. Simon has reasserted control and control of me too. I missed having a strong man behind me.'

'You were excellent today, and Tasha, that was genius. You have quite an eye for self-promotion. How are the injuries?'

'I am mending. My face will be back to normal by the time I go back to University.'

'And how is being married.'

'It is wonderful. I sometimes don't believe it. But I have everything. A handsome and considerate husband, three lovely children, money and I can still study as I want to do. It is a fairy tale. But Annette, what do you know about Odyssey. Are they OK or are they looking to make a sensationalist programme?'

'I think they are genuine. I have seen some of their other work. Alex is quite a fan of yours actually, he was longing to meet you. He described himself as a 'great admirer'.

'We will see tomorrow. I am warming to the idea, but I need to be careful. There are many potential enemies out there. People who are transphobic. I'm undecided at the moment.'

'Yes Trudi, but you are very special. You can be inspirational to others like you and your example can change people's perceptions of transsexualism, just as people coming out in the eighties changed the perception of gay people. You are so lucky to have been born beautiful. I think your example will win a lot of friends.'

'That is more or less what Alex has said. Yes, you are right. If we all live in the dark, then people will think we are creatures of the night rather than, well worthy people in our own right, trying to live a worthwhile life. Thank you Annette.'

Thomas Martin interrupted us. 'Trudi, will you dance, gently, I know you are still injured. But please?'

'Thomas, as you ask me so nicely I cannot refuse. Just be careful, Don't bang into me or let anyone else please.'

He led me to the floor, and we danced carefully. Simon soon cut in and we managed to amaze everyone with the one dance I could do well, the Viennese waltz. It was painful in the extreme but I tried not to show it.

We excused ourselves, told the girls to get a taxi, and we went home. I used four or five pads removing all make up, then a facial scrub to clean the pores. I tumbled into bed and was asleep before Simon came to bed.

I awoke to find an empty bed. [myself alone]

Simon appeared with a tray of coffee, bacon and eggs, toast and marmalade. 'You did not eat last night, so I have made you a good breakfast. Then you need to get ready for Alex at ten-thirty. The girls are going home this morning with the children.'

I ate everything, the only food I had eaten really for twenty-four hours. I showered and washed all the spray out of my hair, straightened it and caught it up in a large grip. I made my face, thankful that most of the bruising had at last disappeared, except for a small line of black above my cheek bone. I disguised it as well as I could. I put on a silk day dress in pale blue and four inch heels.

Simon was in his study, phoning people. I went into the kitchen and surveyed the mess. I put my iPod on with ear phones. I put on marigolds and set about clearing up. I sang along to the songs I knew. I put away all the dishes and dried the cutlery, then cleaned everything down. I was working on the stained sink and letting go to Paloma Faith, '*Do you want the Truth or Something Beautiful*', When there was a touch on my shoulder. I turned to find Simon there with Alex stood in the doorway.

I laughed off my embarrassment, turned back to the sink and swished away the cleaner, then pulled the marigolds off. I washed my hands and dried them. I joined them in to the salon.

'I am sorry about that Alex. I was carried away with clearing up after Simon's breakfast making, and two days of neglect. Can we offer you coffee?'

'That would be nice. I have made a provisional booking for lunch on Bateaux Mouches if that is convenient?'

'That will be nice. We accept don't we Trudi?'

'Yes but first we need to discuss the matter in hand. We don't listen then take your food and turn you down. So Alex you explain fully how you see this project and who you expect to sell it to. If I like the sound of it we will proceed to the next stage.'

'I will make coffee. You can start Trudi, and I will catch up. I leave my phone here to record Alex, just so we have a true record of what passes.'

'So Alex,' I say, 'what do you want to do? How do you see this biopic? You tell me what you want to do, then I will tell you what my conditions are, and what I want in and left out.'

'Good Trudi, frank and straightforward, I like that. Well simply a film biography of your life to date, beginning with your earliest memories, how you came to the stage you are at now. Obviously, as I said last night, we want a truthful account. Any third parties involved will have to give permission for inclusion, and we will leave out anything particularly upsetting to you.'

'What made you come to me? Why my story?'

'Because you are probably the most out transsexual woman since Dana International. The camera loves you, you are studying at the Sorbonne to be a doctor and you also model, and now I know, you can sing too. Who could be more interesting? You have a story, as I understand it, starting from a young age, what we call a journey. There is so much here that we thought it would probably run to three one hour programmes.'

'Who suggested me? Or was it your own idea.'

'That's a fair question.'

Simon entered with a tray of coffee and biscuits. We busied ourselves with the coffee pouring. I reminded him of the question.

'I am a gay man Trudi. I was in love with a man, younger, just out of university and he has chosen to go down your route. That was the seed that started this. I found that you were his idol.'

'But your wording Alex is surely wrong? He, she has not chosen the route, the route has chosen her. It is a compulsion, a deep seated dissatisfaction, particularly with ones physical appearance that compels transsexuals to do what they do. That is basic.'

'Yes, my wording was wrong, careless. What I meant was that she came to a time in her life, an impasse, when she had to make a decision. Could she continue as an unhappy male or follow your path. I do understand.'

'Are you still seeing her?'

'Yes. She still lives with me, but not as a partner. I am supporting her and she works for Odyssey.'

'Thank you for being so honest. Now I think I understand your motivation, besides making money. Have you spoken yet to anyone that knows me?'

'Someone named Ellie, in the BBC. Yes, she is quite a fan.'

'Oh Ellie! A very dear friend, but a little unreliable. What do you think Simon. How do you feel about this? I will make no decision until you make one first on this exposure.'

'I do not see there is any more exposure than is really already known.'

'You have to remember Simon, what happens next July. Do we need this? How do you feel about this amount of public exposure.'

'It makes no difference Trudi. I keep telling you that.'

'Alex, I will be completely honest with you now and let you into a secret, which must remain a secret for the time being. If you divulge what I tell you, to anyone, then the deal is off. In December this year, we are announcing our marriage. That will take place in July.'

'I am not surprised. I took it that you were a couple.'

'Then I am prepared to go ahead with this. You will need information from me, a list of names to contact, a potted history of my life, schools, places, events.'

'I will send a researcher over to interview you.'

'Ah, your protégé I presume?'

'If you like. Yes, I will send her. She will be delighted, sympathetic and interested. Like you she is very insightful, perceptive and a worshipper, a fan. We would also like to put a team with you as you go about your life, here as a model but also as a student, and in your other role as mother to Simon's children, horsewoman, mistress of Beauvonne estate, and of course culminating in the wedding. I presume I will be able to film that?'

'A magazine has the rights. But if your programme goes out some time afterwards, then I have no doubt that you can be accommodated. Simon?'

'We will have to speak to them and put them in touch with you. I would suggest that you do episodes up and until the wedding. Then later a resumé and the wedding itself.'

'Could my protégé as you call her, live with you for some time. She would have a camera, to take natural footage and to really get behind the façade.'

'Provided I own all the footage and have editorial rights over it. I am prepared to do that.'

'Good. Trudi that is really good. But we would also want to do your early life, interview your parents and your brother? Go to your school, speak to some friends who knew you previously. If you could make a list of people to interview, then that will enable you a good deal of control.' I nodded assent. 'Thank you so much. This will be a real coup, and we will make a great programme between us. Simon, do you agree too.'

'I think it will be good. However, perhaps we can go to lunch. Trudi needs feeding. And over lunch, we need to discuss the fee. I know Trudi intends to give the money to a charity, but the money still matters.'

'I am going to set up a charity which deals solely with transsexuals, not transvestites or other trans people, but bona fide people who want to have all the attributes of their non natal sex. So, you need to do your maths carefully Alex. Now I really am starving.'

Over lunch Alex laid out his plans for depicting my life. He thought an opening shot of me walking the hospital ward as a student, in white coat with stethoscope around my neck. Then it would fade to pictures from my early childhood, well they were few, my parents did not take photos often, but I could remember one or two, of a rather fey shy little boy with curly hair and also later in a dress. Then there would be interviews with people that had known me, Heather and her mother, the hairdresser and of course, my family.

He would then pass on to my school days, and Vanessa, Ellie and Wally even. He also wanted me to go back to school and talk though my time there with a tour of it, talk to masters if they would cooperate, but I thought they would. It would be good publicity for the school.

This would be followed by life in Paris and of course the Chateau, and ending with our marriage. It sounded good, but............I still wasn't sure.

'We leave aside the fee at the moment, Alex, because I guess you have to think about that. I know nothing of TV economics, but when you come back with an offer, I will check to see whether it is considered fair. I am still worried about this. I think that my appearance on the runway as a model, might have more instant impact with people as an opening, then move on to my hospital career. Simon please tell me what to do?'

'Trudi darling, the decision is yours.'

'No, the decision is ours Simon. This is a Beauvonne matter. You must say what you feel, what dangers you see!'

'Very well. Most of your life has been covered inadequately by the press. You are already their property. This is an opportunity to give an honest and truthful picture rather than the innuendo and sensationalist half-truths. You know what gay people say, 'out and proud'. I think the same would be good for your people too. You should be proud of your journey. I am proud of who you are.'

'This is so personal for me. I needed you to put it into logical perspective and you have. Thank you Simon. Very well Alex, let me have a contract with the fee included and a schedule, which of course may alter according to how busy I am. If our lawyer has no objections, then I will sign.'

'That is marvellous news. Thank you Trudi. I realise that this is a difficult decision for you, and intrusive. There is one more thing and I don't want to embarrass you. When I came into the villa this morning and you were in rubber gloves, you were singing. I thought you were very good. Why not record a song for release before the programme goes out? I know good producers who would jump at the chance to record you.'

'Really? Oh I do not know. I am a medical student. That is what I want to do. This is all getting too much. No, I don't think so.'

'I will leave the idea there. Perhaps I will bring it up again later. Then I think that is it. Thank you Trudi and Simon. I will be in touch.'

We parted, he to Eurostar and London, and we to the villa and out to the Chateau. Next week I would be back at university. I was looking forward to seeing Jean Luc and Élise again and actually starting work on the wards. It would be a simpler life than my summer had been.

Chapter 13.

A week later and we were all back in the villa, Simon too, so Jean Luc and Élise had my apartment to themselves. We three students found ourselves in different departments under different professors, so our collective learning came to an end. But also there was not so much pressure. The original intake of two thousand students had now reduced to less than one hundred in our year as people had failed or found the going too tough.

We three worked different shifts and catching up with each other was a matter of chance. Summer faded into an autumn that was unbelievably warm. Simon and I slept together whenever I was home, but even as a mere student, there were days when I had to work nights.

Simon went to the States with Wally and from there to Tokyo and Shanghai. Then he was home, leaving Wally to make the visits.

Wally now lived in Paris alone and I did not see him. I was in hospital for eighty hours a week, moving from department to department, learning diagnosis, the detective work of medicine from the sometimes, frequently misleading symptoms patients either exhibited or disclosed. Often their disclosures actually disguised the real illness.

Winter started late, the second week in November, and I had the whole weekend off. Friday night I headed for the Chateau. Simon had arranged a little weekend party, Annette and Gérard, Wally, Sabine. The men were going to shoot. It was not for me. I did not want to kill things, animals, birds. I still ate meat but with an increasing feeling of guilt. I loved the taste of duck, but when I thought of how beautiful a duck is, I felt very guilty.

When I arrived at the Chateau, it was past seven and completely dark. The Chateau showed some light in the porch and the two lamps in the drive were lit. I parked the Mercedes with the other cars before the door. I grabbed my bag and entered.

I looked in the salon and found it empty. I climbed the marble staircase, the same one that Catherine had fallen down, and entered my room. I peeled off my student wear, mini skirt and a loose top and went into the shower. The water descended in a hot comforting stream removing the hospital stench. I sat in the shower tray and let the water cascade over me. I was very tired, and quite emotional. A young patient, a leukaemia victim, had died after a long fight, when she had remained cheerful, hopeful of recovery, her hair gone from her young head. I soaped myself well and rinsed hospital from my nose and the taste of it from my mouth.

I had wanted to cure people. Finding out that I, or medicine is not always adequate, face to face has been a hard lesson. I had cried on the way home.

I dragged myself off the floor and dried. I straightened my hair and did my makeup. Some of the girls, my fellow students, never used makeup. I always did. They sometimes joshed me about it, calling me Modèle Médicin, but I was happier with some, and besides, I just liked it. Those who teased, would have been better with makeup anyway. However, I felt they were not malicious, merely teasing and a little jealous.

I put on panties and a bra and walked into the bedroom. I was busy looking in the wardrobe, when Simon's voice made me turn. He lay propped on the bed, a book in his hand. 'Trudi, Trudi, you should not let me see you like that. I want to make love to you now, but we have to go down to dinner.'

'Is everyone here?'

'Oh yes, they are all here, and Alex and his young friend. A surprise, but it was an opportunity. He rang to say they were in Paris, so I invited them.'

'Oh. Really, I could do without a surprise. I am so tired. It has been a hard week, and today, we lost a young patient.' I tried to hold back the tears but they welled up again. He held me. When I calmed he said, 'Do you really want to go on with your studies? I don't like to see you so tired and overwrought.'

'Of course I want to finish my studies. I just have to learn to handle such things. Don't ever doubt that I want to be a doctor. Now, what shall I wear?'

'I will select something.'

He brought me a figure hugging jersey dress in dark blue, which Simon told me, the colour was zaffre. He studied me carefully. 'Un ange, (an angel). That is what you look like with that light behind you, shining like a halo in your hair. You are composed? Then we go down.'

We found everyone there waiting for us.

'Sorry we are late everybody, but our doctor has had a difficult week. Now, who don't we know. Ah, Alex, your assistant, introduce us will you.'

'This is Helen, Simon, Trudi. She is the one who will shadow you, if that is agreeable.'

'Of course.' I said. It was the first time I had seen another transsexual, or at least been introduced.

I saw a young person of I thought, twenty-two or three, rather gawky, in an ill fitting dress with a terrible hair cut and makeup. Had I looked like that? I hoped not. I was certain that I had made my makeup better than that, but then Vanessa had taught me. There would be work to do.

'Shall we eat. I am hungry and I know Sophie will be after managing the children all day.'

I led the way into the dining room, seating Wally on my right and Helen on my left. Sabine sat next to Wally, then Simon, Sophie and Gérard, Alex and Annette.

The starter was carpaccio of beef, raw, cut very thinly, and served with a light mustard sauce and tomatoes.

'How goes it Wally. Are you enjoying your new work.'

'Very much. The readymade range has created a terrific stir in the market and we are selling the designs in the USA and the Far East.'

'And how is living in Paris? I apologise for not seeing you but the University has been very demanding.'

'I have hardly had time to settle in, but it is fine.'

'Do you hear from Isabel?'

'No. That is over. Really it was never going to work. She is very fiery when she is not sulky. What about you Trudi? Are you recovered from your horse accident?'

'I have mended. I cannot see any trace in my face, can you?'

'You are lovely.' Helen said simply, the first words she had uttered.

'That is very kind of you Helen. And how are things with your work? Are you enjoying what you do?'

'I have had a crash course, Alex showing me the ropes. But keeping up with you will be difficult.'

'What do you do Helen?' Wally asked.

'I am shadowing Trudi making a film about her life. I am taking intimate shots with a hand held camera and finding out her history. Weren't you at school together?'

'Yes we were. Trudi was head girl and I was head boy.'

'So you knew her before, as a boy?'

'Yes. A funny little boy, but yes a boy, a very girly boy, though at the time, I hardly noticed that. It was a shock when she changed. None of us thought she could do it. Well I couldn't have. But she did. Always behaved not like a girl, but a lady. Now she is a great lady and a great beauty.'

I was embarrassed. Luckily the next course came, my favourite chicken dish, Marengo, a favourite of Napoleon and named after one of his bloodiest battles.

An ice cream bombe followed, layers of vanilla, pistachio, and chocolate ice cream. We took coffee in the salon.

Wally chatted to me about news from school. Apart from Wally, the only person I now heard from was Sam. I wasn't really interested in anyone else. He also told me that he was playing rugby for a Paris team. He had lost no time in settling in.

'So what are you doing tomorrow Trudi?'

'I will get up early and go riding, I hope, if Sabine will come with me. Will you Sabine, please?'

'Of course mon amie. It will be your first ride since your accident so you should have someone with you. But I like to ride with you anyway. I rode Sheba twice this week, thinking that you might ride and I did not want her to be too fresh. She is lively, so you must be careful.'

'We must find out where the boys are shooting. We don't want guns scaring us and the horses.'

'I know where they are shooting,' Sabine replied, 'don't forget, I am the estate manager.'

'Of course you would know. I must be stupid. So have you shot before Wally?'

'Very little. Actually, I am a bit apprehensive that I will hit nothing or the wrong thing. Even so it will be another experience to chalk up. Safer than riding anyway.'

'And Alex and Helen, what is your plan?'

'Filming your activities and the Chateau and the grounds. The more footage we have the more we can cut, so we have really good footage to show.'

'And in the afternoon after a late lunch at one thirty, I would like to have some time alone with Helen, to get to know her and to lay some ground rules and set out what I think should be shown. I hope that is alright with you Alex?'

'You are the star Trudi, so we have to dance to your tune a bit, don't we.'

'Well everyone, I am very tired and I must go to bed. I wish you all good night and I will see you sometime tomorrow. Sabine, what time for you?'

'At eight?'

'That will be fine. Good night.'

They all said goodnight and I kissed Simon. I was in bed very quickly. I never heard Simon nor felt him get into bed, but I awoke cuddled into him.

I eased myself out of bed and washed and dressed in riding gear, put my hair in a snood and did my makeup. I was early, but when I reached the stable I found Sabine there already.

'Sabine, you are here already! I thought I would be first and tack up.'

'I am an early riser. Sheba is already for you. Just make sure the stirrups are the right length. You look as though you are riding dressage you are so smart. I feel like a stable girl beside you.'

'Sorry Sabine, I just can't help it. Maybe it is insecurity, but I always like to look my best. I am a bit nervous, will you lead?'

'Of course, then Sheba will follow. Let's go.'

We rode out onto the country road that led to the village. We turned right up a track which took us to the small rise beyond the village, the only hill in a rather flat landscape. We cantered to the top and along the ridge and descended by another track which led to the far end of the Beauvonne estate. We cantered again. 'OK?' she asked.

'Fine, loving it.'

'Fancy a gallop?'

'Lead on Sabine.'

We galloped. Tears filled my eyes from the chill rushing air, and my thighs ached from gripping with my knees. At last we slowed and brought the horses to a walk. I rode alongside her. 'Phew, that was great. Thanks Sabine. Where are we now?'

'On my father's land. Then we turn onto the estate and ride around the other side back to the Chateau. Tell me Trudi, this Wally, he knew you at school?'

'Yes.'

'He knew you as a boy too?'

'Yes he did. We were not great friends, but on a couple of occasions he stopped bullies from hitting me. Then he was head boy and I was head girl. We had a good relationship, I mean like good friends, quite close, like a brother.'

'Has he a girl friend?'

'I don't think so. Do you remember, Isabel? They parted after that week when I had my accident.'

'Oh yes. The sulky girl. He is nice?'

'Wally, oh yes, one of the best. I thought he was laughing at me, but he was just so amused because, I have changed so much since the time we first met at twelve years old. That's eleven years ago. How I hated being sent to that boys' boarding school.'

'And he now lives in Paris?'

'Yes.......Sabine, are you interested in him?'

'I don't think he even notices me. Yes, I find him very attractive. He is big, I think tough but gentle.'

'Sabine, I think you are blushing.'

'Not at all. It is just from the riding and the chill air. Don't you say anything to him.'

'Of course not Sabine, but he may need a little push.'

'No. Do not embarrass me Trudi. If he is not interested, then it is best he leaves me alone.'

'You must eat with us tonight, to make up equal numbers. I want to do something with you. You do not bother too much about your appearance do you? Will you let me do your face at least, not over the top, just a subtle makeover. I would just love to.'

'I don't do that sort of thing.'

'Perhaps you should. There is nothing wrong in presenting oneself the best one can be. Please let me. You can always wash it off.'

'I will let you try.'

'Excellent. I have to do something with Helen too. Where are we now?

'Not far from home, just fifteen minutes away. You have done well.'

'I think so too. I have enjoyed it Sabine. I always enjoy your company, even though you are a tease.'

'You love being teased Trudi, ma belle amie. You like attention.'

We entered the stable yard just as the crackle of gunfire came from the shooters. Alex was lurking in the yard with Helen, camera in hand. We stabled the horses, and I asked Sabine to come to my room at five thirty.

'Alex, can you lose yourself somewhere, while I talk to Helen?'

'Sure. I'll wander about, getting a flavour of the estate.'

'Good. You come with me Helen.'

I took her up to my bedroom and left her looking at my dresses while I had a quick shower. I dried my hair and ran the straighteners through it, then went into the bedroom. I did my make up with Helen watching. It took me ten minutes. I put on a blouse and a heavy woollen skirt.

'OK Helen. Have you had any advice on your makeup or dress?'

'No, well only a bit.'

'Tell me about your family.'

'Dad is a surveyor, mum works in the library. I went to Unie, studied art history and came out as gay, but I also cross-dressed. It was very confusing. I didn't really know what was happening to me. It was bad before puberty, but when my body started to change, it was awful. I hated being what I was. Couldn't tell my parents. I self-harmed.'

'I think I would have self-harmed too, but my childhood was different. At boarding school until I went into the sixth form, I was a boy but a girl at home. I loved my life at home, and that made my life at school bearable in some ways but all the time as a boy, I just longed for my girly things.

'So what made you think you are a transsexual rather than a transvestite? For example, what do you think of your body Helen?'

'I hate it, have always hated it, but only realised why since I suppose I was fourteen.'

'And when did you start cross dressing?'

'Oh way before that. My parents just made a joke of it at first but as I got older, father got angry and I did it in private.'

'And where are you going now. Are you just going to be a cross-dresser or are you taking medication and thinking about surgery?'

'I'm not thinking about surgery, I definitely want it and I am in the programme for surgery.'

'And you are taking hormones etc.?'

'Yes, my GP was good to me and sent me to the clinic.'

'You probably think I am nosey, but I need to know, because it makes a difference to what I share with you and how I think about you and treat you. So what advice have you had about dress and makeup etc.?'

'I went to some lessons at the clinic.'

'Has your mother helped you?'

'No, we find talking about it difficult, on her part and mine.'

'Who gave you that terrible haircut?'

'The hairdresser in my village, well a friend really.'

'With friends like that.....If I can make an appointment, would you like a haircut. I will pay for it. Oh, I forgot, it is Saturday, so everyone will be closed by lunchtime. No wait until we are in Paris and I will have it done properly. In the meantime we must make the best of it. Sit on my stool, I will see what I can do. No first, I think I want to do your face. Here are some pads. Clean your face, everything off, back to basics. If you are going to be around me, then I want you to be the best you can be. Into the bathroom with you. Go!'

She returned to the bedroom with a clean face. I sat her down, moisturised then plucked her eyebrows. I started with foundation and worked through, not allowing her to see what I was doing. Then I combed her hair about and used my tongs to get it to sit in a different way, less punk and more preppy. I stood back and surveyed her. I was pleased with my work. 'Don't be embarrassed by what I say. No don't look in the mirror yet. I have not finished with you. Do you like having you hair done or your makeup?'

'Yes Trudi. I have never had anyone, except for the clinic and Alex and his sister, treat me as a woman.'

'I am doing Sabine too later. Do you wear jeans a lot?'

'I do tend to.'

'Why? Are your legs bad?'

'I don't think so. It's just easy.'

'Yes, but at the moment, your figure is very boyish still. Hopefully with medication you will put some weight on your hips and behind. I know girls figures are much more boyish these days, but even so, they are not like you unless they are half starved. Have you shaved your legs?'

'Yes Trudi.'

'Good girl. Do you mind dropping your jeans? Are you respectable underneath?'

'Oh yes. Now?'

'Oui. Maintenant.'

She dropped her jeans for me and stood shyly, eyes cast down.

'OK.' I opened a drawer and produced seventy denier hold ups in dark blue. 'Put these on!'

I looked in my wardrobe. There were mini skirts hanging there, that I had bought the first weekend I started living in Paris. I brought out a deep crimson one. 'Try this!'

It was not too bad a fit, if anything a bit tight on her waist.

'Now shoes. Do you have any more girly ones?'

'Yes. I have some black patent ones with a four inch heal.'

'You can get them in a minute. OK. Keep facing me and stand up. No that top will not do.' I looked in the wardrobe and produced a more feminine blouse.

'Put this on!' I saw she had breasts at least, so the hormones were having an effect. When she was finally buttoned up and dressed to my satisfaction I said, 'Now you may look.'

She turned and looked in my long mirror. I stood behind her and held her shoulders.

'What do you think?'

'I'm another person.'

'Do you like her?'

'Oui. I love it. So much more girly. I was a bit shy of being so feminine of going over the top.'

'But it is not over the top is it? Transvestites go over the top, they like to dress sleazy, but you are not sleazy. Classy, chic, young, oui? Before, you looked half hearted about being female, in fact you could have been a girl wanting to be a boy.'

'Trudi, thank you. You have been so kind.'

'Go and find those shoes and come back here to me immediately.'

She disappeared. I went through my wardrobe bringing out things I no longer wore but were still good, two skirts four blouses, a coat and three dresses and finally a cocktail dress in pale lilac which I had never worn and did not like much.

I place them all on the bed.

She returned in the heels.

'Walk to me.' I watched. I remembered Vanessa putting me through my paces years ago. It was how long, seven years? It did not seem possible.

'OK. Look on the catwalk, the runway, modelling clothes, we walk like this.' I demonstrated. 'Do that on the Champs and you will probably be arrested or trip up. But as a female, you can tone it down. Look men tend, not all but some, many tend to walk as they sit, knees out. Women walk knees in, toes if anything pin toed, one foot slightly in front of the other. Men have their feet at sort of ninety degrees,' I demonstrated, adding the walk.

It made her laugh.

'Now you have to practice. Are those shoes comfortable?'

'They are a lot better with a stocking somehow.'

'Then wear them all day. Stick to me like glue and get used to your new look. When you sit, smooth your skirt as you sit down. Keep your knees together, or they will see what you had for breakfast. You can cross your thighs, but make sure your skirt is over your legs and not gapping. Or more ladylike is to cross at the ankles and lean your knees away from your feet. You can make one foot pin toed, that will push your knees together, and you can lay your hands in your lap too. Have I been a help? Not too embarrassing?'

'Trudi you have been so kind. Thank you. I will let you have the clothes back.'

'Oh no! You are dressed for the day. And the clothes are now yours and also these on the bed. If you are going to be around me, I do demand that you make an effort and remember all I have said. I shall scold you if you slip.' I smiled. 'Come let's go down and see where Alex is.'

We found that the sun had emerged from the dull November sky. Alex was down the main drive photographing the Chateau while the light was good.

'Trudi, can I take some shots of you in front of the Chateau while the light holds?'

'Of course Alex, what would you like me to do? I could walk towards you, or stand pensively, or probably get my hair to fly in this breeze.'

'All those please. Here, Helen, by the way, you look fabulous darling, take notes of the shots as I shout them out.'

He spent thirty minutes taking shots, repeating them when the light had changed as a cloud passed over. Finally he was satisfied.

'If that is all Alex, I am getting cold and I am sure Helen is. Let us go in and see whether the shooting party have returned. Lunch should be ready anyway. If they are not there, we will have ours.'

The boys were just trooping in through the stable yard entrance as we approached, casting off muddy boots and checking their weapons, to make sure they were unloaded before they snapped the breach shut. They seemed to have a good bag of pheasants.

Helen went ahead to the loo. 'You have given her a terrific makeover Trudi,' Alex said.

'I had a lot of help from Vanessa, from Simon, Marco, Pierre and others. You like what I have done with her?'

'Yes. Terrific. I could not say anything, well didn't like to hurt her feelings, but she needed advice. Thanks so much Trudi.'

'It was partly selfish. I told her that if she was shadowing me, then she had to look the part. Anyway, I had a lot of help and we all need it you know, whether from people or magazines. When we get to Paris I will have her hair done by someone who actually knows about hair. Last time I think she went to a sheep shearer. Looking good will do so much for her confidence. Also, she needs feeding up. At the moment she is a bag of bones, so look after her. Regular good quality meals Alex.'

'Actually it was my sister! did her hair.'

'Oh sorry Alex. Is your sister a sheep shearer or does she have a poodle parlour.'

He laughed. 'You know you are very funny. I am just getting used to your wit. You are quite right. My sister is not a bona fide hairdresser, she just possesses a comb and a pair of hairdressing scissors. But thanks.'

'I know how hard it is being out in the world, searching for an image which has taken girls fourteen or fifteen years to achieve. You need to look after her, Alex. I will do my best to help her. Come I am hungry.'

We all met up for lunch, cold meats and salad and a good claret or white burgundy. In the afternoon, we went our separate ways. I went to bed, glad to have time to myself.

I woke at five, showered and dressed to await my next fashion victim. Sabine arrived promptly at five thirty. I took her up to my bedroom and immediately started on her bushy eyebrows. Her dark hair and eyebrows to match, gave her a glowering look. She made a great fuss at first, exclaiming after each one was plucked. I ignored her pleas and carried on. I continued her treatment by exfoliating her skin with a cream containing apricot shell. Again she protested. I washed her face, then moisturised and applied a foundation. I made her face and painted her nails. I straightened her hair and arranged it in a neat and feminine style. She changed into the dress she had brought, an emerald green dress, which clung to her excellent figure. I was surprised that she had such a dress and even more surprised to find that she had shoes to match. I swivelled her round to face the mirror.

'Who is that beautiful estate manager?' I asked.

'I think that is me. I see what you mean. A little effort can make a lot of difference. I feel quite attractive. I thought I was just plain.'

'You were, but only because you spent no time on yourself. I quite thought that you were a lesbian, because you were so plain. Perhaps you are after all really attracted to Wally. Well that is good, because I told him you fancied him.'

'No. That is terrible.'

'I am joking Sabine. Of course I didn't say anything, but it will be interesting to see how he reacts to you tonight. I think you look gorgeous. Now I am going to get myself ready.'

'Do you want me to go?'

'No, Sabine. I am no longer shy. Being dressed in the models change room, one cannot remain shy. Men have eased my breasts into a dress with the palm of their hand. So stay here.'

She watched me and chatted with me as I dressed.

Chapter 14.

We descended to dinner. Tonight everyone had dressed. When Sabine and I entered the salon, the gentlemen rose. I saw Wally's look of amazement when he saw Sabine. Gone was the tomboy estate manager and in her place, was an attractive woman. I went into the dining room and shuffled the place settings, putting Sabine next to Wally. On my other side I had Gérard, then Helen and Alex. Annette was between Wally and Sophie and Simon was at the end opposite me.

I watched with amusement as Wally started to pay more and more attention to Sabine. She positively radiated sex appeal. And they were soon laughing together, and I saw her touch his sleeve when telling him something. I hoped my plan was working.

Afterwards in the salon I sat with Simon. He whispered in my ear, 'Do you know what you are doing?'

'With what?'

'With Anglo French relations?'

'I am attempting un entente cordiale. I think they are perfect for each other, both single, both intelligent and attractive.'

'You my darling have had a busy day. You have left your mark. Helen looks like a young lady rather than a transvestite and Sabine, almost a beauty. Congratulations. You have done well.'

'I had to do something. If Helen is tracking around after me, I want someone with a little panache. Anyway, I had a lot of help from Vanessa and you, so much from you, my dear man. I had to give back a bit.'

As we spoke, Sabine rose from her chair. 'I should be going. Thank you Simon and Trudi.'

'Are you walking Sabine,' I asked.

'Yes. It is only fifteen minutes.'

'I'll walk with you. I could do with the exercise,' Wally said.

'Oh thank you but I do know the way,' Sabine smiled.

'And I need the exercise. I'll say good night to you all. Come along Sabine, let's get our coats.'

When they had gone, Annette winked at me. I smiled.

'Simon, I think I must go to bed too. Are you coming?'

'I will have to wait for Wally to return to lock up.'

'I will do that,' Gérard volunteered. 'Annette and I will finish this bottle anyway. Leave it to us.'

We went up the stairs hand in hand. Simon kissed me when we reached the balcony. 'You are a naughty genius, and I love you. We make love tonight, yes?'

'Oh yes. You have neglected me lately.'

'You are always working, always at the hospital. I have lonely nights.'

He undressed me, slowly, and gently, until I stood nude. He surveyed me as one might the Venus de Milo in the Louvre.

'A work of art, and I don't mean your posy. Is there anything you have to do before I attend to you?'

'Oui. I have to go to the bathroom.'

I go to the loo and afterwards use the bidet. I use perfume, Miss Dior. I return to find he is already in bed. I climb into bed gracefully, flinging myself over him so I am riding on his hips. He is already rampant and I feel for him, all the time watching his face. I grab his penis, firmly, squeezing him. I lower onto him and grip him with my abdominal muscles, then I start to ride him, all the time we watch each other's faces. I feel as if I am going to come and I slow. I make him jump by pinching his nipple, then I kiss him, and he returns my kiss, his lips roving around mine, so gently because he knows that drives me mad. I press my lips to his and he opens his mouth slightly, allowing my tongue to enter. He grips it with his teeth, but without hurting. His hands rove over the twin mounds of my behind, caressing my smooth skin. Suddenly our roles are reversed and he is on top, pumping away at me, holding me on the edge of orgasm as though he can read my state, and I believe he can. He knows me, and I know him. He keeps me on the edge, almost on the edge of reason for minutes. Just as I think I can stand no more, I climax, and then, only then he quickens and finishes himself. We lie cuddled until we fall asleep.

We woke to a howling gale, rain lashing against the window. I ran to the bathroom and turned on the shower to bring warm water through. I used the loo then entered the shower. I washed and dried, did my hair and still Simon slept. I sat doing my makeup in bra and knickers, when I heard him stirring. I crossed to the bed.

'Hello husband.' I kissed him on the lips. 'What shall we do with our guests today?'

'Never mind the guests, what shall I do with you today?'

'What we must do is go to the nursery and see the babies.'

'Not 'the' babies Trudi, ma belle, *our* babies.'

'Yes, you are right. I do not see enough of them. Come paresseux (lazy bones), rouse yourself.'

'Your French is very good, you can now insult your husband in his own language. Put some clothes on before I am tempted to give you a good spanking.'

'You would not dare. I have never been spanked.' And I remembered that I had spanked, who was it? Oh yes, Dirty David, the tennis coach. I wonder what he thinks, when he sees my name in the press. Those photos I took, whatever happened to them. I must ask Wally.

'I am dressing and dressing warm. It is a beast of a day. No riding. Perhaps we should all go to lunch in Chartres or Alençon. What do you think. We take *our* children and Sophie. Can we?'

'Then go down and tell chef not to cook and book a table. The chef was doing small food for lunch, tell him we will have that for tea. Vite.'

I dressed in a French blue woollen dress and pearls and descended to the kitchen. I gave instructions to chef, and he glowered. Oh well, I supposed, so would I.

I phoned la Rive Droite in Alençon where we had once eaten before. They could fit us all in at one thirty. I went into breakfast and found everyone there except for Simon.

'Je suis désolé to be so late. Simon is just coming. I heard the wind and the rain and buried my head under the covers. As the weather is so inclement, we thought to go to

Alençon for lunch, everybody and les enfants. I hope that is agreeable. I think I will invite Sabine too. I will ring her.'

'I'll do that if you like Trudi,' Wally said.

'Oh, good, thank you Wally. Oh, and I need to talk to you about something after breakfast, if you have time?'

'Of course. I'll phone Sabine now before she makes other arrangements.'

'Thank you Wally.'

Annette looked at me with her amused conspiratorial smile as Wally departed pulling his phone from his pocket. One thing was sure, he had her phone number. It made me feel warm inside.

Simon entered. He looked so handsome and French, silver grey suit, with the faintest blue threads running through it, tie of black and silver and hankie to match. He only needed a Japanned, silver topped cane to rival Maurice Chevalier in his younger days.

I told him all was arranged. I departed for the nursery. The twins wrapped themselves around my legs, and I lifted them both in my arms with difficulty. 'So Sophie, we would like to go for lunch in Alençon, everybody, you and the children, and we will look after them, so you can just enjoy the company. Is that OK?'

'Of course Madame Trudi.'

'Non, c'est Trudi pas Madame. You would like to come with us? I am sorry, you do not have to, I just thought it would be nice to have everyone.'

'I want to come Trudi thank you. Just sometimes I feel, quite lonely.'

'Yes, of course. I should think what we can do about that. Who do we know to keep you company?'

'Sabine has a brother. I have met him about three times. He works on their farm.'

'Ah oui, Laurent. I will phone now Sophie.'

I flew downstairs and phoned Sabine. 'Sabine, you are coming today? Oh good. Sabine, Laurent. Can he come too? Oui for Sophie. You will ask him? Yes I will hold............He would like to, better than walking through the sugar beet? I hope so, I won't repeat that to Sophie. We are going to La Rive Droite in Alençon. We must be there for one thirty. So I suggest you take the Landrover with Wally, your brother and Sophie and little Sébastien. Then I will drive Helen and Alex and the twins. Simon will have to drive Annette and Gérard. Good, I will tell Wally the arrangement.'

I went the rounds telling them all the arrangements. I found Wally and took him into the salle à manger.

'You liked Sabine then?'

He grinned. 'Yes, nice girl.'

'The best. It is nice for her to have someone different to talk to. Thank you Wally.'

'Drop the pretence, Trudi. I can see right through you. I know you too well. There is always an agenda.'

'A good one usually. I hope.'

'Oh yes. But we know you are match making. We laughed about it while we walked to her home last night. That wasn't why you brought me in here though?'

'No Wally. I want you to think back to school. I once gave you a CD for safe keeping. I wondered what you did with it?'

'The tennis coach one?'

'Oh you looked?'

'Not until we had all left school and I was clearing out stuff. I destroyed it Trudi. You don't need to tell me what that was all about.'

'I will tell you. He found out what we did to Stuart, and he was blackmailing me for sex. It was gross. I played along until I could take those photos. Then I had a hold over him. I feel ashamed of what I had to do. It was the most disgusting thing in my life.'

'Trudi, Trudi. You know I love you like a brother. It is all in the past. I still think just as much of you, maybe even more for getting yourself out of that fix.' He kissed me.

'That is the first time you have kissed me voluntarily. Thank you Wally. What a good friend you are. I am so glad you applied for this job. I can't tell you how good it is to have you here. My best time at school was in the Upper Sixth, being head girl to your head boy. I looked up to you, you know.'

'Of course you did.' He laughed, 'But yes it was good. Best year of our lives. Well, I hope not.'

'We better get ready to go.'

Twenty minutes later, I had shepherded everyone into the salon. I would lead in my Mercedes and we would go in convoy. The rain had stopped but the wind was still wild. I had tied my hair up in a knot and fastened it with a leather and wooden peg hair clip.

I settled the twins in their car seats and we all piled in. Half an hour later we parked on the left bank and crossed the river on Pont Neuf to the restaurant that lay just the other side. We were shown up to the first floor, to the banqueting suite and were soon settled after they had found three child seats. Tasha seated herself by my chair. The twins were between Simon and I, and Annette was looking after Sébastien. Helen was between Wally and Alex, then Sophie and Laurent.

It was a merry party. I surveyed them and felt so lucky to have all these great friends around me.

It took quite a time to sort out our choices from the menu, but eventually the waiter had it all down. Simon ordered Champagne and Vichy water, followed by bottles of red and white with the main course. We drivers could have but one small glass.

Simon and I had our work cut out with the twins and Annette needed help from Sophie with Sébastien. The starters were fine, the twins snacking on prawns and apple salad. Sebastien started to sing at the top of his voice and wanted to throw a prawn, but was restrained by Sophie.

The main dishes came and we all said they were delicious too. By the time we had sweets and coffees, it was after four. We returned in pouring rain, the countryside looking dull and uninviting. Alex grabbed one twin, I the other and we ran to the porch. Gradually we all assembled in the salon. We had finger food at six thirty.

I said my good byes and set out for Paris with Alex and Helen. I was on duty at eight in the morning, and wanted to get to bed. Wally was hitching a lift with Gérard and Annette. Tuesday he was off to Los Angeles again. I would phone Sabine in the week and see what she had to say about Wally. It was interesting, but then so was Sophie and Laurent. It would be wonderful if it all ended happily.

The next weeks on the ward seemed endless, but now Simon and the children were in Paris too, life if more complicated, was more rewarding.

Sales from Maison Beauvonne had overtaken production and work had to be outsourced again. Simon had at last secured the factory near Clermont-Ferrand. He was up and down between the Maison and the factory, often with Gérard and sometimes Wally. Simon and Wally seemed to be getting on very well. I was so pleased, but then Wally was just a wonderful young man. I found out from Sabine that he was in touch frequently, and that she joined him at his flat when she could.

I was at last getting used to the wards, finding people who were without hope, being kind to them but not taking those cares home. It had not been easy to learn the knack. Following a surgeon or professor around the wards and being asked to make a diagnosis from a potted history and a cursory inspection, was difficult and nerve wracking. Our tutors could be scathing, and some of our equals were not above laughing, even if they had proved no better in the past. Because I stood out, a celebrity student, I suffered more than most. I had to be better than them and I tried harder.

Christmas approached. I would have to work right up to Christmas Eve, then I had a week off. Wally was going to be with us, as would Gérard and Annette.

Helen had completed her assignment, gathering my past history, doing some camera work. She and Alex were not invited for Christmas, at my specific request of Simon. Our Christmas party was therefore eight of us, and we would all go to the Chalet in Courchevel to ski. Jean Luc and Élise would join us there for three days and Jean Luc's father would be our guide. Wally would need lessons, as he had only skied once before, but Sabine was going to be his tutor.

I arrived home at the Chateau mid morning on Christmas Eve. Everyone else was already there. We ate cold meats and sausages, and rice salad for lunch. I went to bed, asking Simon to wake me at four.

I awoke to find Simon in my bed. It can be the worst way to wake, having finger tips rising up ones thigh, and it can be the best. I had awoken from an erotic dream, not Simon but Wally, and yet it was Simon awakening me, and Simon that I loved. I rolled towards him and our lips met. He smiled and he played with me, his fingers opening me, exploring, his teeth on my breast. I moaned and he chuckled. He came down on me, slowly penetrating until he filled me completely. I wrapped my legs around him, imprisoning him in me, then released. He pumped, slowly, gradually increasing speed until I bucked. He laughed as I climaxed, then continued until he too gasped, thrusting to a finish. I so loved this man. How could I have dreamt about Wally.

Chapter 15.

'I know,' I said, 'smokey eyes.'

'Wrong. Tonight I would like you to enhance the blue of your eyes with blue eyeliner and shadow, with dark blue mascara.'

'So what am I wearing?'

'Silver. When you have washed, then I will dress you.'

I emerged from the bathroom, perfumed and moisturised. Simon rose from his chair and brought forward a corset that tied at the back with long laces. I held my breasts as he wrapped it around me. He pulled on the laces, ever tighter my waist diminishing until I had an hourglass figure. I could hardly breathe, but after a time, keeping a very straight back, I learnt to control my breathing.

He produced the dress. It was a beautiful sheath, pleated up across my hips and continuing under the bust.

The skirt was a long pencil, with a wiggle chapel train. It would be difficult to walk in. It also had what proved to be a dense folded bow on the rear, which looked as though I had a bustle. It was a modern take on a Victorian dress. When he was satisfied that it fitted and I could wear it, he dressed me with my diamond cuff and earrings. Deftly, he pulled my hair back separated it and entwined the different strands into a neat knot. As a finishing touch, he pushed a small tiara into my hair. Only then was I allowed to survey the effect in the long mirror. I looked like a princess. I wanted to cry. How could all this have happened to me? Why did I deserve to be so pampered? How could he love me so much.

I turned to him. 'I look wonderful. Over the years you have transformed me from gauche little transvestite, to princess.'

'All this is only a skin. It is nothing. It merely mirrors the beauty beneath.'

'You are the funniest man. And I love you Simon, to distraction. You will have to hold my arm as I descend the stairs in this.'

'Of course. I will now dress.'

'I am going to check on Sabine and make sure she has everything.'

'Don't worry too much. She too has a new dress, and Wally a new suit. The one he had was just too awful for a Beauvonne representative. I should knock the door first. Your match making may have had good effect.'

I knocked Sabine's bedroom door. It was answered by Wally, fully dressed except for his jacket. He was tall and handsome, a beautiful manly face, and I caught a whiff of aftershave, which I recognised as Polo Modern Reserve.

'A princess to see you, Sabine,' he said.

She was already dressed, in emerald green, her hair straightened, makeup done. She too looked a picture. She rose from her stool and we embraced.

'You look wonderful Sabine. That colour really suits you.'

'And you too. You really are a princess.'

'And Wally, I suppose was assisting you to zip up? I must say Wally, you look so handsome too. I would say beautiful.......' I chuckled. 'It is like when we first walked around the school as head boy and girl, isn't it? If you have all you need then I will leave you. We will be going down to the vestibule shortly for the present giving, so don't delay, then we can get the children to bed and have dinner. See you soon.'

I returned and found Simon ready. We took the stairs sedately. I tried not to look at the treads. Eyes turned as we descended. This year Sabine's father mother and Laurent were there too. I felt very self-conscious, so exposed with all eyes upon us. I wished for the first time that Simon, especially in the company of all our friends, had not made me so exotic.

Sébastien was already in bed, but the twins gambolled about among the legs of the adults and rushed to hug our legs when we arrived on the floor. I was pleased to meet Sabine's parents again, this time as mistress of Chateau de Beauvonne. This was a sign that the slight feud with Simon was at an end.

Didier, Sabine's father, was very like Simon, but I would say fifteen years older. He was quite reserved towards me and I realised that I had some work to do to make him warm to me. Her mother was much more amicable, like Sabine, homely but I realised behind her motherly exterior was an intelligent woman. I spent time with her, answering her questions about my study and my life. Adèle had fastened herself to my leg, and made another subject for conversation, and I felt, made me a more earthly figure than the princess-like doll Simon had assisted down the stairs.

My film idol, Scarlet O'Hara from Gone With the Wind, would have courted attention, but in this company of friends, I just felt too conspicuous.

I circulated, saying to Mireille, Sabine's charming mother, that Simon had dressed me especially, and I felt so over the top.

"I think you look divine,' she said, 'and of course you are a model and Simon is a couturier and a Comte. It is natural that he wants to spoil you and to show you off, dear.'

I thanked her. I excused myself saying I had to check on the table. I made sure that the place settings were as I had agreed with Simon. Sabine's father was on my left and Gerard on my right, with Sabine's mother between him and Wally. Sabine was next to Simon and opposite Annette. Sophie and Laurent were next to each other.

After the champagne, we went into the salon and Simon played Santa, selecting and handing out presents, a role he loved. First the children received their big presents, an electric ride on tractor for André and a sports car, a BMW for Adèle. When they were occupied, with various members of the company protecting the furniture from erratic manoeuvrings, Sophie received her presents, a dress and a beautiful suit from Simon and gold bangle from me. I noticed a tear in her eye as we embraced and kissed.

Simon gave Sabine a long waxed coat and a hat to match, but then produced some beautiful knee high leather boots for her. I gave her earrings, dangly ones in white and yellow gold, with small emeralds set in the end of the two branches and in the earpiece, to go with her dress and colouring. Wally was given a Rolex by me and keys to a car from Simon. Simon instructed him to look out of the window. We all looked and saw the new Mercedes, gleaming in the floodlight that lit the Chateau porch.

The present giving continued with gifts for Annette and Gérard and Sabine's parents and Laurent.

Simon gave me a box, covered in Christmas wrapping. Inside were two boxes. The first contained a diamond necklace. Which he put around my neck. The second was a ring box. It contained a diamond engagement ring, and he put it on my ring finger.

'Ladies and gentlemen, our dear friends. I know that Trudi feels over dressed tonight, my long ears have overheard her say how conspicuous she feels, but there is a reason. It is with great pleasure that I give you Trudi, the next Comtesse de Beauvonne. She has agreed to marry me on 15th July and everyone here is invited. You all know her. Over the 6 years that I have known her, she has proved ever faithful, resourceful, stalwart and perceptive and brave. She held Beauvonne together during my two illnesses and her ideas have made this last year a great success rather than the disaster it could have been. In addition her action has brought me in contact again with my neighbours, my cousin Didier. I present Trudi de Beauvonne.'

Everyone clapped and congratulated us. We were toasted in champagne. At last I relaxed.

The children were taken up to bed, Simon and Wally carrying the children's presents. I helped put them in bed and we sang. The twins fell asleep quite quickly.

Dinner went well. I managed to make Didier laugh with some stories of my life in the hospital and my mistakes in speaking French. He complimented me on the change I had made to Simon and also said how grateful he was for offering Sabine the management of the estate.

The evening had started with my feeling an interloper, now I began to feel a real person, valued for being me and not just Simon's plaything.

The meal was excellent, lobster starter, followed by a cold soup followed by roast pheasant and a sorbet pallet cleanser. At half past one Sabine's parents and Laurent departed and we all went to bed. Tomorrow, Christmas day, we were all off to the chalet. I had no idea how we would fit. This time Sophie and the children would be with us, as well as Sabine and Wally, Annette and Gérard and Laurent. It meant three cars.

We managed to get away before nine o'clock, on a grey day with small flakes of snow flying about in a stiff breeze. We stopped in Thiers for a quick lunch, and pressed on. It was quite late when we finally made the underground car park in Courchevel. Robert collected our baggage and we all piled into the bubbles for Jardin Alpin. The children were asleep and did not wake even when we entered the bubble. We finally had to wake them. Adèle was fractious and I carried her clasped to me under my thick coat.

I was surprised to find the chalet had a new wing of two stories over a new entrance and ski room.

'You didn't tell me you had done this.'

'I thought it would be a surprise.'

'It certainly is. It is just fantastic. Have we new bedrooms as well?

'Two more, and we have a new master bedroom. Look over the door.'

I read the sign, 'Chalet Trudi'. 'Oh Simon. Thank you for naming it after me. Come everybody, let's get in out of the cold.'

Entering through the new ski room with its new ski racks and boot warmers and driers, the heat hit us like a warm blanket. Simon and I took the small lift to the first floor with Sophie and the children. The lounge was now huge, with an open plan kitchen and dining room in the modern style up stairs, with a magnificent view towards the

Saulire slopes and escarpment to the south, and on the other side the valley. A lift had been installed too, to make life easier for Simon and his false leg.

We met everybody and he assigned a room to Annette and Gérard. Sophie and Laurent had said they would share a room as did Wally and Sabine. The new nursery was next door to our room, and Sophie saw that all was in order. The children had a quick snack and went to bed, Sophie helping me calm them down with a story and a song.

We ate dinner of a hearty beef stew followed by crêpes without changing because it was so late. Then we all drifted to bed, tired from the drive and the night before.

Chapter 16.

It is a fact, that any crack in the curtains in the Alps at dawn, will tell what sort of day it is. When I awoke, it was obvious that the sun was coming over the mountain top in a cloudless sky. I was out of bed in an instant, even as Simon stirred and opened sleepy eyes. I pulled back the curtains and saw a clear blue sky. I showered quickly and dressed in base layers. I went next door to the children and found Sophie already there. The twins were dressed, so I washed Sébastien and dressed him. Between us we took them to breakfast, and while they ate yoghurt, bread and jam, we somehow managed to eat the same and drink coffee. The three children were going to nursery, leaving us all free to ski. Sophie and I would have to return by three-thirty to pick them up at the end of nursery school.

Wally entered followed by Sabine, then Simon and the rest of the household. Wally would ski with Liz, who had appeared out of the blue. Simon had of course organised it and she had brought skis for him. Sabine and I took the children down in the lift to nursery, and waited for the rest of the party to join us. We saw Wally struggling down the green run, Liz skiing backwards to keep an eye on him.

The rest of us skied all day, until the light was fading. Sophie and I collected the children while the others did one more run, but by that time the sun had disappeared over the mountaintop and the light was dull and flat. The temperature had dropped a few degrees too. In the chalet, we busied ourselves, giving the children their tea. Afterwards we had a game with them, romping on the floor, chasing them around the room. We bathed them and by the time the others came in from an après ski vin chaud, we were happily eating cake and drinking tea. Wally entered with Liz and flopped in a chair. I poured tea for them as they helped themselves to cake.

'And how did it go Wally.' I asked.

Liz replied for him. 'He did exceptionally well. I can tell he is a sportsman. Natural ability.'

'Did you enjoy it?' Sabine asked.

'Yes, it was good. I can see what people get out of it. Tomorrow we are going over to, is it 1650 Liz?'

'Yes, a little more challenging than these slopes, but not frightening. We had a good time. He is very funny.'

'I was not trying to be funny, but two planks on the bottom of my feet like over large clown shoes, don't help the image." Wally replied with a smile.

I had one more piece of pain de compagne with French butter and Marmite. 'Simon, I am going up to read and rest.'

'Yes Trudi, me also, and to take off this leg. I have found it tiring today.'

We went up hand in hand.

We lay on the bed together, reading a bit. Then we just pulled up the coverlet, cuddled up and had a sixty minute snooze. I was awaked by Simon emerging from the bathroom clad in a towel and walking with his stick. I had not seen him with pain from his leg since the early days.

'Come, lie on the bed and let me look. After all, I am a doctor of sorts.'

He lay on the bed and I examined the stump I had once been so frightened by. There was a patch of redness where the stump had been rubbing. I looked at the socket of the leg, trying to locate just where it met the rubbed patch. There was not much I could do to relieve the pressure.

'Perhaps if I cut one of my fine cotton socks and put a stocking over it, leaving a hole for the sore place, it will be just enough to relieve the pressure there. Can I try?'

'Of course, it's worth a try.'

I found a nice clean white sock and cut it. I fitted that then put a sixty denier stocking over the whole stump. We fitted the leg and he declared it felt better. He would see how it felt after an evening.

We dressed casually and went down. Gradually all assembled, including Liz and Jean Luc and Élise and Jean Luc's father Pierre who was our guide again. Sabine announced that she would ski with Wally tomorrow, and I wondered whether she was jealous of Liz.

Pierre suggested Mont Vallon for next day. I had done it before, a long steep run, whichever side of the mountain one took, but it was more adrenalin than enjoyment. Simon surprised me by saying that he would not ski, his leg being too sore. I decided that I would remain with him.

As we went to bed, I suggested that we visit the medical centre tomorrow and then play with the children in the snow. It would be nice to have a day en famille, just we two and the three children.

Next day after breakfast, we took the children to Le Jardin des Enfants, where there was a toy house in the snow and sledges to play on. We made snowmen and threw snowballs. We lunched overlooking the slopes and saw Wally skiing with Liz, apparently making good progress.

We took the children to a slope-side café. Sunshine reached through the restaurant window and it was unbearably warm. We paid and left, taking the bubble home, which the twins loved. Outside the chalet we made a large snowman and managed to dress it with an old beanie and a scarf as well as the traditional carrot nose. I made snow angels in the snow and the twins made small ones. By two-thirty, the sunlight had faded as the sun passed over the mountaintop. The cold hit and we retreated indoors. We played with Lego, making a crude bed for the teddies to sleep in, then a building with the Jenga, which of course André soon knocked down.

Tea appeared, bread and marmite or jam, and cake, a marvellous orange sponge. The skiers trooped in, first Wally with Sabine, full of joyous chat as they mounted the stairs. After throwing off their ski clothes they reappeared, Wally taking Seb on his knee, bouncing him and making him giggle. Sabine made a building with the twins. Much later the rest appeared, having had a vin chaud or two in the bar.

Sophie and I put the children to bed. I went straight to my room and lay down. Looking after three children was an exhausting business, but I was pleased that Simon and I had done so, even just for a day.

Simon came up. He too felt exhausted he said. He turned out the light and we lay on the bed half clothed. I stripped off and got under the covers. Simon followed suit. At first we just lay cuddling each other, in fact I dozed off, to be awakened by his wandering hands, moving about my thighs. I turned towards him, giggling as he touched more sensitive areas. He mounted me gently, inserted himself deeply, but then just used his hands to arouse me, touching me, mouthing my breasts, playing with clit and anus, his lips tantalising mine until I thought I would burst unless he brought me to a climax. Only then did he start to pump into me, slowly, then ever faster. I came quickly, but he did not stop, I was near screaming when he at last came and we could both relax.

We lay coupled for some minutes then together went into the shower, he hopping along on his good leg. We washed each other and kissed under the streaming hot water. He grasped me to him, so that a pool formed between our chests, and he bent his head and kissed my face all over, his unshaved cheeks rasping on my skin, comfortingly.

As he shaved, still nude, sitting on the bathroom stool, I dried and straightened my hair, then made my face. We were tonight dressing for dinner, and I selected a set of black underwear and stockings. I wore them in front of Simon without any false-modesty, after all, we had indulged already in the most intimate moments. I was proud of my body. I delighted in the fact that he was aroused by it, and I knew that I looked good. I felt good. There was nothing sleazy. It is a fact that women like fine fabrics, lace and feminine designs, and I enjoyed them and the effect they had on men. I did not consider myself vain. I believe that making the best of oneself is not vanity, but a duty. Too many these days have sunk to the lowest common denominator, slopping about in ill fitting, shapeless and dowdy clothes, displaying too much unsightly flesh, underwear and dreadful footwear, even going to the supermarket in pyjamas.

I dressed in the same dress I had left here last year, a fitted black bodice with angled white stripes and a full black mini skirt with a tiered under slip. I wound my hair up and fixed it with a diamante clip. I surveyed the effect. I felt good, the best that I could be, seductive but vulnerable. I would have to be careful not to show my stocking tops, but these stockings came high up on my thigh. I made sure the suspenders were adjusted and fastened properly.

Simon came into the bedroom. 'Stand up,' he said.

I stood and twizzled. He examined me minutely. 'Is this how my wife likes to dress?' he asked.

'Yes.'

'Well, I am so proud of you. You have learned all I can teach you. You are the finished product, not only a beautiful and desirable woman, but also the best advert for the House of Beauvonne. And I love you, my Trudi.'

'And I love you, Simon, husband, tutor and benefactor. Come, we must go down.'

We entered the lounge to find everyone there. Simon spun me round. 'I present the image of Maison Beauvonne, my beloved Trudi.'

Wally was the first to speak. 'That's a very good idea, to use Trudi as the face of Beauvonne. Brilliant.'

'Yes, I think so too,' said Annette. 'It will be a way of branding. We should also go into aromas, perfumes, perhaps Eau de Trudi. Also Trudi, I was talking to Alex. He wanted you to make a single. He said you had a good voice, but you refused?'

'This is all very flattering, but it is too much. I am a medical student and also a mother to these three children as well as a wife. I live in two different places and also occasionally model. That is why I refused to even think about launching myself on the world as a singer. In any case, I could not imagine standing in front of an audience and singing, and there would be a demand, if the single was at all successful, to make an album and to do concerts and tour. No, I refuse.'

'What if you just made a backing number for an advert of say, Eau de Trudi or whatever the perfume is called?' Wally asked.

'Anonymously? I might consider that, but then you could get a thousand people to do that for you, and bona fide singers who need the money.'

'No, I was thinking that, well off the top of my head, a film of you in top of the range street wear in the high street, Regents Street or Champs Élysée and then again, at night, perhaps on Bateaux Mouches, singing the same song, then the logo, Maison Beauvonne, fashion for the World.'

'I like it, Wally,' Simon said.

'Me too,' Gérard and Annette said together.

'This is not fair. I feel you are ganging up on me. It is a good idea, but why me? There are famous models you could film or have a well known singer do it. There are any number of people to choose from.'

'We could. But, I would very much like you to do this Trudi.' Simon said simply.

'Then I can't refuse can I? I will do it, but it will have to wait until I have enough time.'

Robert appeared, saying that dinner was ready. I led the way, glad to escape the pressure.

I revived over dinner and it was a convivial meal. Wally told some funny stories of his travels. We ate well, sea bass then steaks. After dinner, I said I needed some fresh air and was going to get the lift to town and walk around the shops, just looking in the windows. Sabine said she would like to come, and Wally decided to accompany us.

I kissed Simon, put on my snow boots and coat and the three of us went to the lift. I was pleased to see my friends holding hands to the lift, in the lift and as we walked the town, Wally said to me, 'Are you feeling the strain?'

'Oui. I feel like a juggler with too many balls in the air, Wally. To most girls my age, an invitation to make a record would be a dream. I already have my dream, Simon and the children, beyond my wildest dreams of even three years ago. In addition there is the Paris house and the Chateau, my own horse, a Mercedes to drive, and my studies. Lastly I have my dear friends, both of you especially. And there is also the big wedding this year. Five hundred guests, and they are making my dress. To make a record, and videos too? At this time? To resist all that goes with it, being a pop star, making an album, maybe going on tour? I know it may not happen like that, but it could and so many singers go off the rails under the pressure. I don't want to start snorting coke just to get the energy to live. Something will give, and I am frightened it will be the wrong thing.

'I had just about worked out a balance between being mother, wife and student, occasional model. I have rejoiced that Simon is again managing everything, taking the strain off me. Now fresh demands. It is too much.' We had arrived outside a bar. 'Let's go in here for a coffee, I'm freezing in this dress.'

I led the way into a bar. All bars in France seem to be dark and dingy unless one goes to an upmarket Parisian one. We sat in a corner. Wally ordered the coffees. The music playing was the usual mixture of bad French pop and English and American.

'What am I going to do Sabine, Wally?' I ask desperately.

'You have to prioritise. Decide what you most value.'

'You know what I really value, the children, Simon and my studies. Modelling is just a trip, Maison Beauvonne is an excitement and Simon's business. This has all come too soon. We had planned that I would do my medical studies before anything else happened between us. Then Catherine died, and Simon was frightened after his crash and heart attack that the children would be left orphans, so we married. And I would not change that. I am so lucky to have a husband and especially him. And as his wife, I am the children's stepmother, and I could never have had children of my own, and I so love that too.

'I have always wanted to be a doctor. I'm nearly half way through my studies. So those are the important things, Simon, the children and my studies.'

'Then concentrate on those Trudi.' Sabine said.

'But it is not that uncomplicated is it, because I am also married to Maison Beauvonne. You heard Simon, 'The face of Beauvonne and a song to go with it.'

'Perhaps you are panicking a bit,' Wally said. 'You are already married and a mother and a successful student. If you do not let the face of Beauvonne thing get out of hand, you could do that, couldn't you?'

'I suppose so.'

'Perhaps, if the face thing took off, you should think about having a personal assistant, someone to run your errands, look after your diary, buy presents, look after the wardrobe.'

'But if Trudi does not want to do it?' Sabine said.

'Oh, I want to do everything, especially if Simon wants me to. Sometimes, I do just panic. I am not yet twenty-three and I have all these demands and responsibilities. I get frightened of all the work and frightened of failing.'

'Do you want me to speak to Simon?' Wally asked.

'No, it's kind of you Wally, but he would not like that. I can do it, only there tonight, it felt as though everyone was ganging up whatever I felt.'

'My fault. I got carried away. Look Sabine knows I am a great fan of you Trudi. You seem to float through your complicated life as if on a magic carpet, dispensing fairy dust as you go. I think you can do this face thing as long as you don't let it get out of hand.'

'Wally, will you get me a drink please?'

'Of course. What would Madame le Comtesse desire?'

'A sweet greyhound but with a touch of syrup please?'

'What is that?'

'Vodka, and grapefruit juice and syrup or sugar, shaken with ice.'

'Moi aussi Wally.'

'Cor, I don't know. Dad used to buy mum a Babycham and tell her to make it last.' He went to the bar.

'Now tell me Sabine,' I said when Wally was at the bar, 'how is it with you two?'

'I don't know. When he is away, he phones me everyday. He is quite romantic, enough for me. I hope, but who knows what goes on in an English man's brain? They are so closed up. And I am uncertain of myself too. I think it will be difficult to find the perfect man for me. I am just not used to dating I suppose.'

'You have changed. Since I gave you a make-over, you take much more care. You are a very attractive woman Sabine. Does he make love to you?'

She blushed. 'Oh yes, all that is fine Trudi, you matchmaker. Ssh he is coming.'

By the time we went home, we were quite merry. Luckily the bubble was still running. We walked from the bubble to the chalet, arm in arm, my legs exposed in the mini skirt, so cold. The thermometer said minus 23 degrees. I stumbled up stairs and into our room. Simon lay on the bed reading. He smiled as I entered.

'I thought you had run away.'

'I needed to think things out Simon. You know I want to please you and do all I can for Maison Beauvonne, but sometimes it all seems too much....'

'Then you have to tell me....!'

'I needed time to think about it and Wally has helped me. First I need a quick hot bath to warm up'

When I emerged from the bathroom, pink and glowing, I told him of our conversation. 'So Simon, I will do the song and shoot the video, but the things that matter most are my relationship with you and the children and my studies. To do more, I need a personal assistant, to look after my diary, to make sure I have the right clothes, to help me run my life, perhaps to assist with the children too from time to time.'

'Ah, the ladies maid. That can be arranged, of course.'

'I would call her a personal assistant. You agree, just like that?'

'Yes. Do you want to do the selection? I think you should. I will advertise. No, *we* will advertise Trudi. You need to find someone compatible. Now I think we go to sleep.'

We cuddled, but I was asleep within two minutes.

Chapter 17.

I examined Simon's leg in the morning and it appeared to have healed. I padded the stump before he put his false leg on, and he pronounced it comfortable. This was our last day, so we all skied together, Wally doing what he could and meeting us later when we did a more difficult run. We ate above 1650 on the slopes, and the children were there, Sophie bringing them round with Laurent. The twins were fitted out with little skis and a lead. Sophie said they were just amazing. Sébastien travelled in a sort of back-pack.

I sat with Sabine, Sophie and the children, while the rest had a drink at the bar. 'Sabine, I am taking Wally's advice and having a personal assistant, come ladies maid. Do you know anyone?'

'No I don't. It is a pity, it would be a good job.'

'I do, I know someone.' Sophie said.

'Oh yes? Who Sophie?'

'My little sister Nicole. She is a clever girl with a degree in business, but no job. Here, I have a photo.'

She opened her wallet and produced a photo. I saw a smiling girl, quite pretty.

'How old is she?'

'Twenty two in a month's time. She would be a hard worker Madame Trudi.'

'Trudi! Where is she?'

'At home on the farm in Alsace. I could phone her now, to come to Paris, to see if you like her. No commitment, but you would need to pay her fare on the train.'

'Of course. By all means phone her. Could she get *here* tonight? It might be easier than Paris, then we could travel to Paris together if I like her.'

'I will phone now. I'll go outside.'

She came back. 'She will be in Moutier at six o'clock on the bus, but you would need to pick her up.'

'That is possible. Tell her I will pick her up from the bus station. No we, you and I. She has her mobile in case we can't find her?

'Oh yes. I will phone her again.' She phoned from the table this time. 'She is packing. Maman will take her to the bus in Genève. So, it is all fixed. I know you will like her Trudi.'

'I know I will. It depends whether she wants the job or can do the job. I hope so Sophie. It will be such a help.'

We skied home with the little ones and were home by three thirty. The light had gone, which made skiing doubly difficult. Sabine agreed to look after the children while Sophie and I went to Moutier.

We found Nicole, looking like a refugee in a poor coat and carrying a backpack. The bus had been early and she had waited in the cold. She was glad to get in the warm car.

She shook hands with me across the seat back. The two sisters chattered madly in Alsatian patois as I drove back up the mountain. I could see Nicole in the mirror, her face sweetly excited, alight with the joy of the journey and seeing Sophie again. We parked and took the bubble. Nicole was impressed with the size of the chalet. We climbed the stairs to the lounge to find it deserted. Sophie went to see the children were safe in bed. I took Nicole's coat. She was a slim fair girl, pretty, about five feet five inches, skinny jeans and quite a nice sweater. I offered her a drink and she asked for coffee. 'We eat at eight, so we have an hour. I suggest I take you to your room. It is only small and you can wash and rest and change. I will show you the house and where your sister is.'

I took her up and found Sophie, leaving the two of them to sort things out.

Simon was again lying on his bed reading. 'You have brought the girl?'

'Yes, I have told Robert there is one extra for dinner and breakfast.'

'What is she like?'

'Pretty, young, eager. polite. We will see what she is like tonight.'

'I hope she is the one Trudi.'

'It would be nice. I will talk with her after dinner. Leave it to me please Simon.'

'Of course. What do you intend to pay her, how much?'

'Oh, I don't know what the rate is.'

'You need to think about it before you offer the position. Well, remember that she will be one of the household, so it is less. I would suggest €10,000 to start, and say another €5,000 after six months if it works out. Do you agree?'

'Oui Simon, thank you. How do we pay her.'

'She will be on the Maison Beauvonne payroll. She will need a bank account, but I expect she has one. When she is not working for you, she will work for Beauvonne. I leave it to you.'

At dinner I seated Nicole beside me, Wally on her other side and Sophie as far away as possible, so that she would not butt in. Nicole knew her wines, and drank first white with the fish then red with bœuf bourguignon, but only the one glass of each. I asked her about life on the farm and she was much more forthcoming than her sister, telling me about their pigs which ate the fruit they couldn't sell. They also made cider and kept chickens the last being her project.

Her hair was bobbed, two inches below her ears and by her skin, I thought naturally blonde with a trace of red. Made up I should think she would be really pretty in a vulnerable sort of way.

I asked about her degree, and what she had studied. Her course had consisted of some programming as well as computer skills, accountancy, purchasing and contract law. Not much would be relevant to her duties for me but useful for Beauvonne.

After dinner, as the others had coffee and liqueurs, I took her to our bedroom, so we could talk uninterrupted.

'Nicole, I think you are too highly qualified for what I want done. It would be a shame to ask you to do some of the menial tasks I have in mind and which I just do not have time for. The most important thing is for you to be my companion, so when I move from Paris to the Chateau, you can pack things and make arrangements. I need you to manage my diary, for such things as my hospital duty days, lectures and when I have to submit essays etc. Then there is my personal life, fetching dry cleaning, feeding the washing machine and even doing some ironing.

'Simon also wants me to be the face of Maison Beauvonne, on adverts and also making a record, a backing song. Out of that there may be other journeys to make arrangements for and to liaise with people on the times I am available, but also, making sure I have spare time, to be with the children and Simon and also to enjoy myself. It is all quite mundane. I do not want you to be bored.

'On the plus side, you would be behind the scenes at photo shoots and the video and when I record. For me that is all going to be very frightening, I will need someone to lean on. And if I go to a concert or something, you can also come or not as you wish. What do you think?'

'Where would I live?'

'You will live wherever I am, here, or Paris or the Chateau, your own room with us and near your sister. Do you drive?'

'Oui.'

'Good. One never knows when that may come in handy. The pay. Simon says to start 10,000, and after six months, 15,000, paid monthly into your bank. In addition you will be given clothes appropriate for the functions we go to and of course, you live with us and eat whatever we eat. If you want something special, then we can buy that or you can buy it yourself. Now, I have done a lot of talking. Some of the work will be quite menial, like a maid, but some will be for you to use your initiative and skills. It is a bit of a ragbag mixture of duties, doing whatever I cannot find time for myself. If you think this will all be too boring and sometimes lonely, then refuse and I will send you home tomorrow. If you would like to give it a trial for six months, then I would also be happy to see how it goes. Over to you.'

'It sounds a lot more exciting than feeding chickens. Do I call you Trudi or Madame?'

'I am just Trudi to everyone. Oh I forgot. I will need you to sign a confidentiality agreement. As you may know, the media have had me on the front page several times, and I don't like it. So my life is a secret between us.'

'Of course I will sign but I am not a gossip.'

'I do not think you are but these things have to be done. Oh yes and something else. I am getting married to Simon in July. There will be work to do there. Having the invitations printed and sending them and helping make the arrangements. Gérard is assisting, so you will work with him and Annette. There will be about five hundred guests, so we need to book rooms at hotels in Normandy close to the Chateau. That all needs arranging in January. Sabine, you met tonight, will be matron of honour. Sophie will be a bridesmaid and I wonder if you would be too? Then there will be the children to manage and I hope that my friend from England will also be a bridesmaid, oh and another young girl too. Is this for you?'

'Oui, bien sûr, Trudi. When do I start?'

'How soon can you arrange to leave home?'

'Now, I have left home. Mother said that if the job was right, then I have their blessings.'

'Then tomorrow. We will drive to Paris together. You will want more clothes but we can buy them for you in Paris, in fact it would be great fun to go shopping together, and at the Maison Beauvonne we can find you some special things for when it is more formal. Is that OK?'

'Of course. I will phone maman.'

'Trés bon. I am so pleased Nicole.' I embraced her and kissed her three times. 'You have made me very happy. If you have any worries about the work, then you speak to me, no one else. Now let us go and tell the others the very good news.'

We went down to the lounge.

'An announcement everybody. Nicole has agreed to be my personal assistant and general gofer, companion, starting immediately. So we leave for Paris tomorrow. I am very pleased she has agreed.'

Everyone offered congratulations, Simon embraced her and kissed her. Sophie gave her a kiss. I was absolutely thrilled to have someone to lean on.

At bedtime, after I put the light out, Simon and I talked. He asked what I had said and agreed. 'I don't know why I worry, you have sorted it all out. Good. It makes you happy?'

'Oh yes, a weight off my mind. Thank you Simon.'

'Well you should thank Wally too. I am glad he is working for us, in fact all your appointments, have been a great success. I am proud of what you have done for me and for Beauvonne. Sabine and Laurent will drive to the Chateau, oh and Wally, you will take him?'

'Of course. Simon, I feel much happier. Thank you cheri.'

Chapter 18.

Next morning I said goodbye to everyone and Nicole, Wally and I set off for Paris first. Simon was following with Sophie and the children. Annette and Gérard were in another car leaving Sabine and Laurent to make their way to the Chateau.

Snow fell as we left the resort and I picked my way down the mountain, hoping that we would reach the valley before conditions became too bad. A coach before us travelled at a safe and steady rate and I was more than content to stay behind it at a good distance. As we descended the snow became wetter with larger flakes, which the wipers whisked aside to collect in a clump to the side of the screen. I breathed a sigh of relief when we reached Moutier and the duel carriageway. It still snowed but did not settle. I overtook the coach then came up behind grit lorries, side by side. They were obviously expecting a heavy snowfall. With four hundred miles to drive, I hoped conditions would improve.

I asked if my passengers were happy. Wally said he was. Nicole said from the back seat that she was glad to be off the mountain.

'Me too,' I said. By the time we reached Lyon, there were patches of blue sky appearing yet the snow continued to fall. We ran into sunshine, then back into a snow shower. I asked Wally to find a restaurant in Auxerre where we could have lunch and a break.

He selected L'Orée des Champs, in Épineau les Voves. He phoned Simon to tell him what we were doing. After lunch we would have just 100 miles to drive. Wally and Nicole found plenty to talk about while I concentrated on the road in difficult conditions.

We arrived at the restaurant first and were shown to a table. Wally sat while Nicole and I went to the toilette. On our return, we found that Simon, Sophie and the children had arrived, causing a bustle among the staff as high chairs were found. Annette and Gérard also arrived. The food was traditional, country French but good enough. I sat with

Nicole on one side and on her right Gérard who I wanted her to get to know. On my left I had Sébastien, then Sophie, then the twins between Simon and Annette. We did not linger too long. The weather was still very wintry and I wanted badly to get home. I had work tomorrow, starting at eight under a new consultant in obstetrics.

On the outskirts of Paris, we ran out of the snow and progressed under a leaden cheerless sky. Simon had phoned ahead and Madame Gameau was preparing my room for Nicole now I was married to Simon and Mistress of the villa. We turned in just after five having left Wally at his flat.

Nicole and I had just taken our bags from the boot when Madame Gameau and Jerome appeared to welcome us. Simon arrived as we stepped into the lift. I took Nicole to my old bedroom in the apartment. I was sorry to be leaving it for good, for being more remote from my friends, Élise and Jean Luc, who I explained would also be arriving next day. I took some personal belongings and told Nicole I would remove the clothes I wanted. I said she could have any clothes I left, but I would remove any she did not want. We were much the same, size 10s anyway, but I was 10 centimetres taller. I showed her where everything was and how to find me. She would eat with Simon and I most of the time unless she wanted to be alone. Tomorrow she would accompany Simon to Maison Beauvonne and start work with Gérard on the invitations. I had no doubt that Simon would find time to smarten her up and lavish her with some new outfits. I gave her my address book to use for the invitations and my contact details. I had come up with fifty names for myself, Simon had twice as many. There would also be all the Beauvonne staff, fashion contacts and friends, mutual friends as well. In addition we were inviting all the estate staff including Robert and family from the Chalet. I was so glad that I had not that task to do. We began to think that five hundred guests would not be enough. I said we would buy her a top of the range mobile phone at the weekend, one which she could keep notes on and surf the web when necessary.

In the morning I took the Metro to the hospital and arrived well ahead of time. I met up with others in my group and we waited for the great man to welcome us.

He came twenty minutes late, telling us of a difficult birth and then gave us a refresher on the reproductive system of the human female, his words. He pointed out what could go wrong from conception to presentation. I wondered that any baby survived the nine month journey. The afternoon loomed and we were promised a visit to the wards, when we would be taught to listen to the baby's heartbeat in the womb. I was actually quite in awe of all this and not a little apprehensive. It seemed such an intimate action. There were whispers amongst the group, of intimate examinations and how it would be. Some girls giggled and some of the men flushed. On the cancer ward, we had mostly seen people post op or in remission or waiting for diagnoses. It had been a situation of great contrasts, trepidation, hope and relief as well as resignation and realisation of the end. Some days at the end of shift, I would be near to tears.

In obstetrics, it was mostly a scene of optimism and joy. Yes occasional disappointments and some apprehension, but it was very hands on, bulging bellies for all to see. I found it a bit frightening that first day. I found baby's heartbeat at four pm. A rotund and happy fourth time mother put her hand on mine as I moved the stethoscope and guided me to the spot. Suddenly I heard the chuff chuff chuff, at one hundred and twenty plus beats per minute. It was extraordinary. My face lit up and I felt grateful relief for getting me to touch her firmly. We were taught how to interpret what we saw on the screen. I went home a happy girl.

Simon and Nicole arrived just after me. Simon had already got to work on her. She entered in a smart little business suit in deep lilac fine cord, grey stockings and four inch heels. There was a touch more makeup too. Her face was alight. I greeted them both with kisses. Over cups of tea, I asked her how her day had been?

'C'est superbe. Merci Trudi for giving me this chance. I really enjoyed myself.'

'And the invitations?'

'Gerard has completed the list and tomorrow I will go to the printer to get some designs for you to select. Do you have any ideas for the print?

'Like what Nicole?'

'Gold or silver, possibly blue but of course not black. And the font? Perhaps we can look at different fonts tonight on computer?'

'Of course, that is a good idea. Simon, we need to discuss the wording. Can we get together after dinner, the three of us?'

'Of course.'

We ate one of Madame Gameau's stews, with creamed potatoes and French beans, bread for the gravy and a bread and butter pudding to finish. Then the three of us got down to business. Simon suggested the coat of arms of Beauvonne at the top, which was a helmet inside an armorial motto. Below we arrived at:-

Trudi and Simon

Cordially invite

....

to their wedding at Basilique de Lisieux,
on 15th July 2010 at 11.00 o'clock
and to their wedding feast afterwards at
Chateau de Beauvonne.
RSVP Nicole at Maison Beauvonne.
No presents please.

The lettering would be gold. The crest embossed, the printer already having the embosser for Maison Beauvonne. In addition we composed a letter inviting some guests, my parents, my brother and Alison, Sam, Heather and her mother and the Hendersons to stay at the Chateau, as well of course as Annette and Gérard. Others we supplied with a list of places to stay at various costs. The Maison Beauvonne staff would have coaches to take them to and from the wedding. Vanessa and all her family would stay at their villa. I would write to Claire and ask her to be a bridesmaid. So that would be Sabine, Sophie and the children, Nicole, Claire and Sam as my bridesmaids. André of course would be a page, not that he would understand. My brother would be an usher and so would Laurent and Wally.

Simon had booked the Basilique ages ago, and he also had the caterers primed to go and also six limousines. He fetched the menu cards. We decided that the only practical thing would be to have a buffet. A choice of starter: lobster bisque or chargrilled vegetable terrine or cold poached salmon. This would be followed by a choice of main: individual beef wellington, slow roasted Beauvonne lamb, supreme of chicken with a choice of three sauces, or vegetable crumble. The sweets: Normandy apple pie with calvados butter and real custard, raspberry mascarpone or lemon gateau, toffee crunch pie and butterscotch sauce and of course, ice cream. In addition, we would have four wines, a white burgundy, Pouilly Fuissé, a good claret, a graves for the sweet and of course champagne. Simon would use his contacts for that. By eleven we had finished. Nicole would set about arranging everything tomorrow.

Simon and I went to bed tired but happy.

CHAPTER 19.

All that week I spent on the obstetric ward, shadowing the midwives. By the end of the week, I was quite fond of the bulging bellies and my fear of this intimate touching had disappeared, mainly because, the expectant mothers had lost all fear of touch. Their minds were concentrated on the delivery and the joy they expected from it.

There was only one girl who was withdrawn, a young kid of eighteen who was very apprehensive and displayed none of the almost euphoria of some of the other mothers. God, I thought, that was the age I moved to Paris. It was not until the fourth day of my time on the ward that I could find space to sit with her. It was lucky that she recognised me from my disaster on the catwalk.

Her name was Matilde and she came from Amiens. She had come to Paris as a governess to someone in an embassy. There she had been victimised, because she was a European in a Muslim household. She had been forced to wear, what they called, modest dress, a long dress and always a headscarf while in the house. Modest dress had not protected her from the wandering hands of her employer, who had demanded sex under the impression that European girls were without morals and the right of men to take what they want. She had eventually fled the household and worked as a waitress, but finding herself pregnant, had been afraid to return home. She had eventually gone to the police, but by that time her oppressor had returned to his country. She felt without hope, did not know how she was going to cope with a child or how to support them both. I did my best to comfort her, but all I had was words.

I carried that tragedy as I left the hospital, reaching home after ten and more or less climbing straight into bed. Simon joined me and we cuddled. I lay very still. I had come to terms with swollen bellies, actually really enjoying being with these women who were so accommodating in allowing students to examine them. Mathilde was the other side of the coin, and I had brought her sorrow home, something we were told not to do.

'What is the matter?' Simon asked when I remained frozen.

I told him of Mathilde, and how helpless I felt and ill prepared to deal with her anxiety. The priest had been to see her and he urged her to give the child up for adoption, but she could not stand the guilt of that either.

'You cannot be fairy godmother to every patient in trouble.'

'I know, and normally I do not try, but in Mathilde's case, she is something special. I sense a good person. I know you would like her too.'

'Whether you like a patient, should not matter. You are there for their medical needs. That is all. That is your sole responsibility. You cannot delve into their private lives.'

'I think a good doctor should at least understand a patient's state of mind, and she is very troubled at the moment. If we deliver a baby and just put them out on the street, the result could be a tragedy. I believe we should endeavour to give comprehensive, holistic care, not just a plaster and a pat on the head.'

He held me tighter and stroked my hair. 'Pauvre chérie. You are too good, too sympathique. I am coming to see this one tomorrow.'

'Really Simon? You would do that for me?'

'Just this once. But you have to stop being so involved with everyone. Sooner or later, everyone you come across who is at all nice, finds employment with us. It must stop.'

'Yes, of course you are right. And I love you Simon.' I kissed him goodnight, but still lay with my head against his shoulder. I felt him nuzzling my hair and it made me smile contentedly. I fell asleep.

When I went on duty at two pm next day, I went immediately to see Mathilde. I found her room, bare until now, filled with flowers. She was already in labour and I scrubbed up and went to the delivery room. Mathilde was in the final moments, and the baby popped out shortly after I entered. Her baby girl was perfect, and I saw a smile of joy upon mother's face. That part then was fine, it looked as though they would bond at least. They checked her and her baby over and she was wheeled back to her room.

I cleaned up. I had to see other ladies and it was teatime before I reached Mathilde.

'It was nice to see you with smiles to welcome your baby. Have you a name for the baby?'

'Oui. Trudi Simone.'

'Oh, thank you Mathilde. Why Simone?'

'Votre mari.'

'Simon de Beauvonne, not my husband, my benefactor.'

'Oh! He brought me these flowers and a job too.'

'What job?'

'You do not know?'

'No Mathilde. What job, dressmaking?'

'Non. At the new factory in Clermont Ferrand. Running the crèche. It is a dream come true. Thank you so much Trudi. That is why I have to call my baby Trudi Simone Boisseau.'

'Let me see her! Oh she is a beauty.' My namesake was sleeping, in truth, much like any other little new-born baby girl.

'I am so pleased to see you happy. So you have money to get to Clermont? And somewhere to live?'

'Simon has given me a little money and a ticket and an address where I can live until I find somewhere permanent.'

'And you want to do this, run the crèche? You are capable?'

'I am trained. Two years in college and yes, I have the confidence to do it. Monsieur has told me to wear a uniform, which he will provide to give me more authority and he will find other courses for me to do. He is very thorough. And of course, I can have my baby, Trudi Simone with me all day. It is excellent.'

'I am very pleased for you. I must go Mathilde. I will see you before you leave us and I am sure we will meet again after that. Au revoir et bon chance.'

I was overcome by Simon's intervention. It was such a surprise that he would have done this because it had pained me to see one young woman in despair. I needed no proof that he loved me. His indulgence of my whims and his gifts to me, as well as his tenderness were a continued confirmation. The only doubt lay within in my own psyche, that he could love me, a less than complete individual, outwardly feminine and female, but inside.......I went to the staff toilet and found myself in tears. I was repairing my face when I saw Élise enter.

'Hi Trudi, comment ça va?' She looked into my face. 'Why, you have been crying. What is the matter?'

'It is nothing. I am just so in love with Simon.'

'And this is a reason for you to cry? What has he done?'

'He has done something wonderful, because I was worried about something, he has worked a minor miracle. And sometimes I just feel I do not deserve all this goodness, this fortune and spoiling.'

'Why ever not?'

'Well, you know me well. Whatever I look like, I still feel inferior to you for instance, you are born female. I am man made, I sometimes feel, fake, incomplete, inferior.'

'Nonsense. You have so many qualities I do not have, nor does Jean Luc. We could not do all you do. So, you are one of the disabled, just as much as say someone with cerebral palsy. But your disadvantages are much less. Look at you. A beautiful young woman, and one with brains. How many natural born women would love to be in your shoes? Thousands, even sometimes, I am a little jealous of you. I am a plain girl, do you not think I would like to be as beautiful as you, and the Comtesse de Beauvonne, driving around in a Mercedes, money seemingly no object? You also have an adoring husband, oh yes we know you are already married. Now repair those sensational looks and shut the fuck up.'

She kissed me on both cheeks then my lips. 'Trudi, we are in awe of all you achieve. We are amazed. Be grateful that you have a figure, looks and a brain, and an adoring husband.' She slapped me on the rear.

'Ouch!'

'To bring you to your senses. You may be incomplete one way, but you are truly blessed. Now back to work.'

We went our separate ways. I was blessed, I knew that. I needed Vanessa, my surrogate mother. I would phone her tonight.

When I reached home, it was in darkness except for the courtyard light. Simon had left a note to say that he was dining with Wally and a customer. I was disappointed, I wanted to thank him for what he had done for Mathilde. I went into my old apartment and found Élise and Jean Luc there. They told me that Nicole was in her room. I knocked and entered.

'Bon soir Trudi, did you want me to do something?'

'No Nicole, I was just wondering how things are going. Have you the invitations that I am signing personally?'

'Yes, they are in the villa, on the dining table. I have been working on the caterers today as well, making sure that we will get what you both want, and the marquees are ordered and the coaches booked for the staff.

'Also, your little car. I took that to the garage and it will be ready at the end of the week, to drive to the Chateau for Sophie to use. I have bought the insurance, Simon told me how. And that girl, Mathilde in the hospital? I found her some lodgings in Clermont Ferrand with one of the married workers who has two babies of her own. The dress is made and you need to go for a fitting.'

'Have you seen it?'

'Oh no. It is kept like a state secret. I think they would kill me if I peeped.'

'So is that all you have done today?'

'That's it, I thought I had done quite a lot.'

'I am joking. It is indeed a lot. Thank you so much Nicole. Do you know anything about the TV programme. Has Alex phoned?'

'Non, but there was a note. He is on another project but will be in touch next week.'

'Very good Nicole. Impressive. What are you doing tomorrow?'

'Putting stamps on envelopes and sending off invitations. Then I am sitting in on a meeting with the advertiser and Simon, regarding your part and how they see the image of Beauvonne. Simon says that you have the final say on the options.'

'You are a wonder. I hope you have eaten.'

'Oh yes. We cooked, omelette and chips. I know, not Trudi food, but now and again.' she said as I wrinkled my nose.

'OK Nicole, thank you so much. I have someone to ring, so I will see you tomorrow. Bon nuit.'

In the villa, I dialled Vanessa and luckily she was in. We talked for over an hour. It was good to hear her voice and to have news of Eleanor and Claire. Ellie had just departed for Phoenix, Arizona to do a piece on illegal Latino immigration., a safer place to be than in the Middle or Far East. I felt much better after my chat. Vanessa's woman of the world down to earth logicality put things in perspective, just as Élise had done earlier.

I phoned mum and dad. My brother was still at Sandhurst, mum told me. They were fine, leading their dull lives. I did not mention the wedding but asked them not to make arrangements for July because I wanted them to come to France, and to ask my brother and whoever his present girl friend was, to come also. I wanted the invitations to be a surprise.

I went to bed tired out. and did not wake even when Simon came to bed. I slept till the dawn light filtered around the curtains.

Chapter 20.

I felt renewed. I touched Simon and he just groaned. He and Wally had consumed too much food and alcohol with the customer. I worried about it and resolved to speak to Wally, to ask him to restrain Simon from excess.

I showered and dressed for the hospital. I had two hours, so I went in and signed invitations, adding personal messages. I was inviting beside my family, the Hendersons who had looked after me for my last two years at school, and also the headmaster and his wife; Sam, her parents and her brother and his latest fiancée too. My relations of whom there were not too many; Heather and her mother, Élise and Jean Luc, and now Mathilde with her little one. Two old boys from school, Peter and Dick, Vanessa and the rest of the family, even Stuart and his wife. Yes, that might be fun. I wondered if he still held a torch for me.

I scribbled away with my fountain pen, seldom used, kept for just such occasions. When I had done, I took the invitations through to Nicole who was waiting on Simon to go to the Maison.

That done I could go to the hospital for another day of mother care. Today I started on prenatal, sitting in on preliminary examinations. Later I would move to second trimester examinations and then the third, so that I would have a complete knowledge of the full pregnancy span.

The primary consultations I was engaged on were very revealing. The emotions of different patients were interesting and often rewarding. The cost of having a child hardly ever came up and I concluded that the basic urge to reproduce had little to do with logic or practicalities. There was hardly ever a thought of planning. But the next weeks were some of the most enjoyable of my training so far.

As he had told Nicole he would, the following week Alex phoned for an interview. He wanted to show us what he had so far. The Advertising agency also had storyboards for me to see, and they would have a copy of the song, just the instrumental. I said merde. I had agreed to all this but fitting it in with study was hard. I had a three day rest period, so it was coming at the right time, but it was still daunting, becoming a TV star and a singer. I said so to Simon, but his reply was simple and brief, 'You can do it, don't doubt yourself.'

Alex and Helen turned up and showed us what they had. Now they needed some more shots in Beauvonne, of the Chateau and of the estate, riding around it with Sabine.

They also wanted shots of me on one of the wards. I would ask Professeur Rousse if that would be possible. If they guaranteed to pixilate the faces of the patients and staff, I suggested, it might be possible. I looked at my time schedule and said that the Beauvonne filming would have to wait until Easter break. When they had heard about the wedding, it threw them out. They would now be delaying so they could get some shots of that, if of course Paris Match consented to allow them the rights. Helen had improved. My coaching had done something. She was much less gawky and more feminine, in leggings and a little mini skirt, and a sweet little peplum jacket. Her hair was now blonde and straight. I liked what I saw.

Next in was the Agency. We allowed Alex and Helen to sit in and film some of it, but not the content of the advert nor the song. The story board just told my story, of exiting the hospital and stripping off my white coat, then metamorphosing into Trudi the model, collected in a Mercedes limo and stepping out at the opera and on the catwalk and a riding scene too. They had morphed scenes from different times into a storyline that looked real, but was fake in terms of chronology.

At first I thought the song was too sad, but it grew on me. It reminded me slightly of Emile Sandé's Clown. I read the words. They sort of made sense. I would have to sing in

French and English, fine, but also in German and Mandarin and Japanese. Obviously I would just learn them phonetically, reading off an autocue. I hoped that the translator would get it right and I would not be singing something rude and not know it. The sound studio was booked for next week. In the meantime, I was given a recording of the song to sing along to. Oh Simon I thought, but then, it was the least I could do. He gave me so much

The recording session came. I asked Simon to let me go with Nicole, I did not want him there to inhibit me, I was nervous enough. I don't know what I expected, but in the event, it was not as much of an ordeal as I thought it would be. First I sang the song right through in French, making a few mistakes. Then we went through it line by line, conducting me through the glass window. Then I did small parts where it needed tidying up, or my timing was out. It was all spliced together and we listened. They tweaked tracks and where I sounded a bit flat, they changed the pitch. I began to wonder what was real in the pop world.

The finished song was terrific. Nicole was impressed and I was really proud of it, although I was only fifty per cent of the skill. I then sang it in English, easier for me, then the phonetic versions of Chinese Mandarin Japanese and German. We finished at ten thirty. I took a copy on iPod so

Simon could hear. He thought it was brilliant too, but I knew it was pretty well fake.

On my next time off there would be the video to film. They had now scrapped the first version which I had said was naf and decided that I would emerge from the hospital in white coat, stuffing my stethoscope into my bag and it would be raining. Lo and behold, lovely butterfly emerging from a porticoed doorway, in beautiful gown and emerging later, still singing at the Opera, and again in lovely suit swinging down the Champs. It all sounded rather silly, but we would see. Simon was enthusiastic, Nicole was excited and took my hand and shook it. I was touched.

After that I went to Jacques for a wedding dress fitting. The dress came in a locked dress case and I changed in his office with the help of Vivienne the dressmaker. I turned and looked at myself in the mirror. I loved it. It was divine. I felt really beautiful, perhaps the first time ever, I could see in myself what everyone else seemed to see, and I had not even made my face especially. I kissed them both. They made one or two alteration marks and I would have another fitting when it was done. Vivienne and Jacques played about with my hair trying different styles, up and down, coiled and plaited so I would have some idea of which style to choose. It all took a considerable amount of time, but by the end having tried on various types of headdress and tiaras, I knew what I wanted.

I switched my phone back on and found that it had gone mad. There were ten messages on text and another eight on voice mail. The invitations had obviously reached England. I phoned mum from the Maison immediately.

'This is really true, Trudi? You are marrying Simon?'

'Oui maman.' I had lapsed into French with emotion. 'I just love him and he me. He is just the kindest man mother. And father will give me away? You will both stay at the Chateau for the week and my brother and whoever he is with. Oh still Alison! Will he wear his dress uniform? It would be so great if he would. It has all that chain mail on the shoulders. I just tried my dress on. It's wonderful mum, made here in the Maison.'

'You are sure?'

'Oh so sure. Yes. Be pleased maman. Can I speak to father please?'

'Yes dear of course. I am pleased, I just want you to be happy. Here's you father?'

'Trudi. This is very good news. Congratulations to you both.'

'Daddy, you will give me away, won't you?'

'Try and stop me, of course it will be a great honour. I shall be so proud.'

'Oh and daddy, Simon is having a suit made for you and a dress for mother, so you do not have to worry about that. And please ask my brother to wear his dress uniform will you. I can't wait for you to walk me down the aisle. It will be a dream come true. You should see the Basilique, it is beautiful and enormous. You can Google it. Then the reception is at the Chateau and it is going to be so big, five hundred guests, because of all the fashion people.'

'That is all very exciting but the main thing is that you are marrying him for love. That is what this is all about, isn't it?'

'Oh yes, daddy. I have loved him from the first minutes we met and apparently, he me.'

'Then that is all I wanted to know. We would not miss it for the World.'

'Thank you daddy. And please, calm mother down for me.'

I next rang Vanessa, then Ellie and then Sam and the Hendersons and Mr Stubbs. Later, I had a call from my brother who he said was bringing his fiancée, Alison, who he had known for nearly a year, sister of one of his brother officers who was herself in the Royal Army Medical Corps. He would obtain permission to wear his dress uniform, complete with sword, boots and spurs and he agreed to be chief usher on the door of the Basilique.

Wally phoned before I could answer his message. He was so pleased, he said, it was like having his own sister announce her engagement. He was so loving, he made me cry. I went to bed, glad to have a respite from all the emotion.

It was back to the wards again, a lecture and more time in the delivery suite. We were told the dangers of postnatal treatment of babies. Where once they were held upside down to clear throats and lungs and given a smart slap on the rear, now suction is used and if wrongly used can puncture lungs and damage the oesophagus, but done correctly it is much more effective. Treatment always had to be gentle and never forced; we had the message drummed in to us. I knew the dangers already, from a friend whose baby had died from this treatment in the hands of an overzealous young male houseman in England. Always gently, we were told, no matter what the screams were from the mother, birth had to be managed gently, for baby and mother if permanent damage was not to be done.

Then one day I was at the forefront, actually delivering a baby under instruction. I thought I might faint, but at the time, I found it all so enthralling that adrenalin must have taken over. I delivered, well helped, a lovely little boy for a mother who had already given birth to three.

After that I was off to mental health. It was a great change, from a place of hope to one of cross your fingers. I hated it, and had no great faith in what we were doing. The next three months would be tough. I was still learning a lot, just sitting, listening to the victims stories, and I marvelled at the frailty of the human mind, which could so often become obsessed with insignificant, to me at least, events in their drear lives.

It took me back too, to my days of sitting in front of a psychiatrist and sometimes students, explaining why I felt the need to be a girl and so out of sorts with my body.

Nicole was proving her weight in gold. She ran all my errands, did my shopping and even stuffed the washing machine with our smalls. She also helped Sophie with the children, with whom I spent as many spare hours as possible. When the filming came up, she arranged everything to fit in with my hospital duties and made a wall chart of where I had to be and what I was doing. She was a great organiser.

We made the advert. Alex and Helen shadowed making their own film of the filming. In truth, I did not have to act much. Someone dressed me, someone did my makeup and hair, someone told me what I had to do, walk out of a shop, walk down the Champs Élysée, get in and out of a car, walk into the Opera. Smile, look haughty, pout.

If I got it wrong, or the light disappeared or someone walked into shot, then we did it over, and all the time that song went on in my head. At last it was finished, the filming at least. Nicole was always there, completely uncomplaining, carrying, supporting, finding food. A limo picked us up early morning and transported us wherever. I suspected the whole thing would be an embarrassment.

A week after filming we viewed the finished product. I had to admit, they had done a great job. It was quite moody, a lot of black and white, lots of changes of scene and clothes, but the clothes and I always in colour other than when I exited the hospital. My song fitted to the mood and the action. Nicole thought it wonderful. Simon hugged and kissed me, yet as far as my part was concerned, a dummy could have done it. I was no Keira Knightly.

The advert launched the next day, we caught it on prime time. Mother phoned to say she had seen it, then Ellie. Of course she was full of what she would like to do to me and how she had tried to forget me, now I was engaged, but that the advert just reactivated her desire. Wally thought it a great job and wondered how all the gainsayers at school, the skirt lifters and bottom pinchers, elastic flickers and whisperers would feel.

The advert was a smash hit and went viral on YouTube. After a week it had had three million hits. The song entered the English charts at thirty, and twenty three in France. Suddenly I could not walk to the Metro without people stopping me, or a paparazzi chasing after me. I had to be really careful stepping out of a taxi or car, for fear of a camera catching a shot of my nether regions. I started to appear in all the red tops nearly every day, out with the children, walking with Simon or Nicole, emerging from hospital, bag slung over a weary shoulder. I had to make sure that I was always presentable, neat and tidy for fear of appearing in the knocking mags, which just love catching celebs in dishevelment. Nicole started meeting me at the hospital, checking me over and driving me back and forth. At times I had to resort to a hat and dark glasses, sending the children to the park with Sophie or Nicole and joining them later incognito.

If I had known what the exposure would promote, I think I would have refused. The song peaked at number two dropped then rose again. I was asked to do an album. Nicole urged me on. I would think about it I said. An album was a lot of work and I would not do it if it was just one good song and a lot of trash. Ten songs at least and half had to be at least reasonable.

Alex and his gang were also following me about, asking me to walk in and out of the hospital three times, filming while we played ball with the children or I walked

Tasha. Then they followed me to the Chateau, film of me riding, talking to Sabine with the flock in the background, getting into the Mercedes, kissing Simon hello or goodbye.

I did the spring catwalk show, modelling four outfits, a gorgeous fifties style peplum jacketed suit with pencil skirt in navy; a long winter weight overcoat, panther blue over a startling flirt pink mini skirt; a cocktail dress, again fifties with multi layered full skirt in emerald silk with an embroidered bodice in silk thread a shade darker; and of course a wedding dress sort of classic which I actually hated. There was of course much speculation that it was my wedding dress, in spite of my denials. They should have known that the groom would not have designed or seen the dress, but it was at least amusing.

I so enjoyed the whole thing, the preparation, the makeup, the dressing up and hairdos; the catwalk and the ovations. We had a terrific reception, and our biggest ever audience. Suddenly Beauvonne was *the* show to see, and the orders poured in. Wally was buzzing around customers and buyers like a wasp on heat, and Simon was courted by customers who had rejected Beauvonne in the past as being passé.

The party in the evening was lavish. La Poulette and I were the prime objects for the press. After dinner I had to sing the song, well actually mime to it, but I had practised and they told me it looked live. Then the dancing began, a Dixieland Jazz band alternating with a French pop group playing Euro hits. It was very swish. I escaped at midnight leaving Nicole to enjoy the night.

Next day I was back with the mental problems. I had one more week of this before moving on to Urology, problems of the kidneys and bladder etc. Anything would be better than mental health.

Spring came at last. March had started warm, then turned cold again with winds out of the North East. April brought warmer weather, thankfully. Brave girls soon cast off winter clothing, and I went into tights and minis again with little jackets. At Easter I had a ten day break from the hospital. I went to the Chateau with Nicole, Sophie and the children, leaving Simon in Paris except for the long weekend.

I rode with Sabine and found that Nicole was also a rider, more experienced than I, and the three of us had great fun. I was still somewhat wary from my fall, but as the days went on I gained confidence again. I loved Sheba, she was not only beautiful to look at but also had a nice nature. Tasha would run beside us, game for anything. Being with these two girls was an absolute joy and I put the worries and smells and sights of hospital out of my mind.

Speaking to Simon on the phone, I suggested a range of Trudi de Beauvonne underwear as an addition to the outerwear. He thought it a terrific idea.

Sabine informed me that Wally would be staying at her parents home over the long weekend. That was such good news. I kissed her.

'Does this mean anything?'

'I don't know. I suggested he stay with us and he accepted, so I hope!'

'Are you in love?'

'Oh oui, Trudi, I suppose I am. Whether this inhibited Englishman is, I am not sure.'

'And you cannot ask, not yet anyway. I hope all goes well, he is a lovely chap. I would love to see you together. He is my only male friend.'

'I know. I think he would walk through fire for you Trudi.'

'You are twenty-six and he is only twenty three. Perhaps that is the difference. Men are less mature, are they not. He is therefore quite young.'

'Yet he was engaged to that Isobel?'

'No, they were not engaged. He told me they were sort of engaged, because her parents were difficult. I think he was relieved to move to Paris and lose her.'

'Oh, I don't know Trudi. I am not unhappy but my parents ask questions, you know, is this *the* one? They worry that I will be an old maid. Time will tell I suppose.'

Sometimes time needs a little nudge, I thought.

'Perhaps this weekend will help? I hope so Sabine.'

I left her. I would have to speak to Wally and find out his real feelings.

Chapter 21.

Wally must have arrived Friday evening, but of course, I did not see him until mid Saturday morning when Sabine came into the estate office. While she was busy, I invited Wally to walk down to the new lake.

Spring had arrived, though not with any force. Trees and bushes were in bud, but leaves had not yet sprung from those buds. We reached the lake, a great triumph of Sabine's planning and I pointed out the features that were still to emerge.

'So, how was last night with Sabine's family? It felt most strange that you were there rather than staying with us.'

'Strange for me too. I should have been more at home staying with you and Simon, but I like her family.'

'And Sabine? How are you two getting on?'

He smiled beguilingly. 'Oh Trudi, you can be the most impenetrable thinker at times but also the most transparent. Why not just ask me outright.'

'What?' I say innocently.

'When am I going to pop the question?'

'Oh, that. When or is it if?'

'I think it is when. We get on well. I admire her, she is gifted like you and since your makeover, a beautiful woman. Her roots are here, I cannot see her ever moving away. I have been with Beauvonne for six months. I think Simon is pleased with me, but my probation is at an end. I don't know whether I am to be made permanent. If so, perhaps we could make plans, but if I lost my job with Beauvonne, my future could be anywhere.

'The other thought in my mind is that I would not want to be doing this same job in ten or fifteen years' time. What then?'

'I see you have been thinking about your life Wally. The business is expanding, so there will be a need for divisional directors in time. We now have ready made, haute couture, frangrances and next Trudi lingerie.'

'Oh? I hadn't heard that. Is that your idea?'

'I spoke to Simon over two weeks ago. Perhaps he has it in train. I will ask him. Then Wally it is high time we did men's wear, don't you think? Would that make a difference?'

'It certainly would. Will it happen?'

'I will make it happen Wally. Leave it to me. If you were to manage a division, what would you favour.'

'I have been in women's fashions long enough not to be embarrassed by handling them nor talking about them. When I see a Beauvonne creation, I see Euros. The same would be with a bra or briefs or a man's suit. They are commodities to be traded. I like the trade. I like Beauvonne, Simon and of course you, the children and I do love Sabine. I am not always sure that she loves me. She holds back something, like she is inhibited. It is my future career that worries me a bit.'

'Then we have to make you feel more secure. Simon likes you, business, even in these adverse trading conditions is good. The rich always find money to burn. Footballers haven't taken a pay cut have they? I feel sure he means to make you permanent. We must get back to Sabine.'

As we returned, he said, 'You my friend Trudi, are like one of those famed Italian ladies from a great family, the Machiavelli, Medici or Borgia. You Trudi de Beauvonne, are a schemer. I am glad you are on my side.'

'Would you do something for me Wally?'

'Pour poison in someone's wine?'

'No Wally. Not this weekend, but soon, speak frankly about your feelings to Sabine? She is like my sister. She loves you but she doesn't know where your liaison is leading. She calls you her inhibited English man.'

'Then we are both inhibited. It was my intention, as soon as I knew my future is secure to be serious. So do not worry. I will play fair. You Trudi, are like *my* sister. I am absolutely fascinated by you.'

'Why?

'Because you are so many layered, from frivolous girl to industrial magnate.'

I laughed. 'Thank you Wally, you are my only male friend, real friend. Of course you will play fair Wally. I never doubted you. And rest easy, all will be well with your future. We need you.'

We found Sabine coming to look for us.

We kissed and they departed. We would meet later for dinner in the Chateau. I found Simon in his study.

'Simon dearest, when are you making Wally permanent? '

'Oh, review time already? Well of course, I will write a letter this afternoon and he can have it tonight.'

'What about Trudi lingerie?'

'Oh yes, they are already designing the range. I will show you as soon as we have samples.'

'The one thing left we do not do, is men's fashion. I think we should. You dress so well Simon, you could design that, couldn't you?'

'Trudi, you are a true strategist. I will look at that too. I will discuss all this tonight with Gérard and Wally. You are right, we have to expand. We have Clermont Ferrand to keep busy. It is only at half capacity. How do you think of all these things?'

'A logical mind. I could not design a robe, but I can do this. So you think it a good idea, menswear?'

'Absolument. I have been thinking about you and the company. At the moment the company is just me, I am sole shareholder. I own it entirely. I have been thinking to make it a SARL, Société à Responsibilité Limitéee, and appoint some directors. That would give people more incentive and a sense of ownership.'

'Who would you appoint.'

'I had not thought, but we can consider now, between us. First I would be Managing Director. You....'

'Me? I am not in the business.'

'Oh yes you are. All the time. I take your ideas and you have done so much for putting Beauvonne in the news and promoting the name. Deputy Managing Director. The designers have to be Directors.'

'And what about Gérard and Wally, Annette?'

'Ah. Well Wally is Sales. Gérard I suppose I would have to make him Admin but I am not keen. Annette Marketing, though I will have to think about that some more and discuss it with her. She is a bit lightweight, uses no initiative. And Gustav down at Clermont, Production.'

'Do you need to make Annette a Director if Gerard is one. He is not too on the ball either.'

'When it comes to those two Trudi, it is political. I feel I have to include family, Gérard certainly, but I know what you mean. I will speak to Annette, see if she will sharpen up and dangle the carrot of director as an incentive. You are as usual, perceptive.'

'Since you told me about Gérard, I have my doubts about him. Jacques ahs doubts too.'

'I am keeping an eye on him Trudi.'

'Then I think you should lay these plans before them as an incentive. It might be enough to keep Gérard on the straight and narrow. When will the lingerie designs be available?'

'I have asked for them to be ready by the end of next week.'

'And what does the range contain.'

'There are ten designs of knickers with matching bras. The knickers come in a choice in the same design, thong, string and boy. That is already a lot of stock, so many sizes, for one design sixty alternatives.'

'No Simon, it is too much. Cut it to the best five out of the ten designs. We girls will form a panel and vote for them, Sabine, Nicole, Sophie and I. Ten lines is too much.'

'I think you are right as usual. Designers get carried away. Then there are slips, suspenders and camisoles. That is all at present. They are Trudi de Beauvonne, so we need you to promote them. There will be another advert to do for the launch, I am afraid, so I hope you will do that.

'Are you asking me to model underwear?'

'No, no Trudi. You in underwear, that is for my eyes only. But it needs a song, and you will appear fully clothed, probably in a little business suit, saying something like, 'I like to be fashionable, right down to my skin.' What do you think?'

'As I am going to be a director, and in a way this was my idea, I don't like it. Is the song written?'

'It should be by now. Do you remember the iconic images of Nicole Kidman wearing Chanel in the advert? A long feather dress? They are thinking something along those lines, quite moody and mysterious and sexy.'

'For bras and knickers? It doesn't sound right. Wouldn't it be better to have an established star, pop or film actress, someone instantly recognised.'

'Trudi, do you not realise, that you are instantly recognised? You remember last time, the press chasing you? Now you have a top hit behind you, plus your fashion fame. This new song and the TV programme. You are my dear, a star, class A celebrity.'

'I never wanted to be. I just want to be a doctor.'

'I know, but you are now more famous than La Poulette, as famous as Madonna. Unless you disappear to a nunnery, you will remain so. Enjoy it.'

'I want to see the script for this advert and I want the song too, before I agree. Does Nicole know about this?'

'Only in passing. We haven't told her any details.'

'I see. Oh well, I suppose I can do it.'

'Of course you can.'

'I'm going to see Sheba, Simon. I'll see you later at the children's tea time. Don't forget.'

'I'll be there.'

I found Nicole with her sister and the children.

'Nicole, I need to speak with you, please.'

She joined me outside the nursery. 'Have I done something wrong?'

'No Nicole, only Simon has just told me about another song and an advert, to launch the lingerie range. He said that you knew about it, you would have overheard it spoken of. Did you?'

'Oui Trudi. I thought they would have spoken to you first. If I have been wrong I am sorry.'

'No it is not your fault, but in the future, anything like that, tell me, otherwise I find out and it is a shock. Now my days off are going to be filled with all that and I work too hard.'

'Of course I will. I did not realise.'

'I don't think they realise how hard I work at the hospital that is the trouble. Nicole, you have been with me for three months of your probationary period. Are you happy? Is it the job for you?'

'I am very happy. It is all so interesting, a really good experience, Yes Trudi.'

'Then Nicole, I will tell them to pay the fifteen thousand we promised. Find out all the details of this new advert and the song as soon as we go back to Paris, I want the story boards, the lyrics and the music. I don't like the sound of it.'

'Bien sûr Trudi. And thank you so much.'

'You are most of the time in Paris, so a car is pointless. I wondered about a scooter?'

'Ah oui, that would be good.'

'You have a licence?'

'Of course. I have ridden one since I was sixteen.'

'You promise to be careful on it. They are dangerous.'

'Of course. I am very careful.'

'Then as soon as I have a day off, we will buy one.'

'Thank you Trudi, it will be a help.'

'Let us get the children's tea and bathe them after.'

Chapter 22.

Sabine and Wally arrived at seven. I sent Wally to see Simon in his study. Sabine picked up Paris Match and flicked through the photos. Gérard came down ten minutes later, and I sent him to the study too. I amused myself with Nicole.

I asked her how she thought a lingerie advert should run.

'It has to appeal to young people if this is a range to appeal to young girls and women.'

'Simon says dark and moody, like Nicole Kidman advert for Chanel, you know.'

'I think that is so wrong. This is going to be Trudi lingerie. You are young and fashionable but I could imagine you living with say four other working girls in an apartment, and packing for a holiday, or dressing to go out on the town, rushing about in bra and knickers. With a good upbeat tune to sing along to.'

'I think you have something. Nicole, on Monday morning, I want you to make a story board for that idea, you remember how they did the last one? Get one of the art people to do the actual drawings. Then we will have a meeting with Simon and Wally and put it to them. Trudi de Beauvonne is not dark and mysterious, not in underwear.'

'Trudi de Beauvonne is never dark,' Sabine said from the depths of her sofa. 'She is a schemer but inside she is light and fluffy. I know it.'

We all laughed. Annette joined us as our giggles subsided.

'What is so amusing girls?' she asked.

'Oh they were just analysing my character. I am apparently a schemer but light and fluffy inside.'

'I think you are more serious than that, sometimes too serious. You need more time to relax and just be a twenty three year old young woman.'

'I agree Annette, but I cannot see that happening soon. I am too involved with Beauvonne and like anyone in my position, I have a duty.'

We were interrupted in our muses by the men entering. I examined their faces. They were all smiles. Simon caught my quizzical glance.

'Yes Trudi, I have told them that Wally is secure as our sales representative.' He winked at me and remained standing as others sat.

'My friends, I am thankful that I have the perfect marriage, for when I am in default, then my wife gently and ably sets me on the right course. Dumas said, Cherchons la femme, meaning that, when a man behaves in a strange way, it is the fault of a woman. He knew something about women but not all. As much as women, can make men stray, they can also set them on the right road.

'When I met Trudi, I was a sad man without any real ambition, leading a fashion company that had been great, but was in the doldrums. She revitalised me, and Beauvonne. It is she who has appointed you all, not I. It is my opinion that she should be managing director of Beauvonne, but she has this compulsion to help others by becoming un médecin. I respect that ambition. But it is because she woke me up that we are now up there with Chanel and Dior, in fact I believe we are ahead of those great companies. That is Trudi's influence. We are introducing two new ranges in the next six months. This year we have the fragrances already, but soon Trudi lingerie and after that, men's wear.

'As you know, Trudi does not only care for me, but for everyone she comes across, even an unmarried mother in the hospital. So there are going to be changes at Beauvonne. New appointments. I am appointing directors. Trudi, will be Deputy Managing Director, because her input is so great. The designers will be creative directors. Gustav in Clermont Production. Gérard is Administration. Oh, and I almost forgot, the most important because we need to sell what we produce, Wally is Sales Director.'

Gérard sat nonplussed, but Wally was on his feet immediately, hugging Simon and pumping his hand.

'Thank you Simon, after making me permanent, I thought that was as good as it gets. But this news makes a great difference.

Simon stood again, 'Another toast. To Trudi, who has a habit of making things happen round here. Trudi.'

This time I blushed. My stomach did a somersault.

It was a very merry dinner. We ate carpaccio of beef, followed by crab pie finishing off with chocolate fondant and raspberry coulis.

I embraced Wally again when we left the dinner table. 'I waived my wand for you Wally,' I whispered, 'Are you pleased with your knew position,' I asked aloud.

'Very, just what I wanted. Now I shall have to look for a house in the district.'

Wally and I drifted away to the window.

I said, 'Perhaps Sabine will know of something. She knows about this estate, she is the manager, and she also knows her father's estate too, but I suppose it does not have to be in this village. It was a good day Wally, when you applied to join Beauvonne. I am so happy. My life sometimes feels like a nightmare and at other times, a fairy tale.'

I turned back into the room. 'Never forget, everybody, that all the good in my life has stemmed from my dear husband, Simon.' I reached for his hand and kissed him.

Sunday we led a quiet family life, exercising the horses, Tasha running alongside. After that, we had the whole day with the children, allowing Sophie to go to lunch with Laurent and Sabine's family.

In the evening I packed my car and Tasha and I took off for Paris. I started on the ward next day at seven.

The next month passed in a whirl. The Urology department was busy and I became used to inserting a finger to feel for enlarged prostates among other duties. I found male patients largely unemotional, almost fatalistic about their ailments, putting up with discomfort for far too long. They hated the indignity of an internal examination.

Nicole produced her storyboard for the lingerie advert, and we made our case to do that rather than the conception of the agents. Nicole provided me with the song to learn, and this time I was determined to get it right myself, rather than depend on the manipulation of my voice by electronic gadgetry. The recording went well, even Nicole was impressed. I was impressed with her. She had really taken to Paris life, made friends outside Beauvonne and buzzed around on her scooter, but was there for me. In the end, I had a small part in the advert, apart from the song, walking in at the end, fully clothed saying, 'let's go girls,' as they rushed about getting ready.

Lingerie sales went through the roof, a relief because the range was so great. Both designers and Simon and Wally got together on the menswear range. The launch was delayed, and would not now take place until the September show, great winter coats, smart suits and shirts and tasteful socks to match shirts, a first in the industry they believed.

At the end of April my time in urology was over. I found myself in pathology, learning to take samples, finding out about their treatment and watching how they developed in petri dishes. It was so important and busy but I hated it. I wanted to be back with patients. However, the knowledge was essential. Luckily I was only there 6 weeks.

My crazy life went on. Time off was spent at the Chateau when possible, but it was not guaranteed to be a weekend. Sabine and I would snatch time together and ride, often with Nicole when my schedule allowed. Meanwhile the wedding preparations went ahead under Nicole's management of food tastings; wine tastings with Simon; bridesmaid dresses, complicated because two lived in England, Sam and Claire; seating plans in consultation with Simon and I; and some accommodation booking for guests from afar. Nicole was worth every penny. The last week in June, she realised that no flowers had been ordered, for the Basilica or the tables and rooms in the Chateau, but she arranged it all. A professional wedding manager would have cost twice what we paid Nicole for a year.

I had to work until two days before the wedding, so I would have no time. After the wedding Simon had booked a short honeymoon, just a week I did not know where. I hardly had time to think about it, life was a whirl of work, the children, Simon and my friends. I was never alone anymore. In Paris I was pursued by paparazzi after the release of the advert and song. The song took off and shuddered to a stop at number ten, then after the release of the advert zoomed to number one for a week. As a result there were TV interviews. I got better at them, learned to relax and smile a lot, and to be a little funny, self-deprecating.

I loved it all, but it was just the pressure of fitting everything in. I could not have managed without Nicole, who at times had taken me as passenger on her scooter to the next event or work, carving her way around Paris like a native. I found her to be quite an aggressive driver with a truly Parisian attitude.

Nicole, Tasha and I became a frequent sight on the Champs. When we had time we would visit our fashion friends, rival houses or just tour around NafNaf or another young multiple, seeing their trends.

Whenever possible, Simon and I spent time together, in Paris or at the Chateau. Nicole seemed to know when to take off and leave us, but was always at the end of her phone when needed.

June came to an end. July came in warm and sunny, but after a week low pressure brought strong south west winds and rain. We watched the forecasts anxiously. Simon left Paris on the tenth to make sure everything was in order and to welcome my family when they arrived. On the afternoon of the twelfth, Nicole picked me up in my Mercedes from the hospital. My dress was in a bag draped over the rear seat. All the bridesmaids' dresses and André's little uniform were already at the Chateau, and Marco and his team were laid on to do our hair in three days' time. I allowed Nicole to drive all the way. I was too excited to concentrate.

Simon had volunteered gallantly, to vacate the Chateau on the wedding eve, to move into Sabine's room at her father's home and Sabine and Wally would shared a room in the Chateau.

Simon had phoned to say that already established in the Chateau were my parents, my brother Harry and Alison his fiancée, Sam and her family, Claire because she was a bridesmaid and Heather and her mother.

Chapter 23.

When Nicole and I pushed through the door, we could hear laughter and chatter from the salon. Nicole volunteered to take everything up to my bedroom while I went to see my family and other guests. I found Simon playing host, a part he loved. My poor mother looked as if she would die smiling.

Simon came to meet me, putting his arm around me and kissing the tip of my nose and then my lips. My brother rose and for only the second time, kissed me, followed by my father. I kissed my mother and moved to Heather, clasping her to me. I had not seen her in years. She was not as pretty as I thought she would be and I was disappointed. Her mother clasped me to her large bosom and looked deep into my face. 'You'll do,' she said.

Claire was now a willowy pretty girl, very like her mother and we embraced and kissed. Everyone had questions that I did my best to answer, switching from English to French and back again with Simon hanging on to my hand as though I might escape if he did not.

Élise and Jean Luc entered and I introduced them and told the story of how we had worked together for the first three years.

I took mother up to the nursery and we peeped in at the sleeping children. Sophie was in her room, changing for dinner.

We returned to the salon and Nicole joined us. I introduced her to everyone. Simon suggested that we all go to our rooms and brush up before reassembling at seven-thirty before dinner at eight. The Chateau was full of chattering voices as people climbed the stairs. As doors closed silence gradually descended except for a low murmur of voices. Simon and I went up hand in hand last of all. In our room I could at last relax.

'Simon can we just go to bed for a half hour cuddle please?'

'Of course, perhaps you have your shower first, and wash away the smell of hospital. Then we cuddle and after I help you dress. I know we are not dressing for dinner, but I have a lovely dress for you tonight. I so want everyone to see you at your very best.'

I showered and washed my hair which did smell of hospital, and of course I had to dry it. In the end there was not time for a cuddle. One thing leads to another and once my hair was done, then I did not want to spoil it by lying on it. So I did my face. Simon produced the dress, a rich French blue, column/sheath one shoulder dress in stretch taffeta, ending just above the knee. It was lovely and classic without being too ostentatious.

Simon put his silver grey suit on with a tie that matched my dress. He took my diamond cuff from the safe and encircled my wrist, and handed me my diamond drop earrings to replace the plain gold ones I wore every day.

'I will go down and see that everyone is assembled. I will buzz your phone for you to make your entrance. You look fabulous my darling.' He said.

I made sure I looked as good as I could be and awaited his buzz to make my appearance. On cue I descended the stairs as our guests drank champagne and consumed canapés in the vestibule. Heads turned, Simon mounted the stairs to take my hand and lead me down. Harry clapped and others joined in. Once down I just played hostess, particularly looking after my family, Heather and her mother and Claire and Sam and her family. Alison was very self assured and spoke good French too. Father said I already sounded like a frog, then was covered by embarrassment as he realised how insulting he had been.

I stood on the bottom stair and asked for hush.

'I have an announcement about tomorrow. The rehearsal at the Basilique de Lisieux takes place at three.pm, so we must leave here at two latest. Those involved are Harry as chief usher, Jean Luc, Laurent and Wally all ushers and I hear Alison that you have your uniform too, so would you do me the honour of also being an usher? Thank you so much. My father who is delighted to give me away, all the bridesmaids, that's Élise, Sophie, Sabine, Nicole, Sam and Claire, and we should take the children too; Simon and I and the best man of course.

'So that only leaves my mother and Heather and her mother, but they might like to come anyway. So that really means everyone here will go to the rehearsal. Now the dresses, girls can we do them tomorrow morning after breakfast, in the music room, which is here on the right.

That will give us a chance of making an alteration if one is really needed.

'Let's go into dinner.' I sat mother between Simon and Wally and then everyone else, because there were far more women than men, sorted themselves out. I sat the opposite end of the table with my brother and Sam. Dinner seemed to take an age, because everyone talked so much. Harry talked to me more than he had ever done throughout our lives. As a child he had despised me, then we were at different boarding schools and at different ages. At home I was a girl, and played with the girls, while he, four years older was off with his male friends. He shunned me, could not bear the shame.

He had matured. He was nearly twenty-seven, a captain, had been to Afghanistan twice and was lecturing at Sandhurst. He was tall and athletic, six foot one, tanned, his face older than his years and very self assured. He had told me nothing about Alison until today. I now learned that not only was she a lieutenant but also a newly qualified doctor, serving in the Medical Corp territorials. She had already seen service in Afghanistan.

Over dinner, he was sweet, brotherly and complimentary. I asked him whether he was going back to Afghanistan? He shrugged.

'If my unit goes, then I want to go with them, that's how it is. We tend to think that if one of us is not there and a bad situation develops, it would have been avoided if we had the full team. It's a sort of superstition.'

'Brother's in Arms,' I say.

'It is. We live in cramped conditions and work together. It has to be comradely. Officers have to be one of the boys too, while also maintaining leadership.'

'Are you really making a difference? I mean, will the country be a better place after we leave?' I ask.

'The official view or what we actually see? Officially we are winning. Girls are going to school, that is important because it was one of the reasons for going there. We are improving roads, water supply, electricity. The ruins of thirty years of war are disappearing, rebuilding. But we are not beating the Taliban. What happens when we march out? It's a paternalistic society. Women, Trudi, count for nothing. You would hate it. Men hold all the power and enforce it by savagery. I cannot see them moving into the 21st century when the Taliban are ready to regain power, they infiltrate everything.'

'That is depressing. It makes all your sacrifices pretty worthless, doesn't it.'

'We follow orders, but our loyalty is very much to each other.'

'I don't want to think about that anymore, Harry. You have your best uniform for the wedding?'

'Of course, complete with sword, boots and spurs.'

'Thank you Harry. And Alison too?'

'Yes, she has her uniform, but only khaki with gold epaulettes. But she will look very smart.'

'That's great Harry, thank you.' I turned to Sam.

'So Sam, what are you doing now?'

'Looking for a job Trudi.'

'I thought you had one, in the Laboratories?'

'Only a fill in. I hoped it would lead to something more, but so far all applications have fallen into waste baskets. We are told they want scientists, but where are the jobs?'

'This is all doom and gloom. I am really sorry both of you, but this is my exciting time, and I refuse to be downcast.'

'Do you know sister Trudi, you now have the most sexy French accent, in fact you are quite a woman. Why don't you hate me for how I used to treat you?'

'How did you treat her?' Alison asked.

'I was despicable. When she first appeared as a girl, I called her a very vulgar and insulting name. After that I just pretended she did not exist.'

'You disowned me and spat to seal the deed. If I had liked you, it would have hurt, but you hardly registered with me. I had other more important problems.'

'Like what?'

'Like which dress to wear,' I laughed. 'But really, you can imagine my problems, with the neighbourhood children, and then boys' boarding school. That was so gross.'

'That was my fault,' my father said. 'My biggest mistake, but I just didn't understand. Thank goodness she has forgiven me. From this distance, it looks, it *was*, a really cruel act.'

'Forget it father. It all turned out for the best. At that school I met Claire's brother. Through him I met his mother. Through her I met Simon. Through him, I not only have the most wonderful husband, but all this, money, friends, study which I love, modelling which many girls would kill to do, two pop hits, fame, which every no talent wannabe says they want, and a readymade family. I am blessed. The rest doesn't matter.'

'It is good that Trudi has experienced difficult times,' Simon said from the opposite end of the table, 'she finds joy in everything and good in everyone, most of whom, I end up employing. But seriously, she has a tender heart, beauty and a brain, what more could I want. Now I think we take coffee in the salon everybody.'

I sat by Sam and caught up on her news. Michael was married and in the US. Her engagement had come to an end, when the boy had gone to Australia for three months but had not returned. She seemed disillusioned. Her job in the Cambridge laboratory was only temporary, for a specific period and nothing permanent seemed on the horizon. Much as I loved her, my magic wand was empty of inspiration. There was nothing I could do for her.

I moved to Heather and her mother. 'You are so beautiful now Trudi,' Heather said.

'Not much sign now of little Timmy,' her mother said without consideration of my feelings.

'Shush mother,' Heather said, 'she doesn't want to be reminded of all that.'

'What are you doing Heather?' I asked.

'I work in a bank. Getting married next year. Very ordinary compared to your glamorous life.'

'I have been very lucky Heather, and I thank you for that too. You were so kind to me, my big sister, at a time when I was so muddled and sad. I will never forget you and your help, nor your brutal mother, who sent you to get a cane to spank me with. Anyway, no more about the past. I want you to enjoy your time here and perhaps you will come back for a holiday one day, so keep in touch, won't you.'

I went to my brother and Alison. 'Alison, I don't know anything about you, because boys don't bother to communicate, as you probably know by now. You are a doctor?'

'I'm in the Army too. A lieutenant in the RAMC.'

'And do you have to go to Afghanistan too?'

'I have been, and I will probably have to go again. It is a risk one takes, even as a Territorial, but I do like the military life. So what do you do Trudi?'

'I do model, but only for our fashion house, Beauvonne. I have appeared in two adverts and made two records, not my idea. I support Simon, but I am also training to be a doctor, at the Sorbonne and in various Paris hospitals. I am also stepmother to his three children born to his deceased wife. I am always busy. As you know, student doctors have long hours and sometimes, it is very harrowing. So, to enable me to do that, I have a personal assistant, Nicole. I could not do without her. I also live here and in Paris at our Paris house. Life gets very complicated.'

'Do you have time to relax Trudi?' Alison asked.

'I ski a bit after Christmas and I ride. I have a horse, an Arab mare called Sheba, and my dog Tasha and my cat who is over there asleep, Mitzi, so life is very busy and of course the children demand more and more attention as they grow up, but I love my life. I am also Deputy Managing

Director of Maison Beauvonne. It was just an haute couture house until two years ago, when we introduced the ready to wear range. That is doing well. Now we have lingerie and we are introducing menswear later this year. We have a factory in Clermont Ferrand, which is an area of low employment. But I only supply a few ideas, I am not involved day to day.' I suddenly realised that everyone was listening. 'We have just introduced lingerie, and I made the advert for it. So you see, I am really busy and Nicole is my right hand, keeping me on track. My career is important but so is Simon's business.'

'That is what she says, but she is much more than a sleeping member of the board. There are three directors in this room who she has indirectly appointed.' Simon said. 'Also when I was ill, she ran the whole enterprise. A woman of many parts and amazing talent. I have to marry her, or she might take her talents to a rival.'

I got up and went and sat on the arm of Simon's chair. 'Never cher Simon, I love you too much. Anyway, dear friends, I need my sleep, so if you will excuse me, I will go to bed. Bon nuit and thank you all for coming from so far.'

Chapter 24.

After breakfast next day, I at last managed to get all the bridesmaids bar Sabine and Nicole together to try on their dresses. Luckily they all fitted well enough, though they would not have passed for the runway. I filled them in on the arrangements for wedding day and nominated cars for them all. Nicole and Sabine would go in the Limo with father and me. Élise, Claire, Sophie, Sam and the children would be in the second limo. My brother, Alison and mother, Wally and Jean Luc would depart earliest. A mini bus was taking all the staff from the Chateau and estate.

For the rehearsal, we took our own cars. I was dreading it. I was not a Catholic, not even a Christian. I wanted the big day and for Simon as an important local personality, it was essential that we had bell book and candle. I had signed some form to bring the children up in the Faith, but I certainly did not intend to keep that pledge. I would not indoctrinate them. They would have to make up their own minds. My conscience would not allow me to teach them something that I personally could not believe in.

Saint Thérèse de Lisieux, hated pretence, but this whole wedding service would be a pretence on my part. I comforted myself with the thought that as a nun Thérèse would have led a more simple life than mine. In my position, and that of many so called celebrities, pretence is an essential part of being.

We assembled at the door, where a priest welcomed the party and led us in. The interior was even more vast than I had remembered from our previous visit, and Simon, feeling me shudder, squeezed my hand and held it firmly. I heard my mother gasp, and my brother inappropriately whispered 'Christ!' I hoped the priest did not hear.

Simon with Gérard went to the alter end, while I and father, with bridesmaids and the children, formed up for our procession. At a signal from the priest the organ played. I recalled as we made our way to the alter end, that Thérèse had been canonised in 1925, the Basilica started in 1934 and the shell had survived the war intact. It was completed and consecrated in 1954. It was the size of Notre Dame de Paris, but lighter, more open. Here one could breathe, whereas Notre Dame felt oppressive. Outside it was a NeoGothic pile, inside a great and beautiful space. We could not have had a more beautiful setting. We were expecting now, six hundred guests and of course, any other curious onlookers who happened by at the time, plus news reporters and the magazine with the rights. It could hold, Simon told me, four thousand.

I breathed in the scents of candles and old incense. Even as an unbeliever, I was in awe. We arrived at the alter to Michael Praetorius: Es ist ein Ros' entsprungen (or Lo, How a Rose E'er Bloometh), just with the organ, but on the day, the choir would sing the words. As I had no ideas about it, I had left Simon to make the choice. It sounded stately and tranquil, and somehow the words described my life.

We rehearsed the ceremony, father managing not to trip up and learning his cues. Though I had dreaded this, in the end it was not so bad. I managed to repeat Simon's names correctly, and to make my responses in a clear voice. After thirty minutes, it was over. We retired down the aisle to the 'Rondeau' by Mouret.

Several people had by now seated themselves to watch. Simon and I emerged from the cool of the Basilique into the welcome warmth of the sunlit exterior. We said au revoir to the priest, then organised everyone into their cars. An hour later we were home. Tomorrow was Bastille Day, the French national day. There would be parades everywhere, so we would remain at the Chateau, unless anyone wanted to go out to watch.

I went with Simon and Sophie to give the children their tea. Afterwards it was playtime before baths and bed. Simon lay on the floor, allowing the children to romp on him. I was so frightened that they would crush his chest and set off another heart attack, a foolish worry maybe, but

I was ignorant enough about heart surgery to worry. Eventually they calmed down and freshly washed and smelling sweet, they scampered into their beds. Simon read Goldilocks to them, then I sang 'Au clair de la lune'. We left Sophie to make sure they went to sleep.

Down in the salon we took tea with our guests and outlined what was happening tomorrow. The marquees had gone up in the afternoon and the catering staff had erected their kitchens and shipped in supplies to feed the nearly six hundred who were now coming. There were still over thirty-six hours to go. Sabine had designated the car park area, and youngsters from the village were trained to be attendants.

Simon announced, 'Tomorrow you are free to do as you like. It is Bastille day, so there are parades in the towns and cities or you can stay on the estate and relax. The pool is clean and warm. I know that Sabine, Nicole and Trudi will be riding early and there are walks on the estate and the forest. We will do a buffet lunch and tea and supper, then I depart for Sabine's home and will not see you until the wedding, but Trudi will look after you.

'On the wedding day, there will be an army of hairdressers and make up people as well as dressers to help you all get ready. I want to make sure you are all perfect, because this is a Maison Beauvonne occasion.

'Dinner tonight is at seven, and rather special. It is a thank you to you all, our good close friends, for being here.'

I looked at Simon in surprise. I had no idea what was going to happen.

We went to our rooms. As usual on such occasions, Simon dressed me, and of course it was a new dress. This time it was a midnight blue stretch satin sheath, one shoulder strap with radiating lines of white crystals around the breasts and from the diaphragm. It was slashed at the back from floor to above the knee. Simon helped me put my hair up in a classic style, very like Grace Kelly in the film Rear Window, in which she had played a model. He placed my diamond cuff on my right wrist. He stood back to survey the effect.

'Your family will be very proud. We will descend arm in arm my darling.'

Heads did turn as we descended. My brother, my one time bully and archenemy, came to meet us.

'Spectacular,' he said quietly. 'You have made me so ashamed of how I used to be with you.

'Everybody,' he said loudly above the hubbub of conversation, 'I present my dear sister, Trudi de Beauvonne. Please raise your glasses.'

I blushed. I had not expected any such welcome especially from Harry. Mother stood by me. 'You do look divine dear,' she said.

Simon soon summoned us to go into dinner. There were nineteen of us but only six men. Simon had father on his left side and my mother on his right. I at the other end had Wally on my right and Sabine on my left. To my surprise I found that all the places had name cards, and on every place except those of Simon and me, there were little boxes, beautifully wrapped in Beauvonne paper and ribbons.

Simon rapped the table as people sat.

'Dear friends. Tonight's dinner is a thank you to you all for coming, some of you from a very long way. All of you have been good friends to Trudi or both of us. You will each see a small gift to remember the occasion. You may open your boxes.'

They all set to opening the little packages. Each contained a watch, a Beauvonne, but which was a Tissot on the inside. They were inscribed on the back, Simon et Trudi de Beauvonne. Wally gave a short thank you speech.

The first course came, crab cakes. I looked at Sam remembering that Jews did not eat shellfish, but she was happily eating it. This was followed by carpaccio of beef. The plates were replaced by a small sole bon femme. The doors of the dining room opened and a man in dinner jacket entered. He entertained us with card tricks, never uttering a word, just miming and choosing his victims as he walked around the table. He seemed able to produce cards from anywhere, from my hair and Sabine's breast and Wally's shirt front.

The main was of course, magret de canard my favourite. A girl entered playing a violin, she began with a slow and sentimental number, then launched into one of those vibrant, hectic numbers so beloved of solo women violinists, giving her the opportunity to move and shake her long black hair. We finished with a French type of bread and butter pudding. We took coffee in the salon.

At ten, Simon rose from his seat. 'Now ladies and gentlemen, I suggest that we all have an early night, for there will be much to do tomorrow. The makeup and hair for the ladies starts at seven. The cars arrive at nine and the brides car should depart at ten-fifteen. Those of you who are not bride's maids will all find outfits in your rooms. I now leave to spend the night at Sabine's house. I look forward to seeing you in the Basilique. Trudi, you must not be late please. The Basilique will not like it. They are busy too.'

'Simon, you know I am never late.' I kissed him. 'à demain, cheri.'

Soon after his departure, father stood. 'The time by my new Beauvonne watch is ten minutes after ten, so I think we should follow Simon's advice and let Trudi have her beauty sleep.' It was a long speech for my father, nearly the longest I had heard him make ever.

We all went to our rooms. Sam shared my bed. We were asleep soon after our heads touched the pillows.

I awoke to the call of the alarm at six thirty. I ran round the corridor, knocking doors and waiting for replies. The hair and makeup people would have arrived and set up in the music room. For the men it was easy, but for the girls it could take three hours. I was due at the Basilique at eleven. Simon, Wally, Gerard, Harry and Jean Luc were due there at ten-thirty. It was forty-five minutes from the Chateau, so there was not time to waste. I knocked my parents door and was answered immediately by mother. The door opened and I found her already half dressed.

'Don't worry about us Trudi, I will make sure that your father is dressed and ready for you at ten. When is my hair being done?'

'As soon as they are ready for you mother, you will be first in. They will come and wash it here, then take you down. There is a buffet breakfast laid in the dining room, so grab what you can.'

'Very well dear, I will go down soon.'

I kissed her and ran to the nursery. Sophie was up and so were the children. She would leave them in their pyjamas until ready to dress. Nicole was going to help her, so I did not have that worry, but they all needed their hair done too. Nicole was also organising the running order.

I ran back to my room and went into the bathroom. I showered and washed my hair. In my dressing gown I descended to the dining room and ate the buffet breakfast, forcing something down so that I did not feel sick and giddy later. Doors were slamming outside and I heard the gabble of voices and tramp of feet in and out of the main door. I ate two bread rolls with butter and mother's marmalade and drank a cup of coffee. I refilled the cup and went to the music room. Marco greeted me. He took the towel from my damp hair, sprayed my hair to wet it more. He combed it through.

'You have the dress and the headdress?'

'Upstairs Marco.'

'Bring them here, I need to see how they fit on your head before I style your hair.'

I ran up stairs and brought down my dress and the little tiara and veil.

'Bon. Now we see.' Marco tried the veil and tiara. 'So, I will put your hair in a roll at the back of your head, out of the way. It will look classic French and very gorgeous.'

He worked away, first trimming split ends then drying and straightening, so that when pulled back exposing my ears, there would be no loose wispy bits. After an hour he was done. The bride's maids all took their turns, as well as Heather and her mother, my mother and Alison. Even father, Harry and Wally were tidied up. I raced round making sure that everyone was in the production line. To my relief all was well. Sabine reassured me that it was all under control. She was already complete, hair makeup and dress, and marshalled the rest through the process. I had my face done, pretty, no strong eyeliner. They made me look fresh and wholesome rather than artificial.

The boys departed looking pristine, having passed inspection by Thomas Martin, the ready made designer. Father loitered, not knowing what to do. Mother and the other non-bridesmaids, departed fifteen minutes later. Sabine assembled the bridesmaids, father and the children. We would go in the two six seater limousines. Jacques fitted my dress and headdress, my eardrops and necklace. I was ready. Father and I, Sabine and Élise entered one limousine and the rest with the children in the other. They departed and we followed. It was twenty past ten. We were already five minutes late. My heart was beating faster than I had ever known it. I was sure it could be heard, but Sabine assured me that she could not hear it. Father held tightly to my hand.

I watched the countryside go by, wanting to say to the driver, put your foot down, but refrained. Sabine said that there was nothing to worry about. We would be on time, she asserted. My whole life flashed before me; everything that had brought me to this point. My brother's disdain; mother's cruelty that turned to complicit endorsement of my behaviour; father's insistence that I had to try to be a boy and the pain of that; and the bullying, teasing, skirt lifting and kicking after my change. And rape by Stuart and my awful acts of revenge on my enemies.

My life in France had been full of hard work, shock and trauma, triumph and disaster, but at least all the events had been those that every normal person may endure. My life had changed from one of continual oppression in England to a life of love, triumph, luxury and fulfilment in France. My adopted country had embraced me, brought out the best in me, and I found myself surrounded by friends rather than people wishing to drag me down. Sabine, sitting opposite, must have sensed my rush of thoughts. She smacked my right hand quite hard and that jerked me out of the morbid reverie of my past.

'Nearly there,' she said, 'people want to see Trudi le modèle. This is a happy day.'

I smiled. 'Of course it is. I just had so many thoughts of the past and my pain. But now I am very happy. Of course I am, how could I not be?'

As we approached the Basilica, I heard the clock chiming eleven, and the huge bell booming out. I was surprised to find quite a crowd before the steps up to the big west door.

Father helped me from the car and Jacques came forward to arrange my dress for the camera crew and photographers. I posed for a few seconds. Sabine and Élize took up their positions behind me. Sam, Nicole, Claire and Sophie with the children between them walked in front proceeded by the priest and six choristers. A solo treble sang 'Es ist ein Ros entsprungen', taken up by the other five as we entered, and this was answered from the choir stalls on the third verse, when the organ also came in. The Basilica was full. Lisieux had turned out to see and visitors, complete strangers and the curious had stopped to watch. I wanted to cry. I must have faltered, for father increased his grip on my arm and we slowly made our way up the aisle to where I could see Simon and Gérard waiting. Sophie picked Sébastien up as he had started to play about, wanting to run beween the choir's legs. I was nearly overcome by emotion. Sabine reached forward to adjust my veil and whispered, 'Attention, le modèle.'

Finally we reached Simon and Gérard standing before the Bishop of Bayeux. I smiled at Didier sitting just behind Simon's seat. The children and the bridesmaids took their places. Simon turned to me and beamed. The service began. It was far more involved and ornate than I had thought. We seemed to spend a long time on our knees. Incense wafted around and a bell tolled. Finally we exchanged vows and rings. We knelt and were blessed. The prayers seemed to go on for ages. I had a terrible urge to giggle, but suppressed it. At last it was time to sign the register. One final prayer and it was over. Simon and I turned to face the congregation and kissed, to applause from the huge assembly. The Bishop stood before us and my bridesmaids and the children, mother and father, Annette and Gérard formed up behind and on signal from the camera team, the orchestra began to play the 'Rondeau' by Mouret with two trumpets..

The ceremony had been beautiful and solemn yet still joyful, but the Rondeau as we walked in time down to the great West door now wide open, was triumphal and joyous. It was a march of Victory and majesty, and a release from the solemnity of the service. I was able to pick out faces as we progressed, nodding and smiling to them, even touching some hands of people I knew well, then we were out. My brother so handsome in his full uniform, and

Wally and some gendarmes shepherded the sightseers away, so that we were left on the steps with our invited guests. Alison looked absolutely pristine. Gradually the guests were weeded out until it was just Simon and I and the children, Sophie and Sabine lurking to help with them. When the film crew had finished and the photographers finished, we entered the last two limos. Simon and I alone at last, exchanged kisses.

'Thank you Simon, it was wonderful. Now I feel truly yours.'

'Thank you, Trudi cheri. I could not have wished for a more graceful and beautiful bride. Now we can give all our guests a wonderful feast.'

The sun shone and small white clouds wafted across the sky. Across the flat countryside, the horizon was hazy beneath pale grey azure. Clumps of woodland and forest were heavy with leaf and the wheat was turning ever so slightly golden.

I leant into Simon, breathing in his aftershave and the spiciness of his suit. We turned into the Chateau drive and stopped before the front door. The huge marquee on this lovely day, had been opened up on two sides. Waitresses held trays of champagne or orange juice. The seating plans were stationed as had been agreed in five places. At first I could hardly make out individual faces, but gradually as nerves subsided, I saw familiar faces from Maison Beauvonne, my cousins almost strangers, the Hendersons and the Stubbs, Vanessa and Bill, Ellie and John Stuart and his wife. We circulated amongst them. Mrs Henderson was tearful, Mr Henderson avuncular. Stubbs was pleasant in his rather staid manner, and his wife gushing, I think impressed by her surroundings.

Harry looked so impressive in his uniform and Alison clung to his arm, on guard against any other females. Simon and I parted, so we could talk to as many of our guests as possible. Sabine hovered and Wally hovered with her, both keeping an eye on me. Mother whispered that she was hungry, but I said she would have to wait.

I spotted Mathilde come with the staff in Clermont Ferrand. She was happy she said, shyly. She carried her little baby on her hip. She loved her job and new life, and had been home to see her family too. I was so glad for her.

It was nearly three, before Simon collected me and we stood before the great marquee to greet every guest as they went to their tables.

Finally we had done with kissing. My brother was giving a speech instead of my father. He said that he would not embarrass me. Wally was going to interpret for him as Harry's French was elementary. I managed to whisper to Wally to cut anything at all risqué. A string quartet played sweetly in a corner of the marquee. The guests went to the buffet to select their choices, some piling the food on as though they would never eat again. The children ate and were then released to gambol about, popping out from below tables, Sophie and Nicole kept an eye on them, but everyone seemed pleased to tolerate them.

Father rapped on the table and rose from his seat.

'I wish to thank Simon and Trudi for their great hospitality and a wedding event that I am sure will be remembered by everyone. The Basilica was beautiful, and at least for me and all who know Trudi well, emotional. Please raise your glasses to Simon and Trudi.'

Harry spoke next. 'Most of you do not know who I am, so I will introduce myself. Unluckily, I am Trudi's brother. I say unluckily but it is unluckily for her. When we were children, I was nearly four years older. When Trudi appeared, I was not very interested. When she was old enough to be interesting, she was not at all interested in me. I was a horrible boy, and she was very girlie. I treated her with as much disdain and rudeness as a rather nasty little boy could muster. In fact I disowned her and sealed my resolve by spitting. Each time I insulted her, I would find my bicycle tyres flat. We ignored each other, but I took every opportunity to insult her until one day, she turned on me and slapped my face so hard, I thought my teeth had moved in my jaw.

'I am therefore agreeably surprised that I was even invited here today. I am pleased to see that she has become a rather grande dame, indeed formidable, a lady, as well as being a great beauty. I have heard from those close to her, that she has devoted herself to Simon and the children, going to extraordinary lengths, almost making love to Simon to bring him out of his coma, and all the time studying to be a doctor. Life in France has agreed with her and one only has to see Simon and Trudi together to understand that the love they have, is very deep and true. I am truly proud to call her sister and wish her and her new husband good health and much happiness. A toast, to Maison de Beauvonne.'

He walked the few steps between us and kissed me on the lips. It was the seal of approval I had wanted for fifteen years.

I went to the Hendersons and Stubbs family, sitting with Sam and her parents. Mrs Henderson was still emotional, feeling she said, as though her own daughter had just married. It was lovely to see them all again, but school and all that had happened there seemed a very long time ago. They asked me lots of questions about my life and studies and of Simon's coma. They hadn't realised that he had an artificial leg.

Simon came to join me and we circulated together, hand in hand. It was so sweet. We spent a long time with Vanessa, John and Ellie. Then the band started to play and we managed a few steps of the Argentine Tango that we had rehearsed. We soon morphed into just moving and holding each other. To my surprise, Harry and Alison joined us and I danced with Harry. Soon the floor was full. Simon and I left the floor and spoke to people sitting at their tables.

The sun slowly descended over the forest but we were left with a luminous glowing sky. The air remained warm. I found that Sophie and Nicole had put the children to bed when I went to see them. I looked in and found them all sound asleep. Nicole was on watch while Sophie enjoyed herself with Laurent. Simon came up and collected me. Some guests were leaving and we had to say goodbye.

The party went on. At midnight the coaches arrived for the Beauvonne staff going to Paris and to Clermont Ferrand. By two, the last guests had gone except for those staying in the Chateau. They would be with us another two days. I was enjoying their company but I also longed to have the Chateau to our selves again. Mother, Father,

Harry and Alison, Sabine and Wally had tea with us, and gradually we all went to bed.

Simon and I just cuddled and fell asleep. I'd had a marvellous day.

Chapter 25.

I awoke to whispers. I lifted my bleary head to find André and Adèle and Sébastien behind them, having a debate whether they should get on the bed.

'Venir ici!' I mumbled and there was an immediate scramble as the twins climbed up. I hooked an arm around Sébastien and dragged him up too. They inserted themselves under the duvet with many giggles, and Simon turned and grabbed Sébastien, held him in the air and pretended he would eat him. We told them stories, Simon French ones and I translated English ones, making things up where I could not remember. Eventually I got out of bed nude, threw on a negligee and led them back to the nursery. I met Sophie just up, going to see to them.

'I'm so sorry Trudi, I overslept.'

'Il est trés bien. We had fun and you looked after them all day yesterday. I hope you managed to enjoy yourself too?'

'Oh yes, Laurent and I had a super time. It was a great day wasn't it. You must be pleased how it went. And you looked like a princess. Your family were so proud of you. Your father hardly took his eyes from you.'

Between us we dressed the children, while chatting.

'Thank you Sophie. I am so lucky. Even the sun shone for us. I don't know why I am so blessed. Simon had designed a lovely ceremony, with the music and the Basilique, what a beautiful setting. You know I am not Catholic, not even religious, but even I was overcome by, je ne sais quoi, a spiritualism. I nearly cried.'

'But you looked so in control.'

'Believe me Sophie, I was so nervous on the way there, that Sabine slapped me, hard.' I laughed. 'Sabine is very special. She can read my thoughts. Mon père aussi, he gripped my hand hard when he felt me rocking.'

'Peut-être you are human after all, Trudi. I thought you were the fairy queen, touching everything with your little wand making all neat and tidy.'

'Non, ce n'est pas moi. I am like anybody else, but like many en Angleterre, contained. We have, or used to have, what we call the 'stiff upper lip', garder les emotions à l'interieur. Sometimes, I am like jelly inside.'

'Then you have more of my respect, because you appear so cool. Nicole has a surnom (nick name) for you.

No it is not rude, it is a compliment. She calls you Princess Grace, you know, of Monaco, Grace Kelly. In her films she was always the cool blonde.'

'I will take that as a compliment, certainly. She was always one of my idols, even though she died years before I was born. Have you seen Rear Window? I saw that when I was, oh seven I think, and I was so scared but I wanted to be Grace. She was also a model in the film.

'I must go and dress Sophie and be downstairs to look after the guests. You will bring the children down? It is good for them to be amongst us all.'

I found Simon already dressed. I showered quickly and put on a summer frock. I found that everyone was up and in the dining room. Outside the marquee was fast disappearing, and all the other paraphernalia as well. By lunchtime, Beauvonne would be back to normal. Tomorrow we would have contact prints of the stills and the day after rushes of the eight page magazine feature, together with the video before the final edit, in time for our remaining guests to see it.

'Hello everyone,' I said, 'today we were going to Bayeux to see the tapestry and the Cathedral, then lunch at Arromanches before a walk on the sands. Simon has organised the whole thing, including a coach so we can all travel together and drink if we want to.'

John

Vanessa, and Ellie and the rest of the family met us at the restaurant. Lunch was of course sea food, a choice of so much; crab, lobster, sole, herrings, plaice, cod, mackerel and for those who liked disgusting, oysters. I put the latter in the same league as snails, tripe and frogs legs. I would rather eat fried locusts. I ate crab and salad with Gewurztraminer. The children ate sole and chips. It was a wonderful lunch, shared with all my favourite people.

We all walked the beach, the children running freely, Simon and Wally drawing pictures in the sand for them. Tasha ran and ran, chasing seagulls and rounding us all up. The day was gorgeous, a cloudless sky with a slight cross beach breeze. I set the children to finding sea shells and they soon had a good collection. We looked for coloured pebbles and by wetting them, saw the colours come alive.

The coach appeared to take us home. At the Chateau I took mother and father and Harry to play with the children, saying that they are now part of the family. I promised to send photos of them regularly. Father said he was getting a new computer making it easier to stay in touch with us and Harry when he was abroad.

Mum and I helped Sophie get the children fed, washed and into bed. It was such a happy time and I so enjoyed showing off my children to my family. When the darlings were settled and sleepy we went down to join the others for tea and cake.

We had a buffet supper and went to bed tired.

After breakfast next day, a courier arrived on motorbike with rushes of the magazine coverage. There would be bound copies to follow for each of our special guests, Simon's immediate family and my family and close friends.

It was a warm overcast day, so people collected around the very under used pool. Mitzi observed from the top of a wall and Tasha sat under a chair. I was pleased to find that Adèle and André could already swim across the pool. Sébastien loved to splash about, and seemed to have no fear, even doing a few strokes unaided. I found out from Sophie that she had been giving regular lessons but she had said nothing. We would have to review her salary, I thought.

The rush of the video arrived mid-afternoon via another courier. We settled to watch it through in the salon. It was very glossy. I looked perfect, very Grace Kelly, but I could see, if others could not, where I faltered on the way to the altar and father gripped tighter. They had cut much of the service, in fact from well over an hour down to fifteen minutes, but it had managed to capture the music and take in the extraordinary architecture. There was a great deal of the reception and different groups and of our little dance. Harry looked a real swell in his uniform, all the men looked very handsome. The children were caught too, camping under a table and sneaking food to give to Tasha. Mum was caught with tears in her eyes as my brother spoke, his speech taking her back to the difficult days when she did not understand me. I kissed her.

Tomorrow everyone would depart and it would be somewhat of a relief. I was exhausted playing hostess. There was just dinner to get through, a farewell dinner.

We started with Moules Mariniere, mussels in wine sauce followed by Sole Normande, sole in a butter egg and cream sauce, very rich and I warned people that the portions were therefore small.

The main was also a Normandy dish, Canard Rouennaise, duck cooked in blood. It is magnificent, so tasty. We finished with Normandy apple pudding, flamed with calvados.

We sat chatting. Harry whispered that he was expecting to be sent to Afghanistan again. I told him I hoped not. I feared for him in that God forsaken nation. I could lose him, now, when at last he was the loving brother I had always wanted.

The morning dawned in mist. A hazy sun attempted to burn through. The parkland surrounding the Chateau's formal garden, looked mystical. The foliage of the trees of the park were hidden by the mist but their lower trunks were visible. It looked as if huge elephants lurked.

My family and those from England were anxious to get away to Dieppe. Mum and I cried, father tried to be strong. Heather too was tearful but her mother covered her feelings by being exuberant and kissing and hugging everyone in sight, including Simon. Soon only our immediate friends and family remained, Sabine and Wally, Sophie, Nicole and the children, Élise and Jean Luc. I hugged Simon.

'All over,' I said,' now we will just become an old married couple.'

'I cannot imagine you ever being old Trudi, you have so much joie de vivre. I need to talk to Wally. Why don't you and Sabine ride, a long one because we are going to be busy planning the new sales campaign. And then we need to pack for our honeymoon tomorrow.'

'Where are we going, so I know what to pack?'

'Scotland. It may be cold, it may be wet.'

'Oh!'

'You are disappointed?'

'Just surprised. Mm, I am thinking about it. I'll go and see Sabine.'

I found her in the office. 'Bon jour, Mon amie. Comment vas tu.'

'Oh Trudi. I do love you.'

'I am glad you are happy. Simon looks at the detail, that is why he is so good at haute couture. I look at the big picture. He is busy with Wally and suggested that we ride. Can you or are you too busy?'

'I can spend a couple of hours. And Nicole perhaps?'

'I will ask her. Simon has just told me we are going to Scotland for honeymoon.'

'Well that is different. Have you been there?'

'Some time ago. It is wild and empty. I was a bit disappointed at first. I had thought of Egypt or the Seychelles or the Caribbean. But I don't mind. It will be another adventure, and I am sure Simon will have thought of everything.

I collected Nicole and we three rode for two hours, laughing and giggling with the adrenalin rush of cantering and galloping along the rides. It was terrific fun.

On return I went up to pack for Scotland. I took a ski jacket and ski sweaters and thermal underwear, as well as some dressy clothing and casuals. I knew nothing about the trip, the destination, the time or the method of getting there. I felt completely out of control and while Simon and

Wally were ensconced with Maison business, I felt I just had to wait.

I found the girls and Sophie and the children, and we piled into the Range Rover. I made for Alençon and the restaurant Rive Droite. Although we had no reservation, they soon found room. I found out that my celebrity status created a lot of bowing and scraping. I was surprised that the wedding had so soon made me an A grade celeb. The over enthusiastic obsequiousness was intrusive and galling.

We ordered fish salads, with fruit salad to follow, and I asked that we be left alone. It worked. The service became more arms length. As we left, I thanked the maitre and tipped well.

We arrived back at the Chateau to find Simon and Wally strolling around looking for us. A helicopter was in the meadow.

'Where have you been?'

'We thought you were busy planning, so we did what ladies are supposed to do, we lunched at Rive Droite. It was gorgeous, and the children were marvellously behaved.'

'Oh, I see. I did not mean for you to be away so long.'

'Why Simon? What's the matter?'

'No, it is my fault for trying to surprise you.'

'So, what is the surprise?'

'The helicopter. It is waiting to take us on honeymoon. Are you packed?'

'Oui mon cher. Just need to change and pack my makeup. How long have I got?'

'Shall we say thirty minutes?'

'Easy. Come, you can make sure we have everything.' I kissed him and took his hand. 'You are annoyed with me,' I accused.

'No, I am annoyed with myself. I tried to make a surprise, therefore I was dismissive of you this morning, and you quite rightly made yourselves scarce. It is a lesson for me, oui? I must never be off hand with you.'

'Oh Simon, mon homme cheri. Come, and help me.'

We were ready in thirty minutes, giving me time to say goodbye to everyone, especially the children. It was only to be a week, but I felt quite tearful. Sophie and Nicole promised to look after Mitzi and Tasha.

We entered the helicopter and I was extremely nervous. It was my first ride in one and I hardly knew what to expect. The rotor whirred and three minutes later we left the ground, quite gently at first, then rising quickly, but when we turned abruptly onto a course, it felt like being in a fairground machine, as we seemed to swing around as if on a pendulum. I gripped Simon's hand tightly and held onto it for the next two hundred miles.

We descended into Luton, where we transferred to a private jet and ate dinner on board, with champagne. I badgered Simon for a destination and he finally informed me that we were headed for Inverness. We had to go through normal arrivals there and I found a limousine waiting to whisk us to a hotel. It was nearly nine when we finally arrived, yet it still seemed really light. It was a castle and from the signposts I saw it was just outside Fort William. The interior was luxurious, even compared to the Chateau. It was more modern than Beauvonne, but tasteful. The bathrooms were right up to date, and beautiful with slippers and gowns, perfumes and salts and other cosmetics. We were offered dinner, even at that late hour but I declined. We made ourselves comfortable in the suite, bathed and went to bed.

I did not feel much like a bride. I was very tired, but Simon used his ingenuity to arouse my passion, and I soon summoned the strength to respond. We fell asleep, but in the night I awoke with the excitement of this man, who liked sometimes to treat me as his doll and other times would publicly put me on a pedestal. We made love twice during the night. I awoke feeling like the bride I was. I ran a deep warm bath before Simon awoke and was already half dressed doing my hair when Simon finally stepped out of the bed.

In the dining room I found there were several guests and from the stares of others in the dining room, I could tell that my fame had reached the Highlands of Scotland. I recognised a British TV presenter in the room, who had a chat show. He approached the table, presented his card and asked if he could have a few words when convenient? I looked to Simon, as I still had no idea of our itinerary.

'We are here for three nights,' Simon said, 'If you want to do this Trudi, then I am agreeable, but you do not have to.'

'What do you have in mind?' I asked.

'Just a few words now. You are just married so I presume this is your honeymoon? It would be good if at some time you would come on the programme?'

'When would that be, remembering that I now live in France?'

'Not now, the series starts in the autumn again and of course, we would fly you to London and back, with accommodation for two. Can I get in touch?'

I took a card from my bag and handed it to him. 'I would be pleased to do it, thank you, as long as it is in good taste, no innuendo. I am not a show business personality, I am a serious person.'

'Of course. Thank you, I'll be in touch.' He left his card.

'Where are we going today, Simon?'

'We are going on a trip to see some cloth, and seeing the mountain scenery.'

A car stood waiting for us at the door and we drove northwest on the A86, but there was no traffic. We ran in brilliant sunshine through mountain scenery, bereft of dwellings until we came to a large lake on the right hand which was I saw from the map, Loch Laggan. We continued until the first village of any size, Newtonmore and pulled in front of what appeared to be a small village shop set in a typical Scottish cottage with attic rooms.

'Here we are.' Simon said, 'the best shop window of Harris Tweed. Let us see what they have.'

We entered and found bales and bales of the hard wearing cloth, in shades from yellowy brown to purple. It was not for me, I thought as I looked at it, but given another ten years, I suppose I might sport a coat or a cloak made of it at a point to point or some other country occasion. Simon handled the cloth expertly, feeling the quality and the degree of roughness and studying the number of threads.

I wandered about, slightly bored. I wondered frankly why we were here looking at designs I considered passé. Eventually, Simon disappeared into the interior and I stood aimlessly. I came across a light grey tweed, with flecks of black, and I could well picture a skirt in it or a coat, ideal for wearing on country walks around the Chateau. Simon emerged from wherever he had been with the shop manager or owner. They seemed on good terms. I showed Simon the light grey I had found. He also liked it. He spoke to me in French.

'The main problem I have with these fabrics is that they are so scratchy. Unless lined with a good quality lining, they would be uncomfortable on the skin. It seemed a good idea to look at them, while we are touring, but I have to confess, so far I am a little disappointed.'

The manager came forward with a package that I discovered was a swatch of the different weights and designs. We said au revoir and entered our car again. We continued northwest to Grantown and settled on the Craggan Mill Restaurant. It seemed from the menu very Scottish and we had rare Aberdeen Angus steaks. It was very good and we had splendid views of the Cairngorm Mountains as we ate.

After lunch, we continued to Inverness and drove down the side of Loch Ness. We joked with each other about the Loch Monster. *and who among the people we knew it could be* We wandered around Fort Augustus, and looked at plaid fabrics in a shop. They still felt rough to my skin and I drew the conclusion it was the nature of wool. I wondered whether that was why the yarn had fallen out of favour.

We continued our drive south to Fort William, which quite disappointed us. It was larger and more modern than I had pictured in my mind, but the Loch with its boats was beautiful. We continued South to Glencoe, and I told Simon the story of the treacherous Campbells and the massacre of the Macdonalds, and how the Campbells and the Duke of Argyll had sold Scotland to the English. 'Never trust a Campbell' I told him, tongue in cheek. It had been a beautiful drive.

We returned to the Castle and buried ourselves in the luxury of it. The Queen's suite was warm and beautiful. We went down for tea, afterwards walking around the grounds hand in hand, kissing under some cedars. It was very romantic and I considered whether it would have been so romantic in the Seychelles. I decided that the Highlands, because of the atmosphere, the history and the mountains was more romantic than anywhere we had been.

We ate dinner looking at the sun setting over the mountain. The food was good. The TV guy was still there. Simon was very attentive, playing with me under the table and holding my hand above. I was so emotional, as though on a second date, in rapture. I could hardly breathe.

He would not tell me what we were doing for the rest of the time. I suggested that we go to Oban. I had read of it and seen it on television. It seemed to me a sort of mystical place. We decided that we would wander that way and see what took our fancy.

We awoke to rain. We set out for Oban and as we made our way south, the rain cleared. We bought a painting in a roadside gallery, a local scene to remind us of this time together. [highland cattle in a loch with mountains] We arrived in Oban and I was so disappointed. It was not that it was ugly, just much more ordinary than I thought it to be. We looked at the ferry times and on a whim, took the ferry to Craignure. We could drive from there to Tobermory, the name being enough to excite our curiosity.

Simon was quite boyish about this adventure, finding even driving onto the boat, exciting, and when he saw the road to Tobermory was only wide enough for one vehicle in places, I thought he would have another heart attack. Finally we reached the village. I decided that Simon should eat something local. I took him to the fish and chip van on the harbour that I read, had an excellent reputation. We bought our lunch of fish and chips and ate it on a seat looking out over the water.

It was very good. Simon, used to the best of everything, said that while a little greasy, it was excellent.

We went to the pub and washed our hands and drank bitter beer. Simon loved the atmosphere in the pub and asked to sample some of the local whiskeys. Under advice he tried four, and bought a mixed case on the advice of the publican. I drove back to our hotel.

Chapter 26.

Next day we checked out of the castle. Simon drove us to Fort William and we left the car. We took a taxi with our goods and arrived at the Loch.

'Where are we going Simon?'

'We are taking that motor boat,' he said pointing out an approaching launch.

We got in, the boatman helping me enter in my heels. We crossed the still waters until we cleared all the moored launches and arrived alongside a seaplane. I was helped aboard. Another adventure, I thought. I was again nervous. This flimsy little plane with its clunky tin door and great big floats was terrifying. When everything was stowed, the motorboat departed and the single engine of the Cessna sprang to life. It vibrated quite a lot.

The take off even on calm water was a bit bouncy and I was relieved when we were finally several hundred feet in the air. We turned and headed south west as far as I could judge. This was the most intrepid flight yet, flying quite low over the locks and climbing over the mountains. It was fascinating. We saw Tobermory from the air and the little road we had travelled yesterday. We landed at Inveraray for lunch, and to see the seat of the Campbells, the Duke od Argyll's residence.

Lunch was not exciting but Inveraray was a picture beside the still waters of the Loch. We took off again, causing quite a stir. The plane headed north up the coast until we reached Skye, and from there we headed up its west coast. Leaving Sky behind we crossed to Lewis and descended into Stornaway.

At the dock we were met by a man with a trolley who transported our luggage to the Royal Hotel, sitting right by the marina. We were shown into a nice room with a view over the harbour. It had turned cold and clouds whipped across the sky from the northwest. We wandered the town, looking in the tweed shops, but there was little different from what we had seen before. What we did find, which had escaped us, were plain tweeds in a variety of colours, pinks, violet, purple, royal blue, grey and charcoal and a few others too. I wandered the shop while Simon spoke to the manager. It seemed a very jovial conversation and I joined them. Mr McNeish recognised me, produced the magazine with the wedding coverage and shook my hand until I thought it would fall off. He said he would meet us in the bar of the hotel in the evening and tell us more about tweed and tartan.

We returned to our room and enjoyed warm baths and a short nap. At dinner we went for sea food starters and Aberdeen Angus steaks, asking for them to be cooked very rare. Surprisingly, we found them really good. The word seemed to have gone round that celebrities were in town, for the waitress addressed me by name and there were a few stares.

McNeish joined us. He told us of the factory out on the West coast that now made most of the Harris Tweed and said that they were sending a car to pick us up at 09.15. I gathered that Simon had already agreed to this. I did not mind, it was just another interesting little adventure.

Up in our room we found that the wind had gone round, and it was now battering our window. The rain lashed against it and we drew the thick curtains across against the noise. The bay was full of white horses and the boats in the harbour were bobbing on the wavelets. There was a constant tinny clanking from the rigging as the wind shook the wires.

We climbed into bed and my dear husband turned into a voracious sex crazed animal in our large bed. At one time I seemed not to know which way up I was as we performed a number of somersaults. Finally he was exhausted and we lapsed into satisfied sleep.

Next morning after Simon had a large breakfast, the car arrived on time, with a driver dressed in tweed. We traversed the island, first north to the West coast and then south west more or less parallel to the coast. We were welcomed at the factory by the fashion manager and shown the works. Simon looked at all the products and then discussed making even higher specification tweeds for the haute couture trade as well as material for shooting jackets.

They talked a long time and we were shown the weaving floor, the machines clattering away. The noise was deafening. We were given lunch in the cafeteria, a Scottish treat of haggis. I was disappointed in it, and wondered what all the fuss was about for some spiced mince in a bag, but I said it was a lovely new experience, truthful at least in one respect. I wondered why some of these peasant foods, haggis, pizza and risotto received such acclaim.

We emerged into bright sunshine, the wind again from the west and not so strong. We returned to Stornaway by a different route, though the terrain was very similar to our outward journey. This part of the island at least, seemed fairly flat, with a multitude of small lochs, or even just mere ponds, heather and a few sheep mooching about.

Our seaplane was not returning until tomorrow, so we resigned ourselves to another night at the hotel, which we decided was no great hardship. As we sat in the bar that night, McNeish invited us to a ceilidh. I explained to Simon that it was a gathering where people performed to each other in dance or song or told a story, whatever they could do. McNeish accompanied us to the community centre and introduced us to his group of friends, though he seemed to know everyone. I found it difficult to understand their speech and Simon did not know what was going on at all, but when the band struck up playing reels in the traditional way, his foot was tapping and he was obviously enjoying himself. We found ourselves dragged onto the floor to take part in the dance and after the first minutes of embarrassed incompetence, enjoyed ourselves.

I was then persuaded to sing my first song, to the accompaniment of a violin. I acquitted myself reasonably well and received an ovation. After that we were allowed to relax and just enjoy the show, much of which appeared to be in Gaelic. It was though, an excellent and lively and friendly evening. We walked home cuddled together like teenagers. It was after one when I finally climbed into bed.

We awoke to a fine morning. The wind had abated and the low clouds had blown away. After breakfast we packed and checked out. A bolt of cloth had come from the factory to take with us. We were met on the dockside and assisted into the boat that took us to the seaplane. A small crowd gathered to watch us take off and I waived to this friendly town.

I didn't bother to ask where we were headed. It was all just too much fun to bother, a real magical mystery tour and I wondered how Simon had thought it all up.

We landed at Ullerpool, for lunch and a wander. It was another beautiful settlement along the loch side. The pilot found us in the restaurant and said that a new weather front was coming in and we had better move on. In the air again, we headed south and Simon told me we were spending the night in Glasgow, the seaplane's base.

Again a car waited and the driver stowed our growing pile of luggage. We soon arrived at the hotel that looked like a row of terrace houses. Inside it was modern, light and beautiful. We strolled the city centre and I was surprised when Simon took us into an Indian restaurant at just six o'clock. We ate well, the flavours quite unfamiliar. I had eaten Indian several times and mother had cooked a curry from time to time, but this was really upmarket. Simon had seldom eaten Eastern food. Simon found t rather too spicy. It was another new, shared experience.

We took a taxi and arrived at a concert hall. I found that it was a rare Rolling Stones gig, the dinosaurs of rock.

Why Simon had planned this, I didn't know. The truth about our relationship was that music hardly featured as a subject we spoke of. I knew that he liked opera and classical and some modern French music which I dismissed, while I was into classical music and pop and rock. However, it was a coup I knew to get tickets and they must have cost a fortune.

We were really near the stage. Time, drugs and rock n roll had not been kind to these men. These were indeed razzled wrinklies, but the music with familiar riffs and chords was excellent and exciting, even Simon was moving and tapping his feet. I hugged him and kissed him. To my surprise, we did not rush out at the end, but were escorted back stage and met Mick. He was very charming and I understood finally, what had made him a ladies' man for about four decades. He had that cheeky glint in his eye and an appraising look that scanned one in a fraction of a second. We drank a glass of Krug, and departed for our hotel.

Next day we took a private jet to Southampton and from there, helicopter home. It had been a great week. Simon had managed to combine romance, business and excitement in one gorgeous week. I clung to his arm in the helicopter.

'Thank you, it was fabulous Simon.'

'Yes it was,' he said, 'the materials were very interesting.'

He looked into my face, noting my puzzled expression. He laughed. 'Ma chère chérie, you are so easy to tease. It has been a wonderful romantic week, just the two of us, the most time we have had together since San Francisco. Now we have to get back to work, and it is hospital for you again in a week's time. What are you going to do this week?'

'I am going to stay at the Chateau and play with Sheba, the girls and the children, Simon, while I have the opportunity.'

'I have to go to Paris and work. Wally and I have much to do with two new ranges, thanks to your ideas. We are interviewing young designers, to assist Jacques and Thomas and we also have to go to Clermont to look at capacity.'

'Then it is good that I will be occupied at the Chateau and you boys can get on with the business.'

Chapter 27.

Simon and Wally departed early in the morning. I occupied myself with riding early morning, with Sabine and Nicole or just Nicole if Sabine's duties as estate manager did not allow her. Then we would return to look after the children and make Sophie's life easier. Alex came with Helen, who had now improved enormously. They wanted a few more shots of life at the Chateau, and a spoken commentary by me talking about my life to Alex as interviewer, who would always be out of shot. The biopic would soon be complete at last, two months late, but they had waited for the wedding. I could not wait for it to be completed and get some of these people out of my life.

Simon had told me, before he took off for Paris that there would be further adverts and possibly songs to do. I replied that I would comply with his wishes this year, and maybe next, but thereafter they would have to find another face of Beauvonne.

The time with Alex and Helen, took up nearly two days, the weather being poor for filming on the first day and the crew just sat about drinking until filming was called off for the day. However, Alex and I wrote and recorded the voice over, not finishing until nearly nine in the evening. But it was done. They needed more shots of me with the children and in riding gear with Sheba and looking at the estate with Sabine. I insisted that they should show me also studying my medical books.

Sophie and Nicole also had parts. If I had known how long winded it all was, I would never have agreed, but of course, they said they were going to do it anyway. Somehow, I managed to put on a good-humoured front.

It was a relief when the crew and Alex disappeared down the drive.

On Friday after lunch, I was surprised to see two police cars emerge from the drive. I awaited their arrival, my heart beating ever faster, wondering. A man in plain clothes emerged from one and a uniformed officer from the other.

'Bonjour mademoiselle,' the uniform said. 'May we speak to Monsieur?'

'I am Madame Chartrand. My husband is not here at the moment.'

'Pardon Madame. Do you know where we can find Monsieur Chartrand?'

'When I last spoke to him, he was in Paris, attending to business. Have you enquired at Maison Beauvonne?'

'Oui madame. He was there yesterday, but said that he would not be in today, according to M. Gérard Chartrand.

'Perhaps he is in Clermont Ferrand at the factory? Have you tried there? Why do you want to see him?'

'We have a new statement regarding the death of his first wife. We need to put certain questions to him.'

'Perhaps you would like to introduce yourselves? Then we can have coffee and I will see if I can assist you.' I was ice on the outside, but a claw had grabbed my innards and I wanted to be sick.

The uniform with all the scrambled egg on his hat replied. He was gaunt, his cheeks slightly sunken, blue eyed.

'Pardon madame, I am Serge Larock, Colonel de Gendarmerie of Normandy'

'Madame, je suis desolé, I am Pierre Beaudoin, Commandante de Police Judiciaire.'

'Then you had better come in and tell me why you want to interview my husband.'

Nicole had appeared.

'Nicole, would you please make some coffee for us all, including you, and I would like you to bring your phone and record what is said. Nicole is my personal assistant gentlemen. Can you tell me where you are based?'

'I am based in Caen Madame,' the colonel said, 'and because your husband is a well known and important man, I have come personally, I am the senior officer of the gendarmerie for the Department of Lower Normandy.'

Nicole arrived with a tray of coffee and her phone.

'Is your phone recording Nicole?' I ask.

'Oui Trudi.'

'Merci Nicole. Please stay. And you Commandante?'

'I am from Caen also, the senior officer of the Police Nationale,' Beaudoin said. 'Obviously Madame, when someone makes a statement about a crime or an alleged crime, then we have to investigate. Your husband is an important man in France, Madame, so we are being much more circumspect and diplomatic than if we were dealing with someone less important.'

'May I know who has made a statement?'

'No Madame, I am afraid I cannot tell you that until we have made our investigation.'

'Thank you gentlemen. As you know, I am English and I do not understand how the law works in France. Can you tell me the nature of the statement you have received.'

'Oui Madame, because you too are involved. You made a statement saying that you spoke to Simon de Beauvonne the day that he crashed, and when he took the call, he was approximately 170 kilometres from Beauvonne, and that was also the time when Catherine de Beauvonne died. This statement alleges that your husband was in fact just a few kilometres from here.'

'C'est impossible.'

'I can ask you now Madame. Did you speak to Monsieur de Beauvonne that afternoon.'

'Oui messieurs. I dialled Simon's mobile and he answered. It was an extremely bad line and he also told me that he was waiting for a call from the USA, so I rang off very quickly. I do not like to interfere with his business. The next I knew, he was in hospital in Clermont Ferrand. That was nearly twenty-four hours later and I was still in Paris. I left that afternoon to go to look after him in hospital.'

'Thank you Madame. That is exactly as your statement reads.' Beaudoin said.

'Is that all, or is there more.'

'We need your husband to make a fresh statement. Do you know where he is?'

'No, we spoke on Tuesday and he was then in Paris working. He is very busy with new ranges and was with his sales director. I would think that they have been in Clermont at the factory. I expect him home tonight. I can call him on his mobile?'

'May we wait Madame?'

'Of course, but I have no idea how long you may have to wait. Could you not return tomorrow, or we can phone to find out where he is?'

They looked at each other. Beaudoin shrugged. 'It is now nearly six o'clock. Has he said he will be late for dinner?'

'No, but we do not generally eat until seven-thirty. Do you need to stay here all that time, or he can come to your office tomorrow perhaps?'

'The matter is serious madame. You understand that?'

'Mais oui, messieurs. It is very serious. I just think I should phone him and find out where he is and when he expects to arrive.'

Nicole passed me a note on her notepad. It read, 'Shall I try to ring him?'

'Of course you may go to the toilette Nicole.' I said.

She departed.

'May we wait for say half an hour madame?'

'Of course gentlemen.'

We sat for some minutes. They asked about the wedding and whether I was still studying to be un médicin. We made polite conversation.

'Gentlemen, I have things to do. If you are comfortable, then I will leave you for a few minutes. I will ask Nicole to make more coffee. If you need the toilette, it is in the vestibule, under the staircase.'

The Colonel stood and the Commandante followed his example. I left the room and found Nicole in the office.

'Did you find him?' I asked her.

'Oui Trudi. He and Wally are on the way from Clermont.'

'Does he know what this is about.'

'He thinks it is Gérard. He has had his fingers in the till again, stealing thousands of Euros. This time Simon brought the police in and they discovered false invoices. He thinks this is Gérard's revenge.'

'Merde! That stupid son of a bitch. I gave him that job and he was paid generously for what he did.'

'Simon said not to worry. Gérard will retract his statement. Annette has been to see him at the police station in Paris, but it is not good to have the police investigating again Trudi, is it.'

'No Nicole. I wish I could be as confident as Simon. Well done. Can you go and sit with those two? Take a book or a magazine to read. Just let them feel they are not being ignored. Say I am busy with the children. See if they want more refreshments. I wonder what that idiot Gérard has been doing? Thank you Nicole.'

I went to the estate office. I told Sabine what was going on.

'Oh Gérard. Cette imbecile. He likes the horses too much. I expect he has lost money again, just like last time. The bookies threatened to beat him up. I thought he had changed, that this job and Annette would have reformed him, but it seems he is addicted to gambling Trudi.'

'So where do you stand? I don't want you mixed up in this.'

'I didn't see anything. I know nothing. I was in the stables, and the first I knew of Catherine's death that day, was the ambulance arriving. That is all. Do not fear Trudi. I have not even said to Wally what I saw, and I won't. You are the only one I have said anything to. It is best, I know nothing.'

'Thank you Sabine. I am sorry you have this secret.'

I phoned Simon. Wally answered. 'Trudi we are an hour away. Simon says not to worry. Gérard will be taken care of. It is under control. Simon says that these two are on a fishing trip, hoping to catch us on the hop. Annette says that Gérard has already retracted. Ultimately the only person who can save him from prison or a beating is Simon.'

I put the phone down. There was nothing I could say or do. I went to the salon.

'Gentlemen, I have heard from my husband he is still an hour away. May we offer you some refreshments? We have some bread and cheeses and cold meats, ham, tongue, there may be some cold beef.'

'You are very kind madame. I think we would appreciate a little of whatever you have.'

Nicole rose from her chair. 'I will see what we have for these two,' she said, rudely.

As the door closed behind her, I said, 'I hope she has not been rude to you. She has been working very hard and tonight has cancelled an appointment to stay with me.' Nicole and I were bad cop and good cop in reverse.

The food was brought in and plonked down on the coffee table.

'There, enjoy messieurs. Trudi do you want me now or may I go to see my sister?'

'You may go to your sister Nicole. Thank you for your help.'

I waited while the men munched. I switched on the television and found BBC News. There had been three more soldiers killed in Afghanistan. I knew Harry was still in England, but I still shuddered. The Colonel shook his head. 'It is bad. That place will always be ungovernable. They are savages.'

'My brother has been there twice, and he may have to go again.'

'Then I hope he may keep safe, Madame.'

I was relieved when I heard the car arrive. I greeted Simon at the door. He was exceedingly cool, as though these two police were old friends. We kissed and he whispered reassurances and opened the door into the salon, allowing me to enter first.

'Gentlemen, my husband.'

They both stood, The Colonels heels almost clicked. Beaudoin proffered a hand. I introduced them.

'Now gentlemen, what is all this nonsense? Is it that fool Gérard, my cousin? I sacked him because he stole money from the company, but I have forgiven him. He has retracted his statement according to his wife, who pleaded on his behalf. Apparently he got drunk after I dismissed him, and as an act of revenge made up a silly story. I would have thought your office would know by now.'

'We have to check if allegations are made, and as the person who made the statement is in Paris, the news of any change would take time to reach us. However, in the circumstances, we would like you to make a new statement.'

'My statement, messieurs, will not have changed. You will note that I was trapped in my car that afternoon. I had my leg amputated to remove me from the wreck, and then I was in a coma for five days until this lady, my wife, managed to bring me out of it. I still remember nothing more of that day or for that matter, the days immediately before. If that is what you would like, then messieurs of course. Nicole, would you please type on your laptop as I dictate.'

Beaudoin spoke. 'Monsieur Chartrand. Please, we have a statement form here in my briefcase. I will write as you dictate, then you will check and sign. That is all. We are all reasonable people.'

'It is just annoying that a drunken, thief makes a statement in an act of revenge, and then I have my home invaded and my wife frightened. I am sorry if I have been rude. Of course I will make a new statement but it will not have substantially changed. I have had quite a week gentlemen. Business is good, the rich are still spending. We have new lines we are designing and I find that my cousin who is also office manager has gambling debts and has been robbing me blind to save his skin.

'We have looked after you? You have eaten?'

'Oui Monsieur Chartrand, merci. Madame [Trudi] has been truly hospitable.'

'Bon.'

Simon dictated the statement and we both read it through. He signed and Larock and Beaudoin departed.

'Simon, we need to talk. Let us go to the study. Please excuse us Nicole, we have to discuss Gérard.'

In the study, I sat Simon down. He looked drawn and older. 'Now tell me what happened this week?'

'On Tuesday, I had a shock when I saw a bank statement. There was almost €200,000 missing. I went to the bank and the manager produced transfers into a business account that I did not recognise. It was found to be a fictitious business and the statements were posted to Gérard. When I accused him, he admitted that he was drinking and gambling again. I was so annoyed, disgusted, that I sacked him. I threw him out. He went to a bar, got drunk and then went to the police and made a statement. Annette was called and she had the sense to call me and tell me what was in the statement, then she returned him to the police station and he has retracted his statement. They are prosecuting him for wasting police time, but he will just get a fine, as his defence will be that he gave the statement while drunk and embittered. Luckily, he did not say what actually happened, only that he believed I was here in the Chateau when Catherine fell. As usual, he did not want to implicate himself.'

'You were very cool. I have been so worried, the whole place has been upset. Nicole and Sabine have been wonderful, but I felt sick.' I began to sob.

'I am sorry my darling girl. You made that imbecile office manager, and it was a good plan, but Gérard is weak and I am afraid always will be.'

'I cannot think of life without you Simon. If you were to go to prison....I don't know how I would live. So what do we do with him now?'

'I am sending him to Abu Dhabi, to set up a store there. He will have no access to money, bar an entertainment allowance. I will have a Manager there I can trust who will do all the business. I have tried my best with him......................It is most disappointing.'

'And it is disappointing for me, because I put him in that position. I shall never speak to him again. I am sorry I am not stronger Simon, but life without you would be just to frightening. What about Annette? Is she staying here?'

'She has yet to make up her mind. She is a nice person, but needs a rocket behind her. Yet I do not want to alienate her too, because they know too much. She behaved well when she found out what that idiot had done, but she is lazy and not good at her job.'

'I have a suggestion, Simon. We have someone shadow her, someone trustworthy and dynamic, a junior who will be the power behind her and push her.'

'And you have someone in mind, Madame Machiavelli?'

'Oui Simon. You take some of the weight off me. I do not want to do more adverts, but will perhaps do a song if needed. Nicole will have spare time. She has stuck to me like glue, uncomplaining, does my bidding, quickly and efficiently. She has been brilliant over the last three hours. Let us give her more responsibility, another two thousand a year and a car. She is still my PA, but when not needed, will assist Annette. Consider Simon. We do not upset Annette, in fact she will be able to visit Gérard in Abu Dhabi and leave Nicole in charge. If Annette decides to leave, we have cover and we keep Nicole busy and interested.'

'It is a good plan Trudi. I like it. We keep everyone happy. The only thing is long term, how do we ensure that Gérard keeps his mouth shut.'

'That is the remaining problem. But in the meantime, my plan keeps them both happy. Perhaps Gérard will gamble in Abu Dhabi. I do not think those people will be very accommodating.'

'Let us find Nicole.'

We found her in the salon. 'Nicole, we have been thinking about a reorganisation. No do not worry, I think it is good news.'

We settled in chairs and Simon addressed her.

'Nicole, you have been with us for nearly eight months. Trudi has been very pleased with you, very pleased. As you know, it has been a busy time for her, with filming and singing and her studies and of course family life. She would not have managed all that without you.

However. Trudi does not want to do the adverts, so that will take a lot of weight off her and she wants to continue her studies. So there will be much less for you to do, now the wedding is over.

'We need someone to shadow Annette on PR. You have seen so much of the organisation of the adverts and the biopic, that you know what goes on. We would like you to work with Annette, learn all you can from her, but also use your initiative. If you think she is missing opportunities, then speak to either me or Trudi, and we will give you the authority to follow your instinct. Your living arrangements will still be the same, here or Paris. You keep the scooter, but we will also find you a small Mercedes, and we will give you another two thousand. What do you say?'

'May I think about it?'

'But of course. What is your doubt?'

'I am just surprised. I have loved working for Trudi. It has been an extraordinary opportunity, and I have learned so much. But, PR, I know so little.'

'We do not expect you to make decisions right away. I will be honest with you. We now have five ranges. Haute couture, women's ready made outerwear, men's readymade outerwear, lingerie and perfume. Men's underwear is also coming, but we also plan to do shoes and bags. Annette needs help, she is very good, very knowledgeable, but not always dynamic. I want you to be the dynamo, the young innovator. She will teach you much, but your ideas and innovations, above all, your energy, can improve her performance. We do not expect immediate miracles, but Trudi believes you have the ability and I agree.'

'I have thought. It is a great opportunity. This time working for Trudi has been very happy. I accept. Merci. I will do my best not to let you down.'

'Then we are very pleased.' Simon kissed her on both cheeks and I followed.

'We will still have close contact Nicole so do not fear on that account.'

'We will tell Annette over the weekend. And you start with her on Monday, but do not forget, when Trudi needs you, then you have to find time for her.'

'Of course, merci Trudi, I owe you so much.'

'Good. Now let us have dinner and champagne.'

Chapter 28.

After the weekend, I left early Monday morning to arrive in Paris at Pitié before eight. This year, I was permitted to use the staff car park, so I had driven straight there. Normally staying at the villa, I would continue to use the Metro.

Thankfully I had left psychiatrics behind. For the next six months I was in Urgences, Emergency, everything from a cut finger to a road crash or heart attack, the primary care centre where diagnoses were made with instant treatment before moving to a specialist ward. I was going to be very busy and I was pleased to have rid myself of the advert filming.

My status as a celebrity working among ordinary people, good people but only known for their career, was not always easy. Some resented my outside status, and judged me as an airhead, a woman of superficial ambition, taking the place of someone whose only dedication was their medical career. I therefore had to ensure that I worked harder and better, remaining humble and ordinary in the hospital setting, no matter what was happening in my other life.

The professor this time, was Armand Deraveau. He was enormous, seeming to fill most of his small office. He motioned me to sit.

'I have been looking at your record Madame. I am surprised to find you still here, given that you appear nearly every week in some magazine, strutting about on the catwalk. I do not like my staff to wear a lot of makeup, so perhaps you can bear that in mind?'

'Oui Maître.'

'And you must observe the duty roster. We are the spearhead of care. Those who come to us, need immediate treatment. Just because you are needed on the catwalk, does not mean we can let a patient die on a trolley. Do you understand.'

'Oui Maître. I think you will see from my record that I am industrious and responsible. I look forward to learning from you in this difficult department.'

'Flattery has no effect on me Madame. You will follow me today, so that I can see how you work. If I don't like what I see, then you will be restricted in your duties and you will have to stay with me longer.'

'Bien sûr, Maitre.'

By nine o'clock, we were busy. By ten we were full, even some patients sitting on the floor. We had to triage, decide which cases needed urgent attention. I followed Deraveau bustling from one patient to another, a quick inspection and diagnosis, then prioritised for treatment according to injury. It was fascinating to see how quickly he worked and diagnosed. It was not all about the state of the injury but the state of mental strength of a patient as well. Therefore children tended to go to the front of the queue, a pregnant woman also, and the elderly, especially if they had blood pressure or heart problems. After three hours, he made me make the decisions and he watched. Twice he intervened, promoting patients up the list. I felt squashed. He was gruff, changing my judgement without telling me why. As the day wore on, I made only one other mistake, but I felt it badly and recognised that I should have realised by a man's raised heartbeat, that although in his thirties, he was having a hard time with what appeared to be simple injuries from a bicycle accident. By five the place had started to empty and the new shift were coming on.

Deraveau took me to his cubbyhole office.

'So Madame Chartrand, how did you think you did?'

'Not very well Maitre. I should have seen that cyclist was in shock, and there might be complications.'

'Yes, you should, but only if you have been working here a couple of months. Actually, you did quite well, and the patients liked you. You have a good manner with them, but then who can resist a pretty girl. I would like you to shadow me for the next week, then we will set you free to attend some simple cases. You may go. Rest, for tomorrow you will have a twelve hour shift. Every other day, twelve hours. Next week the same but on nights, so no time for playing about in clubs with fashionistas.'

His disdain was galling, but I thought I saw the flicker of a smile from this cynical ageing consultant. Perhaps he was more satisfied with me than I thought.

'Merci, bon soir Maître.'

I was glad to turn into the villa. I climbed the stairs wearily. I was surprised to find Gérard there with Simon and Annette.

'I am going to shower before dinner.'

'We are eating out Trudi.'

'Where, only I am very tired? Tomorrow I have a twelve hour shift.'

'A quick shower, and I promise to have Cinderella home three hours before midnight.' Simon said.

'OK.'

We went to Willi's. One would have thought from Gérard's behaviour that he had done nothing wrong. I was offended by his nonchalance. By the time the sweet menus were produced, he was everyone's best friend, making jokes and saying that he would do big things in Abu Dhabi.

'Do you know Gérard how much you offend me? You turn on the family that feeds you and keeps bailing you out. When I employed you, I trusted you, and yet you first stole from us and then made trouble. I had two police sitting in the Chateau for three hours. I was there, wondering whether Simon, your cousin and benefactor would be carted off to jail. It was like sitting by the guillotine, waiting for my husband's head to roll into the basket. I am so disappointed, and angry with you.'

'I know you must be Trudi. I am disappointed with myself. I am sorry.'

I drew breath, to start another rant, but Simon silenced me.

'Of course Trudi you are right, Gérard behaved very badly, but that is my cousin. I am giving him another chance, and I am sure he will make a success of Abu Dhabi. It will all work out Trudi. Now ma chère épouse, I think I will take you home. We leave Annette and Gérard here. Bon nuit.'

We all kissed, Gerard and I perfunctorily. 'I am really sorry.' He whispered. I made no reply. I was too angry.

'I could kill him,' I said, when we were in the taxi.

'No you could not. We will see what happens in Abu Dhabi. He will of course act the playboy there and do no work, but I do not expect him to. He will be happy and out of the way. So your day was hard? Were you busy?'

'We never stopped, thirty minutes for lunch, that is all, but the mental strain, making diagnosis in front of Maitre Deraveau, is frightening. He does not like me, thinks I am just playing at being a doctor. I just want my bed Simon. I need to sleep.'

I wiped off the makeup and climbed into bed. I was still angry and I thought about Gérard and what I would like to have said. I do not remember going to sleep. I was awoken by the alarm at quarter to seven. I was back in the hospital, bright and shiny by eight and ready for whatever the day brought.

The first four weeks were the unhappiest of my working life. Unsure of Deraveau, and desperately trying to make accurate and quick decisions, as well as my first night shifts was a terrific strain. Six weeks in, I had got to grips with it. Deraveau was positively jolly with me, pushing me to make more and more difficult decisions and nodding in agreement when I made them. His overruling became a rarity, and when he did, he now explained why. My opinion of him as a misogynistic, perhaps transphobic, Neanderthal had changed to one of admiration and liking. I seemed to get all the children to attend to, stitches in cuts, broken limbs, swallowed beads and sometime something much worse, household cleaners imbibed or splashed into eyes. I kept a supply of sweets to calm them, and a few toys for the really afflicted to keep. Some mothers recognised me and even asked for my autograph. Deraveau seemed not to mind that either.

After two months, I was really enjoying it. Although tiring, this was real medicine, dealing with the day-to-day mishaps and illnesses of the human race.

Gérard had gone to Abu Dhabi. I was relieved to have him out of the way. Simon told me that he was apparently living it up, using his entertainment allowance to the full, trying to impress people with far more money than he had.

Annette had visited him twice. She reported that she was worried about his drinking. He was not supposed to drink in a Muslim country, but the law had been relaxed because so many Westerners now went there. He seemed to be travelling into alcoholism.

The police had left Simon alone. He seemed completely unworried by Catherine's death being dredged up again. I was shaken by it. My working life occupied me so completely that I did not have time to think about what could happen, but sometimes, if I woke in the night, the fear I had felt when Beaudoin had turned up at the Chateau, preyed on my mind. In my heart I thought Catherine's death had been a tragic accident, but my brain told me that it could at least have been manslaughter and may have been worse.

I had realised that Simon was a complex character. Generous, good-natured, sympathique, yet a ruthless businessman, driving a hard bargain. The pressure Catherine had subjected him to would have been enough for him to snap. The plan, as had been explained to me, of a fake robbery did not hold up. Why would any thief have taken letters between Simon and I and personal photographs? Catherine would never have swallowed that. Yes she deserved her fate, for she had not only broken her agreement, but unforgivably, flaunted her lesbian lover, and threatened to remove the children permanently. Still, I would rather she still lived.

Simon had accompanied Wally on a World tour of over two weeks. I had made him promise to take it easy and eat properly. They had flown West, first to New York then Los Angeles and Hollywood, across the Pacific to Tokyo, Shanghai, Singapore, Abu Dhabi and home. It was the launch of lingerie and men's fashion around the World. His return coincided with my having five days off after a seven-day night shift. We were together at the Chateau with the children and horses. Simon was riding again, something he had not done since he lost his lower leg.

Sabine and Wally were still together. I was surprised when they announced they had found a house three miles away but it needed a full renovation first. I was pleased they would remain near.

When I came down to breakfast on the third day, I found Simon with his head in his hands. I asked what was wrong.

'It is Gérard. He is dead.'

'How?'

'He was shark fishing and had not fastened his harness. It seems he hooked a large shark and was pulled over the side before he knew what was happening. The boat crew could not find him, but there was a feeding frenzy. They had used blood and offal to attract the sharks. It is terrible. I feel so responsible.'

'Have you spoken to Annette? Does she know?'

'Not yet. I have just had the call from Hassan. I think we should both go to Paris to tell her personally. Will you come?

'Of course. We should go immediately.'

We found Annette in her apartment. She knew something had happened as soon as she opened the door.

'Come in,' she said, 'what has he done now?'

'May we all sit down Annette?'

'Of course. This is serious then?' I sat next to her.

'Annette, I have to tell you that, Annette, my cousin your husband....there was an accident. I have to tell you that it was....... fatal.'

'He's dead?'

'We are so sorry,' I took her hand. 'He fell into the water while shark fishing. He had not fastened his harness.'

'That is typical,' she said, her voice low, 'always the play boy, careless, full of bravado, a real Earnest Hemingway character, looking for that extra thrill.'

'We are so sorry Annette. If I had not sent him out there, then he would still be alive.'

'And in prison, or lying beaten in the gutter by the betting syndicate thugs. Do not feel guilty. He could not help himself. He just liked risk. Even stealing from the business, I think, gave him a thrill.'

I cuddled her. A single tear escaped her eye. 'To tell the truth,' she said, 'his charm had worn thin. It was one scrape after another. There were missing hours when he was gambling, playing cards with a number of sharks. That's funny, the sharks got him in the end, didn't they?' She laughed bitterly. There was no humour in it, just disappointment.

'Come Annette, pack a few things and come to the Chateau with us.'

'No I'm OK. I'm seeing friends later. We are going to the races,' she laughed again, 'it would have been the perfect day for him, placing bets on unlikely winners, being the life and soul of the party.'

'Then phone and cancel. Come with us, please Annette. You are family.'

'I don't know. I don't know what I want to do.'

'Come, you can ride one of the horses, we will make a lunch party. You can help look after the children. We will keep you busy.'

'Oh, the children. Yes, that would be nice. I have some news. I heard two days ago that I am pregnant. I am due in May.'

'That is such good news for you Annette. I know you have been trying for so long.'

'At least she will not have a waster for a father now. She won't have a father. Perhaps that is a blessing.'

'Gérard had a weakness, but he was a good man, and I am sure he loved you.'

'You say that and he betrayed your trust? No, sometimes you just have to face facts and weigh people's character. He was not a good man. He was a foolish one and ultimately his foolhardy weakness has killed him. I'll pack.'

Three hours later we were back at the Chateau. Annette went to her bed for the afternoon while Simon, Nicole and I rode. I told Nicole what had happened.

'How are things going Nicole,' Simon asked, 'only after what has happened and with Annette pregnant too, it is important that her job and the work does not suffer. How ready are you to take over if necessary, or should I advertise for a new PR guru.'

'I am ready to take on her work. I know all her contacts and understand how she works. I would not do things in the same way, she is very relaxed, but I also know not to push too hard. You can only give me a trial. I know I will not let you down. I have several ideas I would like to work out and put to you.'

'Then you have two months and we will review the situation again Nicole, is that fair?'

'Of course, Simon. I will surprise you.'

We rode over to the house that Sabine and Wally were buying. It was a great villa, double fronted with a porticoed doorway and green slate roof. It had extensive outbuildings and an orchard.

'Perhaps I should look for another estate manager,' Simon said, 'it looks as though they are looking to have a large family.'

We rode home. Tonight we were eating early, at seven. The chef was providing a feast, lobster salad, apricot stuffed brie, brandied roast goose, dark chocolate sorbet, apple clafouti.

We found Annette up and helping Sophie with the children who were playing in the salon. She had revived.

Silent on the journey from Paris, she was on the floor with the twins and Sébastien building with Lego and trying to make peace as they argued over how the building developed.

Wally and Sabine were coming, as well as Laurent. We weren't dressing.

I took Nicole on one side and we walked around the formal garden. 'Are you confident about filling Annette's shoes?' I asked her.

'Oh yes Trudi. She is not so good you know. I can do so much more.'

'Good, I am glad you are confident. I do not know whether she will come back to work after the funeral, she may in which case you will still have to play second fiddle. But make sure you learn all you can from her and make sure that you have the details of all her contacts. She did a good job getting celebrities to the shows, but did not seem to get behind the promotional programme. Am I right?'

'Yes Trudi, She seems frightened of these advertising people. I am writing up some new storyboards for men's fashion, perfume and accessories as well as new ones for haute couture and readymade, so you see I am on the ball. Thomas is helping me. He is very good at his job and because he is still quite young, we are on the same page.'

'How old is he?'

'Twenty-eight.'

'Good, I am glad you have everything under control. I have great faith in you Nicole. It was a good day when Sophie suggested you. Is she happy with us?'

'Oh I think so. She is not ambitious like me, nor academic. She loves the children and now she has Laurent, she is happy.'

'And what about you. Do you wish you had a boyfriend? Do I have to get my magic wand out for you?'

'Non merci.' She blushed. 'I am sort of seeing Thomas, only going to lunch and the cinema so far, but I like him. He is good company.'

'But English. Be careful, you never know what an Englishman is thinking.'

'Oh I think I know him. He is very funny when not in the Maison.'

'You will not have much time to look after me Nicole. I will just have to manage on my own.'

'I can still do your diary, which seems a lot less hectic. Oh I meant to say. Alex phoned. The biopic is being shown in three week's time. I have the details. And while I think about it, we need to tell the press about Gérard. I presume we will continue the curse of Beauvonne theme?'

'Yes I think so. We can't expect Annette to do that. Good thought. Can we get something sent to the media this afternoon? Show it to Annette before sending it and say that I asked you to do it. Also ask her if she would like you to notify anyone. The sooner everyone knows, the sooner she can get back to normal.'

'Of course Trudi. I will get down to it now. Thank you for everything.'

'You are going places with us Nicole. We will look after you.'

It was mid November. The light was going and the cold crept over the land. It was good to get inside in the warm. I helped Sophie and Annette with the children. I was still cold when I finally left the nursery and I sank into a deep warm bath.

My mind was worried. I did not like to think too deeply, but Gérard's death was troubling. Perhaps there was indeed a Curse of Beauvonne. Would I be next or one of the children? I did not want to contemplate that. Or Simon? He had already used up two lives. Or does it extend to Wally, Sabine, or Sophie or Nicole?

I thought back to my last words to Gérard, how I had berated him, his betrayal of us, of the family and especially Simon, his benefactor. How humble he had been in the face of my righteous wrath. Yet Annette said that he was up to his old tricks in Abu Dhabi, the daredevil playboy, drinking and bragging.

A dreadful thought entered my head, that Simon had sent Gérard there, knowing his temperament would get him into trouble, even death. Was Simon, so generous in our relationship and with Wally, Sabine, Nicole and Sophie, so Machiavellian, so ruthless behind the gentle charm, that he had sent Gérard to his death?

I let more hot water run into the cooling bath, and scrubbed my skin until I was pink all over. I pulled the plug and stood, just as the door opened and Simon entered.

'I was wondering whether you had drowned, you have been so long.'

'I was chilled after talking to Nicole. You know Simon, at least three of my appointments are working out. Wally is great, n'est pas? And Sabine, delivering and very industrious. But Nicole, she pleases me so much. She is so efficient, hard working, uncomplaining and enjoys the challenges we give her.'

'Yes ma chère épouse, I still believe you have good judgement. And I still have great faith in you too. I was surprised that Annette showed so little emotion. It seems that she had tired of Gérard and his behaviour. Well, when you find someone as exciting as Gérard could be, one often finds that they are difficult to be with. They need constant admiration and stimulus, and that is very tiresome after a while.'

I wrapped my towel around me and sat on the stool to do my toilette, moisturising and then doing my face and hair as Simon sat watching.

'Simon, have you nothing better to do than watch?'

'I never tire of watching you. You are so fascinating, so open, yet so mysterious.'

'I do not think I am mysterious. You see, and that is what you get.'

'But I want to get inside your head and share all your thoughts.'

'All my self-doubts and insecurities you mean? I do not talk of them anymore because you do not want to hear them. Otherwise, I just do my job, here or the hospital or wherever. You know Simon, we need to plan Christmas, it is six weeks away. I would like to have a good party on Christmas eve, all our friends. Nicole, Sophie of course, Wally and Sabine, Annette, Laurent, and Sabine and Laurent's parents, and Thomas Martin and Jaques Paquet. We can let Nicole invite Thomas. I will write and ask Harry and Alison to come too. Oh and Jean Luc and Élise of course, though they may be busy elsewhere. Shall I go ahead?'

'Of course, you are la Comtesse. And skiing after as usual?'

'I hope, though as yet Deraveau has not made the Christmas rota list. If we go, then Wally and Sabine, Nicole, maybe Thomas, Laurent.'

'What is this with Thomas?'

'I think Nicole is rather smitten.'

'Ah, you are matchmaking again?'

'No, just helping. They have been out together.'

I left him to bathe and I dressed. I went down to the salon in time to greet Wally, Sabine and Laurent. Sophie and the children were there. Nicole entered in a pretty dress I had not seen before. She looked very beautiful and innocent. Annette entered in a red gown. Her face was bright.

'Are you having champagne Trudi, only I am leaving off alcohol, for the baby, you understand?' she asked.

'Of course Annette, whatever you wish. Orange juice, or lemonade and lime?' She chose a tomato juice with Worcester sauce.

When everyone had assembled, Sophie and I took the children up to bed. We spent twenty minutes telling stories and singing to them, then they snuggled their sleepy heads down onto their pillows and we left.

The gathering was very gay considering the bad news we had had. The food was wonderful too. All in all, the day had not been as dismal as I had feared. Annette was positively gay, smiling and telling jokes. I could not fathom her attitude at all. Only my thoughts troubled me. It was so convenient that Gérard had died far from French soil and law enforcement, so convenient too that there was no body to examine. It was a perfect way of ridding ourselves of this troublesome relative. Was it just too perfect to be true? The good advice on taking up an offer is always, if it looks too good to be true, then it is. Yet the only person who had reason to design such an end, was my husband. Surely it could not be?

Chapter 29.

Monday and I was back at work. I now loved Urgences. One never knew what would appear next, so the work was very varied and never boring. Another factor I liked was that it was very person to person. I needed to know something of these patients' lives as I treated them. Of course, it was usually a once only meeting, but it was very intimate in our little cubicles, and I was often treated to a window into their lives. I found it fascinating, not always pleasant, tales of brutality and of neglect or worse.

It was heart rending at times yes, but oh so rewarding, seeing instant relief for many of the afflicted. It was not only the minor injuries I was involved with either. Sometimes, when we had a critical case, everyone was involved. If I had not the skill to do complicated procedures, I could at least insert a finger into a wound to stem the blood. The gore and mess no longer affected me, and I had managed to adopt a remote attitude to the patients misfortunes, so that I did not carry grief home with me.

It was exhausting, the twelve hour shift system worked but one needed to pace oneself. Nights were mainly easy, except for weekends, when we would have a crop of knifings some drunks and household accidents. It could be quite terrifying, and we had two gendarmes on duty all the time. Worst were the domestic abuse cases, tearful, hopeless victims. Once or twice the abuser had followed to the hospital and they were unpredictable. If it was an African patient, it was not unknown for a dozen relatives to turn up, crowding into the waiting area, trying to see into cubicles or an emergency room. Somehow Deraveau and his staff made order out of chaos.

Autumn turned to winter. Deraveau demanded that I work Christmas day and the day after, in return for Christmas Eve and a week off after the official holiday. It was a bargain I took. We would celebrate Christmas on the twenty-fourth, then I would depart for Pitié Salpêtrière early on the twenty-fifth, returning on evening of twenty-sixth.

Simon and I found time to Christmas shop. We now had a long list to give to. We tried to give the children presents they could use and which provided some sort of learning. Adèle wanted a particular doll with its six changes of dress, from jodhpurs to ball gown. André wanted an iPad, having been shown Nicole's. We decided they would both have iPads. Sophie was teaching them to count and to read, so they were well advanced. We bought three Welsh ponies for them, all chestnut. They were very pretty, about eleven hands.

The girls would all have jewellery. The men, Wally, Laurent, Thomas, Jacques and Jean Luc we just gave money to buy whatever gadget they hankered for.

Simon and I were the problem. We considered we already had everything, certainly all we needed. I went back to the shop where I had bought Simon's de Gaulle cuff links to see whatever else I could find. The shopkeeper showed me several items, but nothing took my eye.

By luck I picked up a horse whip which had come from, he told me, the estate of Jean de Lattre de Tassigny, a famous hero of World War 2. The handle was ivory, mounted in gold, obviously a ceremonial item of a famous cavalry officer. It had de Lattre's crest embossed in the gold. It cost a mint but I was very pleased with it.

The days in Emergency went quickly, five on and three off. Occasionally I would not get home, if there was a bad road accident or disaster, like when there was the gas explosion in a dilapidated block near Porte de la Chapelle. It was horrific. Deraveau was marvellous. I was now his pet and commanded to follow him everywhere. I was learning so much, at last feeling like a real doctor although I was only doing a lot of the menial work, an injection, providing medicine with instructions, a bandage here and washing out an eye or extracting a pea from an ear.

On the twenty-third, I left work at seven and was at the Chateau before ten. I went straight to bed.

Christmas Eve, Nicole and I brought in the tree Sabine had left for us and dressed it. We decorated the vestibule, salon and salle â manger with holly that had abundant beautiful berries, and with mistletoe which grew on the poplars. We used no tinsel, but had lovely glass baubles for the tree. We set the table. Simon busied himself with the menu and wine. We gathered all the presents and put them under the tree.

I asked Nicole what she was wearing and she showed me a gown that Thomas Martin had made for her. It was beautiful, a deep cerise, cut low on her beautiful straight back, with a V neck and embroidered with sequins and pearls. She would look terrific. She had really blossomed, gradually filling Annette's shoes as the pregnancy progressed. Nicole had attended to the launch of perfume and menswear, and according to Simon, had done a marvellous job. He had given her a further rise.

So that Sophie did not feel the poor relation, she had a small Mercedes, and my poor little mini that I had hardly driven, resided in an empty store, chocked up and in mothballs. I could not bear to part with it.

Wally looked in with Sabine, hand in hand and looking very much a couple. Wally had grown much more sophisticated, but I could still see the charm he had possessed as head boy. My heart always gave a little jump when I saw him.

Those in the house, Sophie, Nicole, Wally and Sabine, Simon and I, Annette and the children ate lunch, a warming prawn curry that I had made and frozen a week before. We had dishes of nuts and different fruits to throw into it to cool the spices. The children always ate what we ate, something the French normally do and I insisted upon.

I rode out with Nicole, Sabine and Simon for two hours after lunch. Sabine and Wally went to her parents to prepare for the evening with us. We all played with the children, keeping them amused.

We took them to the stable to see their ponies, to choose and pick names. Sébastien called his Jo-Jo, which for a two year old was not bad, André called his mare Hercules, insisting on it. Adele said she would think about it. Thomas and Jacques arrived in time for dinner.

Finally it was time to bathe the children, putting them straight into their pyjamas. We bathed and got ready. Simon produced my dress, a retro number, long, sleek art nouveau, like the spirit of ecstasy in deep lavender. It was pure silk and felt wonderful. I could wear no underwear, Simon said, because it would have created lines.

We descended early, so we could welcome everyone. I remembered my first Christmas here, when Simon had been sent to fetch me, and how shy I had felt. Now I was amongst people who were friends, even Sabine and Laurent's parents were friendly, their feud made up with Simon now that Sabine worked for him, and I think Didier gave me credit for that. Soon everyone was assembled, and the children gambolled in their pyjamas amongst the guests, with Tasha also putting in an appearance. Mitzi sat at the top of the stairs, well out of the way.

We drank champagne as usual. Sophie and I took the children up after they had received their presents, and told them to go to sleep before Father Christmas arrived or they would receive no more presents.

We returned in time for the present giving. As usual, Simon and I waited till last. He gave me an SLS AMG Roadster. It was second hand, even so it cost an enormous amount of money. However, he was very pleased with my riding crop gift with its history. The dinner was very merry, now everyone knew each other and the food, crab salad followed by turkey was terrific. This year I had imported Christmas puddings from Fortnums, two enormous ones and it was brought in flaming. It was accompanied by mince pies, brandy butter, crème anglais, clotted cream and an ice cream bomb. It was a terrific success.

I had to be up early to drive to Paris, so I was off to bed before midnight, leaving everyone else still enjoying themselves.

I drove my new car to Paris. It was extraordinary, but so low that I could not see anything over the hedges. The day went well, not too many patients, but a little boy with a bad burn down his leg from a kettle was distressing. He was admitted so his wound could be given the best treatment.

The next day was also quiet. I kissed Deraveau goodbye. It was a relief when I could take off my white coat and get in the car for the Chateau. There was no traffic, but the night was very cold, so I drove carefully. It was a relief to reach the Chateau, spend a few moments with everyone and go to bed. Tomorrow we were trekking off to Courchevel at dawn.

There was a hectic rush in the morning getting the children up and dressed, everyone rushing about packing last minute items, up stairs, down the stairs and up again as something else was remembered. Luckily we had Nicole to help. Sabine, Wally, Sophie and Laurent were going in one car, Simon and I and the children in Simon's big Mercedes; Annette, Nicole and Thomas in Nicole's new car. We arranged to meet at Thiers as usual, so did not travel in convoy. Simon said that was too dangerous, in any case, we were in touch by mobile.

We all arrived within ten minutes of each other, in the old town of Thiers high up in Puy de Dôme. At nearly 1,000 feet, the air was crisp and cold, and we were pleased to reach the snug warmth of the restaurant. It was a very merry lunch party. The children were spaced out between us, and those not driving, indulged in the local wines. I was driving the next stretch so did not eat heartily as I found a heavy lunch made me sluggish.

The roads were empty, and we made good time, arriving at Courchevel 1850 in the dusk. Robert and his wife welcomed us once more, and there followed lots of hugs and kisses, chatter and laughter before we were all in the bubble lifts to Jardin Alpin.

The chalet had grown again, having had the basement garages converted to a small pool and sauna. We all went to our rooms to unpack and prepare for dinner. When we met up in the salon, we watched the forecast on television. The morning was promised to be sunny with clouds gathering in the afternoon. We ate steaks and went to bed early.

I awoke to hear a shutter banging. I went to the window to see whether I could fix it back. The window was completely covered with snow and when I went to another window, I saw snow lancing down, almost horizontally. There would be no skiing for us today.

I went back to bed and cuddled into Simon. We had not made love for two weeks. I remembered our bedroom exploits of previous years and wondered whether his lust for me was wearing off. I need not have worried. He stirred at length from a deep slumber, and gradually came alive. I took him in my mouth and he groaned with pleasure. He entered me gently, then his passion grew and grew and he pumped away until we were satisfied.

After breakfast the party resigned themselves to remaining in the chalet. We played board games and cards and entertained the children. In the afternoon we coated up to go to town, but found the snow deep and the bubble not working, due to the high wind. We took our coats off again. Robert phoned to say he could not get in to cook, so we would have to fend for ourselves. Sophie and Nicole suggested cooking a dish from Alsace, baeckeoffe, which they said needed fifteen hours cooking, but they thought they could speed it up. It was they said a delicious stew of mixed meats. We left them to it. Simon and I chose to make the starter and Annette and Sabine with Wally's help would do the sweet. We all set to.

It hardly stopped snowing until nightfall. With the children bathed and tucked up, we could feed ourselves. Our salmon mouse starter went down well. The baeckeoffe was delicious, very tender, cooked for eight hours and the sweet, apple and calvados tartlets finished off a good meal.

We had a backgammon tournament, a new game for me, and I lost easily to Wally. Nicole popped the DVD of my biopic into the player. People stopped playing to watch. Even though everyone there was a friend and knew my history, it was embarrassing. I crunched down into a corner of the big settee, trying to hide. They were all so kind and complimentary but I hated it. Sometimes I appeared so haughty and cocksure that I felt quite ashamed, yet sometimes I appeared diffident and taciturn. It was a relief to go to bed.

Again we awoke to snow, but the wind had dropped so it was possible for the bubble to run. Robert made it in, having waded through two feet of snow from the lift head. It was a good thing we had left the kitchen tidy as he was not in a good mood.

By the afternoon the weather had more or less cleared. There was sun and shifting cloud. We ventured out with the children and made snow men, but the snow was too deep for them to run about in it. Jean Luc and Élise appeared out of the gloom and Jean Luc set about making an igloo for them. He organised us all and we soon had a fine little snow house. The children loved it. As darkness fell we retreated indoors for a tea of fresh bread, honey, jam, marmite and a lemon drizzle cake.

We had a great bath time with three tired happy children.

We managed three days of skiing, and it was back to work. Sabine and Wally heading to Beauvonne with Laurent, and the rest of us off to Paris. The following day I was back in a white coat repairing damaged people.

Chapter 30.

I had been back at work five days. It was a busy morning, the sixth of January. I was surprised to find Nicole in the waiting room. I smiled then frowned. 'What are you doing here?' I asked.

'Trudi, I must speak to you, it is very important.'

'I'm working. I can't get off until after one.'

'I have some bad news and it cannot wait.' I could see from her face that she was very anxious, her voice had sunk to a low note with a tremor.

I took her to an empty examination cubicle. 'Tell me quickly then Nicole. How can I help you?'

'It is not me. The police have arrested Simon again, at Maison Beauvonne this morning. I tried to phone but could not get hold of you.'

'Why have they arrested him Nicole?'

'Apparently Gérard left a letter with his solicitor which was to be forwarded to the police if he should mysteriously die. That is all I know.'

'Has Simon's lawyer been contacted?'

'Oui. I contacted them and they are attending to it. They say that they think he will be released on mise en liberté sous caution, (bail), but I thought you should know immediately.'

Somehow I remained calm. It was as if I had always expected this, and so it was no surprise. Even so, I sat down while I considered the situation. Nicole took my hand, stroking it with her other hand.

'I will have my phone on silent Nicole, so if there is news, text me. I do not think there is anything I can do at the moment.'

'They want to speak to you too. They have asked me to inform you that they will ask for a formal statement.'

'About what? I know nothing of Gérard's appointment in Abu Dhabi.'

'I do not think it is his death there they are investigating. It is something else.'

'Merde. I thought we had finished with all this. Damn Gérard, that weak minded imbecile. Il me fait chier, (he pisses me off), even though he's dead. C'est le bordel.' (This is a mess).

'I am so sorry Trudi, but I had to tell you.'

'Of course Nicole. I trust you implicitly. I want you to go to the police station, to make sure that Simon's lawyer has attended and to keep me informed of what develops. Tell them that I will go there after work. I am off for three days from tomorrow anyway. Do not make any statement to anyone. We know nothing if the media ask questions, until we find out exactly what is going on. Tell Annette that this is my instruction.'

'She is not in the office Trudi. She called in sick.'

'Oh, so you are left holding the reins. Perhaps we are better off without her at the moment, after all she is

Gérard's widow. Maybe that is why she has called in sick. Merde, I wish I had never appointed either of them. I know I am in good hands with you Nicole. So no statements, except we do not know what the police can possibly want. You can do this. Let me know what is happening by text. Thank you Nicole, you are doing a super job.' We embraced and she departed.

I went back to work. The rest of the day was difficult, my mind on Simon and whatever stupid Gérard's note from the grave had said. I ate no lunch. I drank water, but even that was difficult to swallow. I was consumed by a dreadful fear that this time, Simon would not shrug off the probing questions of the examining magistrate.

Nicole phoned at just after four while I was snatching a quick cup of tea. 'Trudi I am at the Police. They want you to make a statement tonight. I will pick you up from the hospital. What time?'

'I shall finish at six, so about six fifteen Nicole. Can you bring me something to wear? Perhaps that tea dress, the blue one and shoes and a jacket, oh and tights please? And Nicole, did you see Simon?'

'Non Trudi. They would not let me see him but he was with the lawyer. The lawyer will be there at seven tonight for you too, and she hopes you will be able to see Simon after you have made your statement.'

'Good Nicole, I am so grateful. I'll be ready at six fifteen.'

The rest of the afternoon was hard work. I told Deraveau what had happened and he made sure there was cover for when I disappeared after six.

Nicole was dependable as usual and brought my clothes in so I could change. I redid my makeup and I felt ready to meet my fate. So far I had no idea what Gérard had written in his message from the grave. Nicole had no idea either. I wondered what sort of statement I could make if I knew nothing.

Nicole delivered me to the Police and I reported to the desk. I was shown to an interview room and waited there with a female officer until the lawyer came. I had not met this one before. I was surprised to find a woman entering the room and she immediately asked to be left alone with me. The officer departed. The lawyer introduced herself as Mademoiselle Antoinette Dupois, a senior partner from Simon's lawyers, who specialised in criminal law. She was around forty, quite attractive and neatly dressed in a charcoal wool suit.

'I know who you are of course,' she said. 'Apparently the letter left behind by Gérard Chartrand stated that in the event of his death it is likely that Simon had ordered it. Your husband has of course denied it. The Abu Dhabi police have arrested the boatmen, but they have denied that they could have saved Gérard and maintain that he refused to put his harness on while shark fishing.'

'I don't know anything about any of this. What can I say?'

'You knew Gérard. You just have to say what his character was and that the first you knew of his death was when the news was broken to you.'

'What of Simon? Surely they cannot hold him? There is no proof he has done anything.'

'The police are being difficult, there is after all the history, Catherine's accident. However, if you corroborate Simon's story, it will be difficult for them to hold him.'

'Let us get this over then and we can all go home.'

Antoinette opened the door and spoke to the officer. Two male detectives entered.

They identified themselves as Inspector Alain Barre and Olivier Roux.

After the preliminaries, Barre got down to business.

'Madame Chartrand, tell us why Gérard Chartrand was in Abu Dhabi?'

'He was there to help organise the new Beauvonne boutique.'

'Whose decision was it to send him there?'

'It was of course, the instruction of Simon de Beauvonne. He is the managing director.'

'And why was it Gérard Chartrand who was sent.'

'He was available I believe and as a member of the family it was thought too, a good place for him to go. A perk.'

'I put it to you that Gérard was sent there because he had abused his position as office manager.'

'I think that might be so. I had heard that Gérard was gambling again and time in Abu Dhabi would perhaps get him back on the straight and narrow. But although I am deputy managing director, I do not take part in the day to day running of the Beauvonne enterprise. As you know, I am studying to be a doctor, and tonight I have come directly from Pitié-Salpêtrière. I work long hours there.'

'But as deputy managing director, you must be kept aware of what is going on?'

'Non. As you may know, my husband has only one leg, but more important, he had a heart attack seven months ago. He has been worried that he could die if he had a further attack, although the doctors are optimistic. He has a defect which cannot be mended surgically unless he has a transplant. He is monitored by the hospital. To be truthful, although we have married for love, it was also for that reason, so that if anything happened, I would take over as head of the business and be the children's stepmother, to ensure that their inheritance is safeguarded. I did help manage the business while he was ill, and it was I who made Gérard office manager and some other appointments too at that time. Now Simon is well, I leave everything to him, except for the most general suggestions.'

'What sort of suggestions Madame?'

'I suggested Beauvonne should do lingerie and menswear, but after the suggestion, I left it entirely to my husband to consider ways and means and the range and marketing. It is normal in such households as ours, is it not, for a wife to make suggestions about the business, but leave the decisions to the husband. I did help with the TV advert, against my wishes, but when it is a family business, how could I refuse. My husband knows that my ambition is to be une femme médicin, so it is unusual for him to consult me.'

'You are telling me that you were not party to sending Gérard to Abu Dhabi?'

'Oui monsieur.'

'You were not told about the move?'

'Of course I was informed by my husband but by then Gérard was already on his way. To be quite honest monsieur, Gérard had been naughty. He had borrowed money from the company to pay gambling debts. It was not the first time he had embezzled. He lost his previous position and Simon as his cousin, more or less supported him. I made the mistake of giving him a position of trust, not knowing of his previous record. In the circumstances, and because he and my husband had grown up more or less as brothers, they are cousins actually, my husband was charitable. He sent him to Abu Dhabi where he had very little responsibility, where he would be away from his gambling contacts and also where he could enjoy himself. It is a tragedy that this has resulted in his death. We have been distraught and shocked.'

'Do you think it likely that a man fishing for shark would not wear a harness?'

'No, I do not, not for normal men. But Gérard was not a normal man. He was full of bravado. He would be the fastest skier in the party, the fastest driver on the road. If he went horse riding he would take a bet on jumping a fence. He gambled with his life and with money. It was his character to do so. That is why he was in Abu Dhabi, because there were too many gambling opportunities here in France. There is nothing sinister.'

'Why would Gérard have left a note with his avocet (lawyer) to be sent to the police upon his death, making certain allegations against your husband?'

'I do not know. My husband had been very forbearing with his cousin, I believe, getting him out of trouble on various occasions. Until the recent problem, I knew nothing of Gerard's behaviour, that is why I gave him a position of trust which he apparently abused.'

'Madame, the allegation made by Gérard Chartrand against Simon Chartrand is very serious and concerns the death of Catherine Chartrand. Why would your husband's cousin make such serious allegations?'

'I don't know what the allegations are, nor why he would make them, unless all these years, when he has been indulged by Simon he was actually jealous or embittered. Simon had been so good to him. My husband has been stern with him at times, of course he has, when someone goes off the rails, one has to be stern and strict. If Gérard bore a grudge for that, then perhaps. He would not be the first delinquent relative to turn on the hand that has raised them, would he? What is the allegation?'

'It concerns the whereabouts of your husband at the time of Catherine's death. You made a statement concerning her death.' He passed me my signed statement.

'Would you read that Madame, out loud for the recorder please?'

My heart pounded. I read the statement.

'Is that still correct to your knowledge?'

'Oui monsieur. I have made two statements which say the same thing. As the statement says, I phoned my now husband on his mobile that afternoon. He did not want to speak as he was expecting a call from New York. It was also a very poor line, I could hardly hear him. What do you want from me? I have nothing to add.' I suddenly, probably through tiredness, burst into tears. There was a pause while I searched for and found a handkerchief in my bag. I recovered myself.

'I have told you nothing but the truth. Gérard Chartrand était un imbécile. Pardon monsieur, je suis bouleversée pour mon mari. He is not a well man. His heart disease has been under constant monitoring. I demand that he be released.'

'Very well Madame, that is all for you. Unfortunately Monsieur Simon Chartrand will remain with us tonight, but we will release him tomorrow on bail. He is well looked after. You are at liberty.'

'Why not release him now? He is not a well man. If you want proof of that, then contact Professeur Rousse at la Pitié.'

'We have questions still for him. That is all for now madame.'

'I implore you monsieur. He is a man of substance, he is not going to abscond. Release him to me now and I will guarantee to return him here tomorrow. May I speak to him?'

'Non Madame, tomorrow.'

Outside I spoke to Antoinette. 'You are looking after Simon while he is questioned?'

'Of course, but they will not start again until tomorrow. I thought you were very good, that is why I did not interrupt. It was better to let them take your statement without interference. It means we have nothing to hide. I expect I will see you tomorrow?'

'And Simon. Will they release him? He really is not well.'

'I do not see they have any reason to detain him. I will speak to them now. It is the word of an unreliable wastrel against a respected business man. I think he will be released tomorrow.'

Nicole drove me home. I was dead on my feet.

Chapter 31.

I awoke to find Nicole by the side of my bed, shaking me. I struggled to shake off the dullness of sleep which had been filled with so many demons. I was tired and befuddled.

'What Nicole? What time is it?'

'Nearly five. The Police just phoned me on my mobile, because that was the number they had. Simon has been taken to Pitié. He has had another crise cardiaque.'

I was out of bed in a flash. I threw on whatever clothes I found to hand, skinny jeans and a T, my leather bomber. I found Nicole waiting for me, her little Mercedes ready to go. I managed to put on a little makeup as she drove through the still quiet streets of early morning Paris. I felt sick. A sob escaped as Nicole drove into the car park at Pitié. I managed to find my pass and show it.

We ran the corridors to the cardiac department. We were shown into Rousse's empty office. I wanted to run the corridors and search for Simon, but Nicole hung onto my hand. After several minutes, Rousse appeared.

'Trudi, come I think we have managed to save him for the time being. He is conscious and wants to see you.'

I rose and brought Nicole with me. We followed Rousse to and ICU room. There was no policeman in sight. I entered, leaving Nicole at the door. Simon was propped in bed, wired up seemingly with every machine monitoring his physical condition. Rousse left us after lowering Simon's oxygen mask. Simon looked a good colour.

I kissed him and took his hand. Carefully I laid my head on his shoulder and he managed to wrap fingers into my hair and stroked me. I tried to hold myself together, but my throat tightened and tears started from my eyes. I bit my lip and he turned my head and saw my distorted emotional face.

'I'm going to be OK my Trudi, but I will not be very well for a time. I know that you will look after the children and the business. You are a great comfort to me, a great relief to know that if anything really bad happens, you will take care of everything. It was a good day when we met at that fancy dress party and you thought I was in fancy dress, because I was in riding clothes.'

'I loved you from that moment Simon. You made me whole, gave me a wonderful life, indulged me and taught me so much. It was a very good day when we met, but each day since has been better. Rousse says you will get better, but you must do as you are told.'

'I will. Promise me, that you will finish your training and become a doctor.'

'Of course. And you will be my first patient.'

Rousse appeared and Nicole entered behind him.

'It is time to leave Trudi. He must rest.'

Nicole took Simon's hand and kissed it. 'Look after my wife Nicole.'

'Bien sûr Mâitre.'

I kissed him and we left. In Rousse's office we waited for him to appear.

At length he entered. 'I hope Trudi that he will make a good recovery, but he has this weakness. We may have to consider a transplant, without it, the outlook is not good. For the moment, he is stable and out of danger. I think you should rest and come back this afternoon. By that time we will have done more tests.'

'I would rather stay.'

'No. There is nothing to do. He is sedated now and will sleep. You need rest too. Nicole has told me that you spent the evening after a working day, with the police. Go home, rest and come back later.' He gave me a few sleeping pills.

We started home. On the way, I asked Nicole to take me to Pont de l'Alma. She managed to park on the side of the road, watching for traffic police. I walked to the Seine, then across the bridge. The Bateaux Mouches were moored up. The rush hour had started and traffic whizzed about. I thought of our meals on the Bateaux and everything Simon and I had done. I let the tears run and leant over the parapet, sobbing. It was very cold, the wind across the Seine penetrated even my bomber jacket. I wanted it to, wanted to feel pain as if being punished would somehow expurgate whatever sins we had committed and deliver Simon safely to me. I rocked with the deep distress I felt. I found Nicole by my side, her arm around my waist, and the car behind me on the kerb. A police car had stopped too, and an officer was approaching. I pulled myself together, dabbed my eyes and got in the passenger seat. Nicole spoke to the policeman. She joined me in the car.

'Let's go home Nicole. We will help Sophie with the children, I will try to sleep for an hour or two.'

At the villa, I tried to bury myself in domestic life, but it all seemed meaningless. With the aid of a pill, I fell asleep. I awoke at two, fuzzy, my mind more tranquil from the effects of the drug. I dressed quickly and made my face. I would have some soup, and head for the hospital.

Nicole met me as I opened the door of the bedroom, Simon's and my bedroom. I could see by her tearful face, that there was bad news. Simon had died at 13.47.

This has been an emotional journey, killing Simon has been difficult.

There is another Trudi novel.
'Trudi after Simon' [without]

Made in the USA
Charleston, SC
25 June 2013